Realm Travellers

The Deep Tarn

M.J. Raco

The Realm Travellers Series:

The Ancient Gateway
A Parallel Dimension
The Forbidden Passage
The Deep Tarn

MJ Raco, author of the fantasy/adventure series Realm Travellers, is an orthoptist by day, a novelist by night. MJ lives in Sydney, Australia, has three adult children and two grandkids she adores. She has two exceptionally large ginger rescue tabbies she's allergic to, but wouldn't part with for anything.

The daughter of a great storyteller, songwriter and poet, she grew up surrounded by mythology and parables from the scriptures. Her love affair with fantasy began when she was gifted her first Enid Blyton book at the age of seven. Escaping into a world of endless imagination was her happy place, and she hasn't stopped venturing there since.

When she isn't saving sight, babysitting or tucked away tapping on her archaic laptop, MJ spends her time reading, cooking and making plans to see the world—especially ancient worlds!

Realm Travellers—The Deep Tarn
M.J. Raco
Copyright © 2024
Published by Alkira Publishing, Australia
ABN: 32736122056
http://www.alkirapublishing.com

ISBN: 978-1-922329-74-5

DEDICATION

Follow your dreams!

PROLOGUE

Once, not so long ago, five Aussie teenagers, of supposed minimal description, happened upon a mysterious portal that transported them to another dimension … to a world from a time, long gone … an ancient realm. Here, Max, Jack, Peanut, Ruby and Kenny discovered, through a sequence of trials and tribulations, that they're, in fact, not *quite* so ordinary.

Before the realm, Maxine Darcy-Rutherford (Max) was the girl at school you steered clear of. She was a troubled sixteen-year-old with a sharp attitude and an even pointier death stare.

But Max was fractured. Her world splintered to pieces after the death of her mother. The life of Doctor Grace Darcy came to an abrupt halt the day she fell victim to a senseless motor vehicle accident.

Max was twelve.

It was just Max and her father. The Three

Musketeers were no more.

But Professor Edward Rutherford struggled to come to grips with the loss. His one true love was gone … forever.

How did he cope with such a heartache? Regrettably, he didn't. His unyielding grief just about shattered their little family.

Thankfully, they had Annuska.

Lifelong carer to Max and housekeeper to the Darcy-Rutherford's, Annuska, or Annie to those who know her best, was the glue that held them together—albeit tenuously. And this fragility lasted a long while; it lasted three years.

In her school life, Max remained, at best, indifferent to the goings-on around her. That is until something poked her. In these instances, she could turn quite prickly. On one such occasion, when Max was flung into a randomly selected peer group for a five-day school camp, things didn't go down too well. At least they didn't at the beginning …

More on that later.

Moving forward.

Also allotted to this fated, thrown-together, eclectic group, were level-headed (and hockey jock) Jack Braden and his best buddy (and equally talented, if not more so) Charlie (a.k.a. Peanut) Brown.

Tall, lanky, bespectacled geek (but super smart)

Kenny Chen and newcomer to the school, strawberry-blonde, amber-eyed *bombshell* (according to Peanut) Ruby Arlington were also tossed into the mix.

With the minority (well, Max, really) begrudging this mandatory grouping, the teens did their best to get along.

To Max's utter dread, Jack volunteered to be the *go-between* to try to bridge the differences. Why? Because that's what Jack does best—he mediates.

From the outset, this *niceness* about Jack irks her. Why? She has no idea … he just does—he somehow gets under her skin. But as time goes on, and on closer inspection, Jack's annoying peculiarities became less and less irritating, and unexpectedly more *interesting* …

The journey begins.

High-school Camp, Day One: Jack's efforts miraculously begin to show promise. Bridging manoeuvres take form. Rigid barricades fragment, and rays of hope peek through the cracks.

High-school Camp, Day Two: Sudden and unexpected events turn their whole world upside down. While navigating a seemingly harmless camp activity, the five teens fall through an undiscovered portal and find themselves captured and imprisoned in a world from another dimension. A primitive world full of brutality, one they have a chance to survive only if they learn to work as one.

Rapidly, their petty grudges become insignificant. Their focus changes. They learn to put aside their differences to work towards escaping the confines of the medieval fortress and making their way home … as a team.

And there *is* a way home, but they learn that to achieve this they must compete in deadly ancient-world challenges. An almost impossible task.

Pitted against a squad of four older, well-honed opponents from South Africa (also victims, from an alternate portal), and purely for the benefit of entertaining the nobles of the realm and their cohorts, Max, Jack, Peanut, Kenny and Ruby begin the battle of their lives.

And then from adversity comes strength.

In an effort to pull together as one, the young team of five Aussies unearth, quite by accident, that by entering the realm, they've inexplicably acquired *superpowers*. Max discovers she can *heal*. Jack learns of his power of *invulnerability*. Peanut finds he's capable of *vanishing*. Kenny's brain transforms into a human search engine—he becomes *Master Google*. And Ruby learns to craft a barrier of sorts, conjuring a *shield* from thin air.

They swiftly call upon these defences to help battle these hostile adversaries.

Initially a team of five, the now-four South African troop have in their arsenal Ryker, a military trained, green-eyed, *muscle-clad,* human anomaly; Edra, a resplendent, auburn-haired, athletic *speed freak*; and deceptively diminutive, sharp-eyed twins Banji and Ulan—both skilled in *mind-reading* and communicating telepathically. Jeopardy understated, personal headspace, a non-entity. Each private thought, never again your own.

Having spent four torturous years trapped in the realm, the opponents are more than ready to take on the fresh meat, win the challenges, and go home.

The games begin.

The rules? There are none. It's simple. The team that bests the other in five challenges wins the chance to oppose the realm's champions, *The Invincibles*. And if possible, the team that claims victory over these herculean-like beings receives the gift of freedom, the prize.

Again, *simple.*

But not all that's plotted comes to light.

Having suffered extensive injuries in near-death challenges, the nine victims of the realm, against all probability, form an alliance and become one.

The Ancients are blindsided.

Our heroes' plan to escape appears to be a good one, but not all make it. Ryker and Max get left behind. Max loses crucial seconds as she battles to save Jack from a life-threatening arrow to his chest.

The consequence? Guards descend to foil their getaway. Jack and the others make it through the portal in time. Max and Ryker don't.

Ryker, now loyal to Max for saving him in an earlier chariot-race catastrophe, snatches Max and forges an escape into the forest. Here they remain hidden and wait.

Back in Oz, the survivors regroup and begin rescue strategies.

Meanwhile, Ryker and Max call upon an alliance made with a group of outcasts of the realm to assist them in evading capture. The incentive to help them in this? A promise of a better life.

And among those good people of the forest is the beautiful, dark-eyed and exceptionally capable Aelianna.

Ryker and Aelianna immediately form a connection—a bond that proves to be a distraction for them both. This distraction creates unexpected complications they could do without.

Meanwhile, Max, marked and valued for her rare ability to heal, becomes a target—there's a price on her head. Betrayal prevails.

Recaptured and imprisoned within the fortress walls, Max is coerced to exercise her power to repair and save the lives of the numerous wounded in a challenge that had gone terribly wrong (wrong only for the people of the realm, not the newly allied friends). One of the victims of this tragic elephant stampede is none other than *Pius*, the Ancients' noble ruler himself.

Ryker battles to rescue Max. And with Aelianna's capable support, he does.

And then, at the eleventh hour, military intervention brought about by Jack and company arrive to fight off the Ancients' retaliatory attack—dodging arrows fired from airborne Invincible *Vyvian*; fending off *Archimedes* and his ruthless mind control; and battling to remain upright against *Shant's* devastating twister.

Ruby, with her infallible shield, emerges from the depths of despair like a phoenix. The aggressors are defeated, and at the finish, the friends are victorious, vowing never to set foot in this vicious, barbaric world again.

So why is it that Ryker schemes to return to the realm some months later?

One word. *Cancer.*

While trapped in the ancient land for four years, he was separated from his dear mother, and now she is dying. And who better to heal her than his new best buddy, Max, the miracle healer. But this can only come about if they return to the realm where her powers can be reignited.

They hatch a plan. It should be a quick in-out operation. But all plans fall to the wayside when Ryker clasps eyes on beautiful Aelianna once more.

A new archenemy appears on the scene—Wulf.

Wulf has designs on having Aelianna for his own and does everything in his power to do away with his new rival, Ryker. The two steers lock horns in a fight for alpha-male dominance. Ryker is captured, tortured and thrown into the bowels of the earth, only brought to surface at Wulf's command for battle.

During the clashes, Ryker struggles to stay alive, let alone protect Aelianna and her family as he swore to. But an opportunity presents itself during one of the challenges, and Ryker makes his escape. In his desperation to get away, he stumbles across an expanse of the forest he'd never previously entered, a place no one would willingly choose to enter. Its frigid and ominous atmosphere alone is enough to make anyone turn tail and run.

But it's here, through a twist of fate, that Ryker chances upon his former teammate, Jaeger. The taken fifth member of their group, now a ghost. Dead and unable to pass to the other side. Stuck for all time in limbo.

Ryker considers that perhaps Jaeger hasn't crossed

over from spirit to eternal being because his presence in this ancient world was never meant to be, as it is for them all.

And it's the emptiness he sees in Jaeger's eyes that makes him vow to take him from this place and return him home, given the chance.

Hence, a new mission takes form—to rescue Jaeger. And with help from his new-found Aussie friends, Ryker does.

But it's not until they cross the threshold of the portal on their return that they discover another facet to the mystical phenomenon that is the ancient gateway. Before their very eyes, and to their complete and utter astonishment, their long-lost, deceased friend miraculously and inconceivably returns to life.

The magic of the portal surprises them once again.

I
THE CEREMONY

MAX

Max stares at the scissors in her hand. Her hold tightens around the cold metal. Flashbacks fill her head, taking her back to the ancient realm—reliving the trauma she once went through. Her pulse gathers speed. She drags in a few deep breaths, trying to find calm.

Her friend, the beautiful Aelianna, sits patiently before her, dressed in white satin, aglow with anticipation, her big brown eyes bright, her smile radiant.

Max lets out her breath. Her lips curl and the tension fritters away. This is Aelianna and Ryker's big day. She can't ruin it for them.

Her best friend, Ryker, freshly shaven and with his hair trimmed in typical buzz-cut fashion, stands off to the side. He's dressed in a smart, teal-coloured, three-piece suit, his arms folded, his expression troubled. With them are Ryker's parents: tight-laced, no-nonsense Vice-Admiral Denvon Engelbrecht and his radiant wife, Isebel. As too are Max's family: her adored father, Edward, and of course, their beloved Annie.

And guest in the Engelbrecht's home in picturesque Johannesburg is newly acquainted civil celebrant Sarah Matthews.

Again, Max looks down at the scissors, then glances at Ryker. Their eyes lock, his green eyes dark. The negative energy radiating from him is palpable. She forces a smile and does her best to ignore him and focus on what's about to happen. But Ryker's brow furrows deeper; his jawline tightens. She can almost hear his teeth grinding.

Tension fills the room.

Aelianna must sense it too, for she reaches out to touch Ryker's arm.

He turns to look at her; his eyes soften.

Max exhales. *Okay, it's time.*

She prepares herself but is easily distracted by the memory of her own ceremony. Absentmindedly, she tugs at her shortened brown hair, remembering the time her beautiful long black ponytail was hacked off with a pair of rusty, ancient shears—a customary ritual before one is to wed, she'd been told.

The marriage took place—her husband, Herodus, the then head gate keeper. It was a necessity at the time. An intentional undertaking to keep her alive. For who else would save the multitude of wounded if not her?

And the person put to task with those rusty shears? None other than her best friend's bride-to-be, Aelianna.

Max's eyes narrow; her lip curls. As much as she loves Aelianna, it's payback time. 'Let's do this!'

Aelianna squirms with excitement. This ritual means everything to her, and Max knows it. The cutting of the bride's hair tells the world she's no longer unattached. It signifies a married woman. Once done, she and Ryker will be as one forever.

Max sighs. *So romantic!*

But a quick glance at Ryker reminds her of the dispute they'd had earlier. 'Why hack off her hair? It's barbaric and, not to mention, criminal! Look at her beautiful hair!' he'd hollered. 'I think we should just call in someone to make it official. A celebrant. That'll do. Right? After all, we're living in the present, not the past.'

But it was Aelianna's look of dejection that

weakened his protest. Max didn't even need to raise a brow at him.

He can be such a caveman!

Max shakes off the memory. She then gingerly takes a few strands of Aelianna's long dark hair, brings the scissors to it and gestures to Aelianna, asking if a ten-centimetre snip from the end is enough. Aelianna frowns and shakes her head. Max inches the blades a little higher. Again, Aelianna shakes her head, then bumps the blades up to the level of her chin, just as Max's hairline is.

It shouldn't surprise Max, but it does. She gulps.

Aelianna smiles.

There's no getting out of it. The deed needs to be done. And then without another thought, Max shuts her eyes tight, and the blades grind. Silken strands fall limp in her hand. Her eyes pop open. She inhales sharply.

In contrast, Aelianna is all joy. She claps her hands, her smile contagious.

Encouraged, Max grabs another strand, this time with a little more ambition.

Snip!

Then … grind, snip, grind, snip!

Soon, all of Aelianna's tresses have fallen to the floor. Max steps back to survey her handiwork and smiles. Aelianna looks just as beautiful as she did before, if not more so. And the goofy look on Ryker's face tells her that even he agrees. Max rolls her eyes and shakes her head.

And now for the final touch.

Max takes the delicate pale orange film of tulle the bride herself had prepared for the occasion and carefully pins it to the top of Aelianna's head. Tiny muted gold pearls sewn at the crown catch the light streaming through the window as she secures it.

Done.

Max pauses to take it all in and sighs, a vision of loveliness before her.

Ryker kneels by Aelianna's side, his eyes bright. He takes her hand and smiles.

The ceremony is now ready to begin.

2

THE TRIPLE C

JACK

Jack struggles to get a firm grip on the bulky cardboard box he's carrying up the winding staircase to one of the many spare rooms at Max's house. The box, overloaded with electrical and computer gadgets, barely allows him to see where he's going. Behind him, Ruby carries a smaller flat box tucked under her arm. It contains a brand-new computer monitor. Peanut, Max and Kenny trail, carrying various loads of their own. They're abuzz with excitement; they're setting up *The Triple C*—the Central Communications Cooperative, a base where they can keep tabs on anything suspicious that's potentially *realm* related.

Since their recent return from the ancient world, the teenagers have been eager to investigate the possibility that other undiscovered portals exist. They know of two: one in Blue Ridge National Park on the south coast of Sydney, and one on the outskirts of the camping reserve at Kruger National Park in South Africa. But are there more? If so, they must be found and destroyed. These portals are fraught with danger.

At the top of the staircase, Jack pauses a moment, props the box on the hallstand there and wipes his damp fringe from his eyes. He then continues, leading the gang down the long, wide corridor, past Max's bedroom, to a room two doors down from it. It's the quietest room in the house. They'll have all the privacy they need here.

He pauses at the entrance of the room and calls over his shoulder. 'Hey, Kenny, where do you want this stuff?'

Kenny, one of the two masterminds behind this setup, shouts back from down the hallway. 'Um, I guess anywhere's fine. I'll sort it out in a sec.'

Jack carefully lowers his box onto the carpeted floor in one of the corners of the near-empty room. A sudden commotion from the passage behind him has his attention. He goes to investigate.

His freckle-faced best mate, Peanut, and pocket-sized girlfriend, Max, have locked horns for the umpteenth time today. Jack and Ruby share a look. She shrugs.

He groans. *I don't believe it! They're at it again!*

'Watch where you're goin', squirt!'

Max's eyes widen. 'Me?' She struggles to balance her load, narrowly averting a disaster by propping her box on her knee and resting it against the wall. Colour flushes her face as she prepares to strike back.

Peanut doesn't give her a chance. 'Oi! Precious cargo here!'

Max looks him up and down, her brow raised. The corner of her lip twitches. 'You can say *that* again!'

Peanut pauses and frowns, then realises her meaning. 'What? Not *me*, you twit, the *stuff in the box*. I nearly dropped it!' He pauses to look around. 'Man, how big is this place? If I'd known you were taking us to woop-woop, I'd have taken a lighter box!'

Max mumbles something under her breath. Jack catches the word—*wuss*.

'Hey!' Peanut cries out. 'I heard that!'

Jack groans. It's time for *another* intervention. 'Will you two quit it?'

Peanut gives him a stink-eye. 'She started it!'

Jack stops short. 'I *cannot* believe you just said that. What are you? Five? Just pull your head in, will ya?'

Max smirks and pokes out her tongue.

Peanut splutters. 'Oi! Did ya see that? And you call me a *five-year-old*!'

Impatient to enter the room, Kenny groans and sidesteps the feuding duo. 'Guys, you *do* remember that we're a "communications *cooperative*", right? So, how about we start looking like one? We've got work to do.'

Jack frowns.

Peanut and Max exchange a sheepish look.

'And just in case you're interested,' Kenny calls out over his shoulder, 'there's been a missing kid's case reported. This time in rural New South Wales. A place called Mahlee. I think we should look into this one. It's not that far, just a little over two hours' drive from here.'

Peanut's eyes light up, all prior grievances forgotten. 'Cool! I'll drive. I've been hanging to go on a decent road trip now that I'm officially on my Ps.'

Jack shakes his head, incredulous at the workings of his best friend's mind.

He shrugs and follows his friends into the room to help set up *The Triple C.*

As everyone sets down their boxes, Jack takes a moment to appreciate the space provided for them by Max's dad, Professor Rutherford. There's ample room for their rookie setup. A large, expensive-looking, bare mahogany desk and traditional leather swivel chair dominate the room, both positioned in front of the closed double French doors, which open to a small Juliet balcony overlooking the Darcy-Rutherford's well-manicured lawn and gardens. Opposite the desk sits a large, well-worn leather Chesterfield sofa.

Jack moves to look from the cushioned window seat adjacent to the doors. From here he has a good vantage of the roof of the clear glassed-top greenhouse. He sees movement within the small structure and smiles, knowing it's Annie, the Darcy-Rutherford's housekeeper.

But Annie is more than Max's housekeeper. She's family. Annie became part of the household before Max was born, Jack was told, and has shared in each and every one of the Darcy-Rutherford's experiences. She helped deliver Max into the world almost seventeen years ago. She had cuddled and soothed her the day Max cut her first tooth. She watched on with pride as Max took her first steps. And she was there to pick up the pieces when Max's twelve-year-old world was shattered by her mother, Grace's, death. Grace was like a daughter to Annie. And on that tragic day, it's been said, a tiny bit of her died too.

And now, Annie is fundamentally the reason why Jack and the gang have all survived the aftermath of the ancient realm. Annuska Hedke is, and always will be, everyone's pillar of strength, and now, everyone's beloved *oma*.

Looking down at the top of the greenhouse, Jack imagines Annie pottering around, wearing her distinctive floral apron, trimmed with lace, idly humming out of tune, her focus immersed on whatever she's doing. Whether it's tending her cherished crop of brightly coloured tulips or gathering ingredients for tonight's dinner—her famed Hungarian goulash, apparently. The thought of it arouses his senses. His mouth waters; his stomach growls.

Jack chuckles, then turns his attention back to the room. Empty boxes and polystyrene packing foam are strewn everywhere, the new equipment, out and already in the process of being hooked up. He blinks a few times. *Geez, that was quick!*

He'd better pull his finger out and offer to help.

'There, that should do it!' Kenny jumps up from under the desk and presses the button to fire up the computer. He swipes away his shiny black fringe, his narrow, dark chocolate-coloured eyes alive with anticipation. 'Give me a sec, and I'll pull up that story.' He dives onto the padded leather swivel chair and starts typing.

Jack smiles. Not only does he marvel at Kenny's enthusiasm but also at his incredible transformation. Since their experience in the realm, Kenny has come to form. A year ago, he was a timid, awkward teenager that hid behind his thick, dark-rimmed glasses and shied away from bringing attention to himself, preferring to blend into the background. Sadly, he was too easily overlooked and often not heard. But today, he's bolder, more confident and eager to take the lead.

Although it was a toss-up as to who initiated the formation of the Cooperative—Peanut stands firm that it was *his* idea—it was Kenny who started paying closer attention to the nightly news, looking for clues of other portals existing elsewhere in the world. It became his mission to track down and bring an end to the existence of these treacherous gateways.

And it was Max who suggested they set up something at her place where they can look into these disappearances without their parents becoming anxious.

Professor Rutherford was impressed by their initiative and enthusiasm and promised to support them, but only on the provision that it didn't interfere with their studies, and that they ran things by him first before taking anything on. If it so happened that they came across something that raised a flag, only then would he take it up with his friend Gerard Thompson, the deputy director general of security at ASIO.

'Max, you're the greatest.' Kenny laughs. 'There's

no way in the world I could've set up anything like this at my place. You *all* know Mum …'

Peanut snorts and launches into a few karate moves, slaying the air with rapid open-handed strikes, throwing his leg out repeatedly in enthusiastic sidekicks. 'Yeah, ninja tiger mum. Small but deadly!'

Ruby jumps clear out of his way. 'Settle down, Goku, you nearly whacked me in the head!'

Peanut bows respectfully before her, his hands clasped in prayer. 'Fear not, precious one, these hands are precision-built fighting weapons. No head whacking unless provoked.' He looks up and gives her a wink. Ruby fights to hide a smile and nudges him.

Jack grins at his friends. They're finally getting along again. Too often of late, they'd warred over the smallest of issues.

Jack turns his attention to Max. She appears troubled by something. 'Hey,' he asks her. 'Everything okay?'

Max's focus is on Kenny. 'Kenny, just so we're clear on something, what we're doing here is strictly between Dad, Deputy Thompson and us, right?' she says. 'Even Annie needs to be left in the dark about all of this. Okay?' She turns to look at the others.

Kenny nods, his eyes wide. 'One hundred percent!'

Ruby marks a cross over her heart as a sign of her pledge. 'Absolutely. Poor Annie, I think she's just about had enough of this realm stuff. We were lucky to sneak all of this in while she was still outside.'

'I know! Look, Annie's one tough cookie, but I think even *she's* reached her limit.' Max sighs.

Oblivious to Max's concerns, Peanut rummages through some of the boxes strewn on the floor, then hesitates. 'Man, where did you get all this stuff?' He looks at Kenny, a huge grin reaching from one ear to another. 'If I didn't know better, I'd say you've been picking Ryker's brain!' He pauses to study a small black gadget, turning it over in his hand. His eyes widen. 'Wow, you're kidding me! A police scanner? Man, that's just totally awesome!'

Jack stops. He turns to see the colour drain from Max's face.

'A scanner?' Max faces Kenny in a panic. 'Is that legal? You said we weren't doing anything that'll get Dad into trouble!'

Kenny whips around and glares at Peanut. Peanut flinches and holds his hands up defensively. 'Hey, you're the brains in this setup. I was just asking.'

Kenny adjusts his glasses and clicks his tongue. 'Relax, Max, it's not a *scanner*, it's a *two-way*. We're not doing anything that'll stuff up what we're setting up here. I swear.'

Peanut snorts and nudges Max. 'Yeah, chillax, will ya? You heard the man. Nothin' illegal in it!'

Jack clips Peanut on the back of his head.

Peanut swings around to glare at him.

'I reckon you've been hanging around Ryker too long,' Jack says to him with a grin. 'Peanut, this ain't no military covert operation. We're just keeping our eyes and ears peeled for any disappearances. And seeing if they're somehow linked to these portals. Remember?'

Peanut scowls and rubs at the sting.

'And I think it's a brilliant idea,' Max says. 'There may be hundreds of these portals all over the place, with stacks of people falling into them, like we did, and disappearing without a trace. If we can help somehow, then why not?'

'We'll be able to keep up with current news events all over the world using news aggregator apps,' Kenny says to them as he busies himself surfing the internet.

Ruby's eyes widen. 'A what? Kenny, you'd better explain that one.' She looks over at Max and scrunches up her nose, her freckles blending into the flush of her cheeks. 'Is that a dumb question?'

Max frowns. 'I'm clueless too. And it's not *dumb*, Ruby, it's just that Kenny's so *smart*.' She laughs, then turns to Kenny. 'So, Kenny, fill us in. What's a *news aggregator?*'

Peanut runs his hand through his messed-up ginger mane. 'And keep it simple, will ya? My brain kinda hurts when you start with all this hi-tech, cyber stuff.'

Kenny laughs. He skims through some information popping up on the screen while he explains. 'Well, it's really not that complicated. In fact, I guarantee you've all had some experience in what they do already.' He goes on. 'The app compiles news from a wide range of sources in one place for easier access. So by using this as the base computer, the aggregator customises what searches are relevant by automatically personalising our feed based on our search history. For example, if we're looking for breaking news on kids that've gone missing, then it eliminates the tedious task of watching every news report all over the world to find what we're after.

'It happens all the time,' he continues. 'How often do things just randomly pop up on your phone or laptop while you're browsing, and it's exactly what you've recently searched for? You probably thought it was a coincidence, but it's actually a form of this information sifting that I'm talking about.'

Jack grins; his excitement escalates. 'Don't you just love it! Kenny, you're the best. It'll definitely make our job a whole heap easier. The sooner we find these portals, the quicker we can shut them down.'

Kenny's cheeks colour. He adjusts his glasses, leans into the monitor and continues his search.

'So, Max, we've got Ryker and the others on

board too, yeah?' Jack asks this because he knows she spoke to Ryker last night.

Max's eyes light up. 'He's so keen,' she tells them. 'You've got no idea. It's like it's his new assignment. *Operation Portal Shutdown*. He just wants to make things safe out there. He feels he owes the world that much, now that he has his mother back and well.'

'So how *is* Isebel?' Jack asks with a crooked smile and his brow raised.

Max bites back a smirk. 'Miraculously *healthy*.' She gives him a wink. 'As you can imagine, she has the doctors bamboozled with her recovery. There's not even a trace that she ever had cancer.' She looks towards the door, then lowers her voice to a whisper. 'Thanks to Dad.'

'Man, if they ever find out what happened—' Ruby starts.

'But they're not going to. Right?' Max cuts in. 'Dad's neck is on the chopping block if that ever leaks out. Even Annie has no idea what happened when we went to South Africa recently. And we need to keep it that way. Okay? We were there for Ryker and Aelianna's wedding, and that's all.'

Ruby holds her hand over her heart and sighs wistfully. 'Oh, how romantic. I can't believe they're married.'

'Eew, gross!' Peanut cries out, his face screwed

up like he'd just sucked on a lemon. 'Can't imagine anything worse!'

Jack falls back. *What the …? He didn't just say that, did he?*

He flicks a glance at Ruby. Her eyes darken; her cheeks colour.

Uh-oh! This isn't going to end well.

And then, to Jack's mortification, Peanut keeps going. Giving an impromptu performance, he drags his leg as though weighed down by a heavy load. 'I've got *one* word for ya … ball 'n' chain!'

Jack smacks his forehead and groans.

Like a flash, Max zooms in on Peanut and pokes him in the chest. 'For your information, that's *three* words, you twit! And watch what you …'

Jack dives forward. He takes Max by the shoulders and carefully moves her aside to step between them. His eyes fix on Peanut. He clicks his tongue and shakes his head, then turns to the others. 'So he's got a *big* mouth! What's new? Let's just drop it and get on with what we need to do here.'

Peanut crosses his arms and frowns. There's silence.

Tactfully, Jack changes the subject. 'And Max, you don't have to worry about anything. Your dad's secret's safe with us.' He looks for reassurance from the others. 'Right, guys?'

Always ready to have Jack's back, Kenny steps up.

'Hey, they won't hear anything from me.'

Jack turns to Ruby. All the fire from her now gone, she shrugs and gestures, locking her lips. 'I guess, *mum's* the word. Right?'

Max inhales sharply.

Jack knows where her thoughts have gone. *Mum* isn't a word Max can hear without dredging up mixed emotions. Five years on, she still struggles with the loss of her mother.

He pulls her into a side hug and presses his lips to the top of her head. She wraps her arms around his waist, snuggles in a little closer, then looks up and smiles. He gives her a wink.

Peanut clicks his tongue and rolls his eyes. 'Oh, *p-lease*!'

Ruby turns on him, her hands fisted on her hips. 'And what exactly is your problem?'

Peanut sticks his finger down his throat and pretends to gag.

Jack groans. *Here we go again!*

Ruby's eyes darken.

Peanut's hands shoot up defensively. 'Okay, okay, we get it … they're into each other,' he says with a laugh. 'They don't need to keep ramming it down our throats!'

Ruby growls. She shoves him before storming off to the other side of the room.

Peanut startles. 'Oi! Are you nuts? What was that for?'

Ruby turns to look at him, flushed. '*Don't* get me started, *Charlie!*'

She then busies herself, stomping on the empty cardboard boxes and ripping them into smaller pieces. 'Just be thankful this isn't your head!'

Jack snorts. Peanut whips around and glares at him.

Oops! It's time for another distraction! Jack clears his throat. 'So, Kenny, what was it that you heard about those kids? D'ya think it's linked to a portal?'

The diversion works. Peanut shakes off his mood. 'Hey, yeah! Cool! So how many kids are we talking about?'

Jack peers over Kenny's shoulder. He watches him enter '*MISSING KIDS, MAHLEE*' in the search engine. Several articles from the town's local paper, the *Mahlee Post*, pop up reporting on three kids who went missing two weeks ago. One of the headlines reads, ***A prank gone terribly wrong!***

> *… It has been reported that the three children, Shaun Tailor, Liam Cooberong and Bec Jones, spent the night in the abandoned 1912-built St Hubert's Orphanage on a dare.*

Police say the derelict building has, over the years, consistently attracted vandalism since its closure in 1978.

Riley Tailor, the older brother of missing fourteen-year-old Shaun Tailor, confessed to the local police that he and his friend William (Bill) Flaherty foolishly dared the younger children to spend the night in the notoriously rumoured to be haunted building.

'I know it was stupid,' Riley tells the Post. *'But Billy and I … well, we figured they'd be safe. We even stuck around for a few hours before we went home, just to make sure they were okay. In the morning, we couldn't believe it—they were gone. There was no trace of them. Not their swags … no nothing. We kind of freaked out and called the police.'*

Police have searched the building and the vast grounds of the property and have found nothing to indicate

Peanut looks up from the article, his eyes wide. 'So, what d'ya reckon? Worth checking out?'

'It's haunted!' Ruby says from behind him. 'I'm not too keen to poke around a place like that.'

Peanut snorts. 'What's the big deal? We've dealt with ghosts before. Remember? Jae, Seb and Eddie …'

Ruby shoves her hands in her jeans' pockets and shrugs.

'And you've got to admit, Ruby, it *does* sound interesting.' Kenny turns back to the computer. 'How about we check out the building's history? Maybe knowing a bit about it and its past might help.'

So they spend some time reading as much information about the old orphanage as they can. They learn that it mainly housed boys from the ages of five to sixteen.

'Hey, look at this.' Kenny points at something on the screen. '*Initially the building's capacity was intended to house approximately one hundred children,*' he reads, '*but at times that number was exceeded more than two-*

fold. Early accounts state that the standard of living was appalling, and outbreaks of disease were commonplace. One such incident was documented in 1919 during the Spanish influenza pandemic, when numerous lives were lost, ultimately reducing the orphanage's numbers.'

Max frowns. 'Those poor boys! I can't imagine what they had to put up with. Living on top of each other. Barely having enough to eat. Freezing in the winter. And being deprived of the medical attention they needed. It's no wonder it's haunted.'

Stiff from being hunched over Kenny's shoulder, scouring through the information, Jack steps back to stretch. 'Yeah, makes you appreciate how lucky we've got it today.' He rubs the back of his neck. 'So what do you reckon? Worth having a look?'

'Well, there's not much there that screams *realm*,' Ruby says with a frown. 'Don't get me wrong, I feel bad for those kids and all, but I'm not seeing the link.' She shrugs. 'I need to see red flags.'

'Wait on! What's this?' Kenny loses himself in something that's caught his attention. Jack watches on with interest. Kenny suddenly jerks back, eyes wide, and reads out what he's found, his voice unsteady. *'In light of the recent disappearances, authorities were forced to treat the reported account with the utmost urgency … and although these children were never found, there was never any evidence to support any mismanagement of the residents of the orphanage …* ' Kenny taps the screen excitedly, his mouth moving but no intelligible words coming out.

'Wait. What?' Jack moves in closer to the monitor and skims over the report. 'Hang on a sec, is this still the report on the same kids—the ones that went missing recently?' He has a better look.

He stops and swallows hard. 'What the …? This report is dated 1927!'

Kenny opens another tab on the computer and frantically starts typing. 'And look, there's more,' he says, eyes wide. 'Check this out.' He points to another archived article he's come across.

Jack skims over Kenny's new find. 'Wow, you're right! It looks like more kids have gone missing from this place.'

All four jostle to get vantage of the screen. The report mentions another two orphaned children having vanishing back in 1936.

They stare at each other in stunned silence. Max is the first to speak, her words irrefutable. 'Ruby, you asked for flags. I think we just got them.'

Peanut jumps up. 'So are we going or what?'

Jack turns to the group. They all need to be on board or it's not happening. Max looks hopeful. Ruby chews her lower lip. Kenny continues to investigate. Peanut twitches with excitement. Jack can't hide a smile.

Peanut groans. 'Come *on*, guys! Let's *do* this!'

Admittedly, the articles have spiked Jack's interest. And although he's just as eager as Peanut to get the CCC up and running, he holds back from reacting to think things through. In the past, Peanut's knee-jerk reactions have landed them in hot water. He doesn't want a recap of any cock-ups like that.

Kenny turns in his seat. 'What do you guys think? It's already been a couple of weeks, and the police haven't found anything.' He shifts uneasily. 'Surely the cops would've come up with something by now. It sounds like they've hit a brick wall. Maybe they're missing something we can help them with.'

And that, right there, tips the scale in favour of going. 'I agree. How about we check this out?' Jack suggests.

Peanut jumps up and fist-punches the air. 'Woohoo!'

Max grins. 'Count me in!' She looks at Ruby. 'Ruby?'

Ruby hesitates. 'Well, I guess so.' She sighs. 'I wish I had my shield. I kinda feel naked without it.'

Peanut's thoughts visibly take a detour. His eyes bulge and his jaw drops. Jack is quick to shut his mouth, but clearly not fast enough. Ruby's eyes turn to slits. 'You'd better get your mind out of the gutter,

Charlie, if you know what's good for you!'

Jack chuckles. 'So I guess we're all in, then.'

Peanut shakes off his apparent wayward thoughts, jumps up and hoots. 'You betcha! Come on, let's go hunt down some portals!'

Just then, there's a knock at the door. Silence fills the room.

Max's eyes widen. She mouths, *Annie*.

Jack gasps. Annie would've heard Peanut's outburst.

'Maxy?' Annie's happy, sing-song voice calls through the door.

Max hesitates a moment, draws in a deep breath, opens the door and steps back. 'Wow, is that for us?' She moves aside to let Annie in.

Jack is quick to take the tray overflowing with sandwiches. 'Perfect timing, Annie! My stomach was growling.'

Peanut claps his hands. 'Food! You must've read my mind. Annie, you're the best!' He then startles Annuska by grabbing her by the waist and swinging her around the room in an impromptu waltz, humming happily to a classical tune.

Even if Annie had heard the remark, Jack figures, by the time Peanut finishes spinning her around, all her thoughts would be well and truly muddled.

Annuska presses her hand to her lips and giggles.

'Oh, Peanut! You are sveeping me off my feet,' she says in her thick Hungarian accent.

After a few more turns, she breaks from his hold and fans herself, out of breath. 'But now, ve must stop before I get it too dizzy.' She staggers to the nearby sofa and plonks herself down.

Her glowing smile assures Jack she's none the wiser.

Peanut gives Jack a secret wink, clearly impressed with himself.

Max snorts.

'So, let's eat!' Peanut dives for the tray. 'Ooh, my favourite! Schnitzel sandwiches. Annie, if only you were a few years younger ...'

Annuska barks out a laugh and clicks her tongue. 'My goodness! De tings you say!' She struggles to get to her feet, then turns to Ruby, wagging her finger. 'You vatch it dat one—he is too cheeky.' She laughs as she exits the room. The door closes behind her.

Max collapses on the sofa and lets out a drawn breath. 'Guys, that was *way* too close. Quick thinking, Peanut. I think you just saved our butts.'

But Peanut becomes too engrossed in eating to accept any accolades. After the first mouthful of Annie's scrumptious sandwich, he falls back into the Chesterfield, closes his eyes and moans.

3
OUCH!

PEANUT

Peanut groans inwardly. *What's wrong with me? Why do I keep doing this?* He sits back into the Chesterfield sofa and shuts his eyes, doing a good job of pretending to enjoy Annie's schnitzel sandwich, but really he's blasting himself. Once again, he's stuffed up. He takes a peek and sees Jack offering Max and Ruby the tray of sandwiches before taking one for himself and passing it on to Kenny. Ruby smiles at him, her face bright as she takes one. Peanut groans some more. It's been a long while since that killer smile was directed at him. Far too long. And that's all he wants. That's all he ever wants. For Ruby to smile at him. To tell him she really likes him and cares for him. And to remind him that he matters. But he knows, deep down inside, he hasn't done anything lately to truly deserve it.

Suddenly Annuska's legendary, mouthwatering schnitzel sandwiches taste like cardboard—the same cardboard he watched Ruby stomp on earlier …

He swallows hard. What was he thinking? Pulling the old ball-and-chain routine? He may as well have announced to the world that being hitched was the worst thing imaginable. Fundamentally a death sentence. No wonder Ruby flew off the handle.

But it was a gag, a joke … simply his way of bringing a smile to her face.

Peanut rubs his forehead and moans. But it was stupid.

The irony in it is that Peanut couldn't be happier for his two friends. After all that Ryker and Aelianna have been through, no other couple deserves happiness more. So why does he do and say things he doesn't really mean? Is getting a reaction to his jokes more important than sparing someone's feelings?

He looks at the way Jack treats Max. Okay, Jack isn't perfect, but Max adores him. So how is it that Jack gets it *right*, nine times out of ten, and him *wrong*, just as often? Peanut shakes his head. Although maths has never been his strong point, he can't blame his deficiency of smarts on that one.

But somewhere along the way, he must've missed the memo, that's for sure. And he'd better find it super quick if he wants to salvage what he has with Ruby. This, he already knows. But how?

Absentmindedly, he takes another bite of his sandwich and chews. He takes a moment to study Jack out of the corner of his eye. There's nothing forced about what Jack does. Thinking of others before himself is natural. That's the sort of thing Jack does. So why doesn't Peanut ever think of doing the same? Why can't *he* be the bigger person for a change?

He has no answers. It's like it's in Jack's DNA. He just knows Jack would literally give his last dollar if anyone needed it. That's the kind of guy he is. Peanut pauses to consider if he'd do the same. His lip curls. *Well, maybe not my* last *dollar …*

He chuckles at his blatant frankness.

Okay, so they're different. Almost polar opposites, really. But somehow their friendship works. For his relationship to Ruby to progress, there need to be some changes, and taking a leaf or two from Jack's book isn't a bad way to start.

4

UGGH!

RYKER

Ryker and Aelianna are at the dinner table. They've finished their meal and are discussing the conversation they had with Max yesterday. They keep their voices low, careful not to stir up any unease from Ryker's parents. Although supportive of this new development the Aussies have come up with, they're still a little wary of just how much of Ryker's time, and more to the point, involvement, will depend upon its success.

Ryker takes Aelianna's hand and squeezes it. His hand feels massive, wrapped around her delicate one. Compared to him, all that's Aelianna is diminutive—except for her heart and inner strength. Here, she's undoubtably his equal, if not more.

She withdraws her hand to blow her nose, now a little puffy and red from constant rubbing. She sighs.

Ryker frowns. She's been struggling to shake off a summer cold that's taken hold. He touches her forehead. 'How are you feeling? I guess the paracetamol is keeping your temperature down.'

Her lids heavy, eyes glassy, she smiles despite her obvious weariness.

He smiles in return, then gives her a wink. 'My warrior maiden.'

Warmth colours her porcelain skin at the compliment. His heart skips a beat. He can't believe it—this gorgeous vision in front of him is real. And against all odds, she has chosen to leave her home and family to be with him. He strokes her flushed cheek. She leans into his touch, then turns to press her lips to his hand.

These past few months, since their return from the ancient realm, have been the happiest he can remember, teaching her the ways of the world and loving her reaction to everything foreign and technological. Not only has he this *goddess* by his side, he also has his mother back—cancer free and loving life again. His family, once again whole. And now, with the addition of Aelianna, life couldn't be more perfect.

He thinks back to Max's conversation last night. *The CCC would be up and running by now.* He does a mental checklist of things he needs to do tomorrow to set up the link with them. His mind races, envisaging the discovery of more portals and shutting them down. What the authorities do with them once they find them, he has no idea. As far as he's concerned, it won't be his problem. Between the Australian Defence Force and the SANDF, they'll somehow work that out.

He smiles as he thinks of his Aussie friends. *That Kenny is a genius! It goes without saying that he'll be our go-to guy for information. And of course, Jack will keep things in check. He's perfect for running an outfit like this.*

As much as Ryker would like to take the reins, he's determined to take a back seat in the running of the CCC. He knows his father would have reservations about him doing more than that.

But truth be told, since their return, he's been restless with his studies, and more than once has considered dropping out of college to join the armed forces. Of course, news like that won't go down well with his parents. And upsetting them is the last thing he'd want to do after what they've been through.

So he'll stay the course. He'll captain the CCC in South Africa, investigate the possibilities that other portals exist in his part of the world, and then report them to the authorities. He won't be alone in this. Banji and Ulan have expressed an eagerness to help. And now, with Jaeger back, he can count on his and Edra's support too. So it won't fall on his shoulders alone. The South African base will theoretically be overseen by the old gang, and of course, now, to some degree, Aelianna.

The sudden, loud vibration from his cell phone on the table almost makes Aelianna fall off her seat. She clutches at her chest and laughs.

Ryker chuckles, then squeezes her hand before answering it. His eyes light up when the caller ID indicates it's Max FaceTiming him. He presses to connect. 'Well, hello, beautiful! Were your ears burning?' He glances at Aelianna and is surprised to see a look of deep concern on her face. He laughs, realising how literally she would've interpreted his words. 'It's okay, Lia'—he chuckles—'it's Max. And her ears aren't on fire.'

Aelianna squeals; her eyes brighten. She dives onto Ryker's lap, and he pulls her in close so they can both be seen on the small screen.

Aelianna takes the phone. 'Hello, my dearest friend! I have truly missed you.'

'But Aelianna, we only spoke yesterday.' Max laughs.

''Tis not the same.' She takes the phone from Ryker and turns it over in her hands, frowning. Her shoulders slump. ''Tis as though you are entombed within this tiny contraption! If only I could embrace you as I long to do so.' She strokes the screen with tenderness and sighs. 'Alas, it is what it is, and I must be grateful for seeing you in this tiny, untouchable form.' She giggles. 'Tell me, are you well?'

Max, in her excitement, tells them that they might have a lead to a case and to expect some details from Kenny soon.

Aelianna's face lights up. 'Perhaps an opportunity to visit home? I so long to see my family again.'

Ryker stiffens and gives Max a pointed look. If he had it his way, Aelianna would never step foot in that hellhole again. Her passive involvement with the CCC pushes the boundaries already.

'Oh, hon, we won't actually be going back,' Max is quick to tell her. 'What we're doing,' she continues carefully, 'is locating these gateways to secure them and prevent more kids from falling through. That's all.'

Aelianna frowns. 'But if an unfortunate child has entered the realm, unbeknownst to the danger, should we not follow and retrieve them?'

'There are people who can do that for us,' Ryker interrupts, shifting in his seat. 'People like Captain Logan and the taskforce. Remember? And Father has formed a squad to do the same here.' He tightens his hold on her hand, then strokes his thumb over her delicate skin repeatedly, his thoughts elsewhere. 'Aelianna,' he says quietly, 'I thought you understood. We can *never* go back.'

Ryker watches as the sparkle in her eyes fades, and he immediately regrets being so blunt. He's gone and done it again. Turned Neanderthal on her. The heated discussion he and Max had only the other day about his apparent possessiveness comes to mind.

'Max, just drop it, will you?'

'How can I drop it? You're being pigheaded, and not to mention, acting like a caveman! Why can't Aelianna help? She's amazingly clever. Believe in her! You never know, she could turn out to be your best asset.'

'Look, I don't want to talk about it.'

'I can see you don't, but I think we should,' she'd persisted. *'What's eating you? Do you think she might be tempted to return for good? Is that it?'*

Ryker didn't have a comeback to that. He'd just gritted his teeth and said nothing.

'So I'm right, aren't I?'

Of course, she was right. Ryker had lost her once; he couldn't risk losing Aelianna again.

'Oh, Ryker!' Max sighed. *'Don't you know how much Aelianna loves you? And not only you, she loves her new life too. Can't you see that? I hear nothing else*

when we talk. It's understandable she misses her family, but she never, ever, wants to go back to the forest to stay.'

Hearing it had made him feel like a jerk. And knowing that he's thinking it again now makes him flinch. In the time she's been here, Aelianna has not once shown him any cause to doubt what they have together. So why the insecurities?

He shakes his head and makes a mental note to (as Max so eloquently put it) pull his head in!

Ryker looks at Aelianna, squeezes her hand and sighs. 'I'm sorry, I'm being inconsiderate. Forgive me?'

Ryker chances a look at Max on the phone; her expression is severe. He shrugs. 'Max, give me a break. I'm trying. Okay?'

Max's eyes soften. 'You'll get there, Ryker. I know you will.'

Later that night, lying in bed, thinking of all the kinds of stupid he's been lately, Ryker's phone pings, alerting him to an incoming message. He reaches for it. There's a text from Kenny. He sits up with interest. At his side, Aelianna sleeps peacefully. Thankful the tone hadn't disturbed her, Ryker breathes out a sigh and opens the message.

*Hey Ryker, you may have heard
from Max already, but we've come
across a lead to some kids disappearing*

Ryker lets out a drawn breath, relieved it isn't a lead that requires his immediate attention.

He stops, a little surprised by his reaction. Although eager to help, he realises with sudden clarity that he needs more time to get his head around what committing to the CCC really means. Just how much is he prepared to invest in this? And how involved is he willing for Aelianna to be?

He could easily put the phone down and ignore Kenny's text, but he can't. He rubs his brow and re-reads the message. His mind races. Adrenaline kicks in. And then his curiosity gets the better of him. He opens the media links Kenny sent him and very quickly dissolves into the information he finds there.

5

THE DOGHOUSE

MAX

The adventure begins. *Finally!* Crammed in the back seat of Peanut's mum's Suzuki Jimny with Ruby, Kenny and an overladen food basket on her lap, Max sits back, closes her eyes and sighs. Who would've thought coordinating a short trip away with her friends would be so draining? It goes without saying that the five sleeping bags, two tents and five backpacks stored in the back of the small four-wheel drive are essential. But additional space for the multiple food baskets, lovingly prepared by Annie, proved to be something they hadn't considered. So now, with every possible nook and cranny occupied, Peanut behind the wheel and Jack riding shotgun, they're off.

Despite it all, Max grins with anticipation. Who knows what they'll find? Not that she's expecting much. Chances are they'll uncover nothing at all, but hey, just spending time with her friends is enough to put a smile on her face. And that's saying something. Because not that long ago, Max considered herself an outcast, avoiding all forms of social interaction like the plague. She grimaces at the memory and shrinks further back in her seat.

But that was before the realm, she reminds herself. A time when she was at her lowest. Friendless and bitter.

Things are different now.

She looks at each of her friends, an inexplicable warmth filling her belly. 'So ... is everyone's alibi tight?' she asks as they head towards the Hume Highway to begin their two-hour journey inland past the Southern Highlands to their destination—the small rural town of Mahlee. 'We're going *camping*, and there's nothing more to it. Right?'

Although Max's father has been kept in the loop about the workings of the CCC, the rest of the parents have deliberately been left in the dark, especially regarding this new venture; the topic of the realm is still a bit too sensitive for rational consideration.

And so Max promised her father she'll keep

him up to date on everything they get up to, on the condition that he, in turn, promises not to reveal anything to the other parents. Especially Kenny's.

Peanut twitches in his seat and cranes his neck to look at Max through the rear-vision mirror. 'I can't believe it! We're actually gonna check this place out! Like real private detectives! It'll be like the good old days … you know, like back in the realm.'

Ruby snorts. '*Good old days?* Are you nuts? Since when was our time in that place *good?*'

Peanut pulls up at a set of red lights, turns to look at Ruby and gives her a lopsided grin. 'It brought us together, didn't it?' He waggles his eyebrows. 'I'd say it has its merits.'

Max snorts but quickly realises her mistake and slaps her hand to her mouth.

Too late. Ruby whips around to face her. Her eyes narrow. 'Hey, whose side are you on?'

Unfair! They're both her friends, so Max would rather remain neutral on this one. With lips pressed firmly together, she does her best to look remorseful.

She exchanges a look with Peanut in the rear-vision mirror. He shrugs, his eyes sparkling. Max shakes her head. She's got to hand it to him, Peanut is nothing but determined.

Ruby's ongoing frustrations with Peanut come from a place Max is well acquainted with and, to a degree, understands. And now, for some reason, he's gone and done it again. Done something that's clearly put him back in Ruby's bad books. Though not privy this time to the how, when and where, Max has a fair idea *why* he's there. And going by the murderous look on Ruby's face, Max knows she should stay well clear and say nothing further. Aware that her relationship with Jack inadvertently stirs up problems between her two friends, Max needs to tread carefully.

Ruby notices how comfortable Jack is in showing his emotions and clearly wants Peanut to be the same. What Ruby fails to understand is that, although the two boys are as alike as chalk and cheese, what Ruby and Peanut have is basically the same as what she and Jack have. Same, but different. Peanut's struggle to display his feelings and reassure Ruby that she's his everything is his only failure.

Max sighs. She's at a loss as to how she can help Ruby any further with her supposed relationship problems. Despite Max's repeated pep talks, instead of the situation getting better, the tension between her two friends appears to be escalating.

Unfortunately, Ruby's insecurities have had a two-fold effect. Not only are they affecting the relationship she has with Peanut, but they're also causing friction between him and Max. Which explains why they've been at loggerheads lately.

Watching Ruby torment herself daily clouds Max's judgement and, ultimately, her perspective. This creates an animosity towards Peanut that Max struggles to contain. So, without meaning to, every now and then, their six-foot, never-serious, goofy friend cops Max's mounting exasperation.

Wedged against the car door, trying to figure it out, Max closes her eyes and works at the growing tension in her neck with a gentle massage. Sitting in such tight proximity seems to have amplified everyone's reactions.

'Hey, did anyone have any problems getting away?' Kenny asks, being tactful in diffusing a potentially volatile situation.

'Piece of cake.' Peanut laughs. 'My folks are cool about stuff like this, but they did grill me on the importance of safe driving. Man, I can't tell you how many times they reminded me not to drive anywhere past curfew.' He groans. 'Geez, give a guy some credit! I'm not a complete moron.'

'Same,' Kenny tells him. 'Although it's not as bad as it used to be, my parents still treat me like a kid. I'm lucky they let me come at all.'

'And without a chaperone …' Ruby laughs. 'So how did you manage to come without Leonard?'

They all know how stern Kenny's parents are and more so since his involvement with the realm travels.

Kenny shrugs. 'Yeah, well, Len's done with babysitting me, so these days we tell our parents whatever they want to hear, just to get them off our backs, then we do our own thing. Len's probably with Ming. And to answer your next question,' he says with his finger in the air, 'no, our parents *still* have no idea they're seeing each other.' Kenny groans. 'So what hope do I have? It'll be ten years before they let me date!'

Although finding this kind of strictness unfamiliar, Max respects it and is grateful to Kenny's older brother for covering for him. A trip like this wouldn't be the same without Kenny.

Jack cranes his neck to look over his shoulder. 'You can't complain, Kenny. They're finally cutting you some slack. Three months ago, they wouldn't have let you come on a camping trip with us. That's for sure.'

Peanut sniggers. 'Hell, no! Man, after that last trip, it was like we had to go through a security check each time we'd visit. Dude, what's with the thousand and one questions?' He shakes his head and chuckles. But then his hands shoot up. 'Hey, don't get me wrong, I like your mum an' all, but *man*, is she *scary*!'

The corner of Kenny's lip twitches in a crooked smile. Colour taints his cheeks. 'Tell me about it!'

'Oi, is anyone else hungry?' Peanut asks suddenly.

'I'm starving, and there's a Maccas coming up.' Before there's time to answer, Peanut flicks on the indicator to turn into the fast-food driveway.

Ruby splutters. 'Un-be-lievable! Too bad if someone had *other* plans!'

But Peanut drives on, oblivious to her reproach.

Max knows Ruby was hoping to stop on the way for a picnic. She'd baked some chocolate chip muffins—Peanut's favourite—and packed a flask of Italian coffee. It was meant to be a surprise.

Max reaches for Ruby's hand and squeezes it.

'I'm not overreacting, am I?' Ruby asks five minutes later in the women's bathroom. 'I mean, look at the difference between your guy and mine. Just now, Jack offered to get in line to place your order. Mine, on the other hand'—she laughs humourlessly—'couldn't get to the counter fast enough to put his order in first. He nearly knocked me to the curb in his hurry to get there!' Ruby sighs. 'Look, I'm all for gender equality and all, but come on! The guy is clueless! It's not like I expect him to pay my way or open doors for me. That's not what I'm saying.' She shrugs. Her eyes soften. 'A little courtesy and consideration isn't too much to ask for, is it?'

No, Max doesn't think it is. But it's up to Ruby to set the bar to a level she'll be happy with. Nothing outrageous, just something achievable. If he gives her anything less, then she needs to pull him up on it. 'Ruby, it's up to you to show people the way you want to be treated. Do you remember that line out of *My Big Fat Greek Wedding*? You know, where the mum, Maria, talks about being the neck that *turns* the head?'

Ruby frowns. 'Yeah, but I don't get how that's going to help Peanut.'

'Okay, let's look at it this way. Earlier, when Peanut nearly bowled you over, instead of cursing him under your breath, you should've called him out on it and asked him to get you a burger too. Peanut would do anything for you. You know that. He just needs to be shown how to do it. Turn his head, so to speak. Get it?'

Ruby huffs. 'I guess so.' She shrugs. 'Come on, we'd better go order something.'

On the way back to the table, Max notices two meals set aside for them both. She first looks at Peanut—he's downing his burger faster than she'd think was humanly possible—and then at Jack, who's waiting to catch her eye. He gives her a wink.

She smiles. 'Thanks, Jack. That's so thoughtful.'

Ruby sighs. 'Yeah, thanks, Jack.'

Jack chuckles. 'Don't thank me, Ruby, it was Peanut.'

Ruby's jaw drops.

Max nudges Ruby and giggles. 'Careful, you'll catch flies.'

'Hey, I hope you're okay with a Big Mac?' Peanut grins at her. 'I know it's your favourite. And I thought you'd like some fries too. And water instead of a coke. Right?'

Ruby glances at Max, her eyes wide. Max nudges her again.

Ruby reaches for Peanut's hand and squeezes it. 'Perfect. Thank you.'

Peanut sits a little higher in his seat, clearly happy with himself. 'Hey, I'm just about ready for dessert,' he tells her. 'You want somethin'?'

Ruby blinks, her jaw drops. 'Um, just a coffee would be great.'

'An extra strong capp, right? Skim milk?' He gets up to go. 'Anyone else? My shout.'

Again, Ruby's jaw drops.

Kenny snorts. 'Nah, we're good, buddy. Thanks for asking, though.'

Max and Jack exchange a look. She raises her brow at him, silently asking if he had anything to do with Peanut's remarkable transformation. Jack shrugs, indicating he hadn't, but the mischievous twinkle in his eyes and lopsided grin says he may have. Max glares at him from out of the corner of her eye, calling him out on it. Jack chuckles.

Max grins. It doesn't matter where the credit lies, she's just thankful for the change. She couldn't imagine the next few days without it. A totally unbearable time for everyone, for sure.

6

THE JOKERS

JACK

The second leg of the drive to Mahlee proves to be more enjoyable than the first. On form and firing on all cylinders, Peanut entertains them with his shenanigans, telling them one joke after the other; Ruby, his most avid fan.

As they drive, Jack debates what to do when they first arrive—have a snoop around the orphanage while there's ample daylight or try to locate the two boys responsible for the prank. Although he's itching to see the derelict building firsthand, he settles with the more rational decision to find out as much as they can by talking to the primary mischief-makers, Riley Tailor and Bill Flaherty. He wonders whether Kenny had any luck locating the boys through the internet.

Max turns in her seat to face Kenny. 'So where do we start, Kenny?' It appears that Jack and Max are on the same wavelength.

Kenny slaps his forehead. 'Argh, I forgot to tell you. Last night I got in contact with Riley … you know, the missing boy's brother.'

'No way!' Peanut cries out excitedly. 'How d'ya manage that?'

'Well, believe it not, it wasn't that hard,' Kenny tells them as he leans forward and passes a piece of paper he retrieved from his shirt pocket to Jack. 'I just looked him up in the phone directory. Fortunately, Tailor is an uncommon spelling for a surname—there's only one family in the region with that name.

'So I rang,' he continues, 'and as I started to explain who I was, something weird happened.' Kenny lowers his gaze. His cheeks colour. 'Riley kinda went all goofy … like he was starstruck or something. He knew all about me … saw me on the TV and said I was a hero! Can you believe it? Me? A hero?'

Peanut chuckles and looks back at him through the rear-vision mirror. 'Don't ya get it, buddy? We're famous!'

Kenny blinks several times and shakes his head. 'Well, anyway, he's agreed to meet up with us. And he reckons we might be onto something. A portal into another dimension isn't so far-fetched, considering the way his brother and friends have vanished. There's literally no trace of them. It's got the cops stumped.'

'Well, we've got nothing to lose,' Ruby says. 'A fresh set of eyes might just be what they need. With what we've been through, and what we know, we might see something they've missed.'

Although it's a good thing they now have a direction, Jack worries that information about their visit will leak out to the public. He knows only too well from experience what the press is capable of. And information like that will definitely jeopardise the assignment. 'Kenny, you told him to keep what we're doing to himself, right?'

'Yeah, don't worry.' Kenny laughs. 'I know what the likes of Trina Portabella can do. They'd stuff up our investigations in no time.'

Ruby moans. 'Pl-ea-se! Don't remind me about that woman! She'd sell her own grandmother for a story.'

They all laugh, except for Max, who scratches her head. 'I don't get it. Where was I when this happened?'

At the time of their encounter with the Channel 8 news reporter, Max was trapped in the realm with Ryker. So Ruby takes a moment to explain, clearly eager to embellish the details of the experience.

Meanwhile, Jack enters the Tailors' address into

the GPS.

Before too long, they arrive at the designated meeting point—a park down the street from the Tailor residence.

As they roll to a stop, Jack scans the near-deserted park and spots two boys close to their age sitting on a table in a sheltered barbeque area. Their feet rest on the bench, their heads slung low. Two discarded bikes lie on the ground nearby.

The boys hustle when they notice Jack and Kenny get out of the car. One of the boys hails them. He's tall and slim with light brown hair. His expression is welcoming. He makes his way towards them. The other, slightly taller, boy, takes his time coming out from the shadows. He pauses to slick back his long fair hair and adjust his jeans before making a move to meet them.

Kenny leans into the car. 'That's them … Riley and the other kid involved in the prank, Bill.'

Ruby jostles to get out, her long legs slowing her progress. 'Wait for us. We're coming too.'

Together, the friends approach the two boys, keen to hear firsthand what happened to the missing kids.

The boy with the light brown hair reaches them first. He's a bundle of excitement, bouncing around with nervous energy. 'Kenny? Wow, I can't believe you guys are really here! Celebrities, *here* in li'l ol' Mahlee!'

Jack holds back from laughing. He masks a snort with a cough.

'We spoke last night,' the boy continues. 'I'm Riley.'

The boys bump fists as a way of greeting, and Kenny makes the introductions.

The other boy, Bill, now caught up with them, ogles Ruby, openly showing a keen interest. He takes Ruby's hand in his when being introduced, holding onto it a little longer than what's socially acceptable. He lets out a slow whistle. 'Now ain't ya just somethin'! You're way prettier in real life.'

Ruby's eyes narrow. She snatches back her hand.

Peanut stiffens beside her. His eyes narrow. He steps forward, glaring down at the slightly shorter boy. Although similar in build, Peanut's puffed-out chest makes him look twice the size of the other boy.

Riley, quick to step in, grabs Bill by the arm and yanks him aside. 'Don't mind Billy-boy, here. He's had a crush on Ruby since he saw you guys on the telly.'

Bill's head whips around so fast he flinches as if from a crick in his neck. His cheeks flush pink. He slaps Riley on the back of his head. 'Mate! Why d'ya go and tell 'em that for?'

Riley rubs at the sting. 'What? These guys are here to help us find my kid brother. Remember?

There's stuff we need to do, so quit mucking around.'

'Okay, now that's sorted,' Max says with a certain tone of authority in her voice. 'Let's get on with it.'

Riley is quick to go over what happened the night of the prank. 'So apart from the footprints on the dusty floorboards the next morning, it was as if they were never there. And like we told the cops, we'd stuck around outside for a few hours, thinking they'd freak out and come running. But they never did.' Riley looks down at his feet. 'We figured they must've been okay, so we left.'

'Yeah, they definitely had more guts than what we gave 'em credit for,' Bill tells them. 'Especially that Bec. I've gotta hand it to her, she's one tough nut. I had money on her being the first to crack. I reckon I lost that bet.'

Riley pulls out his phone and shows them a photo. 'This is them. Just before we left 'em. Shaun, Liam and Bec.'

Jack takes the phone. He sees three kids, around twelve to thirteen years old, arm in arm, grinning with excitement at what they're about to do. The boy to the left is dark-skinned with green eyes, the other, on the right, is very much like Riley, dark eyes with light brown hair. In the middle is Bec, her curly blond hair tied in a messy ponytail, her blue eyes alive with mischief.

'Bec's not your typical girly-girl, you know. She's always up for a challenge—one of the boys, really.' Riley chuckles. 'She'd give any guy a run for their money. In fact, I'd back her over my own brother any day.'

At a flick of a switch, Riley turns sombre, rubbing fretfully at his forehead. 'Look, I just hope they're okay. Wherever they are.'

Bill clamps a firm hand on Riley's shoulder. 'We'll find them, mate. Don't worry. With these guys on board, those pains-in-the-necks'll be back before you know it.' He turns to Kenny. 'So tell us about this other world you guys fell into. Do ya reckon this is somethin' like that?' Bill looks at them, optimism in his eyes. 'If it is, then there's hope. Right? You guys look like you did okay, so there's a chance Sheep and the others are okay too. Yeah?'

Kenny frowns. 'Sheep?'

Riley smiles a crooked smile. 'Billy nicknamed Shaun *Sheep* … you know, based on the animated character.'

Billy scowls. 'Yeah, only because he kept calling me *Goat*!'

Riley jerks his head in Bill's direction and chuckles. 'Those two are always at each other's throats.' His smile wanes. 'Well, they used to be …'

'So … how about we head out to the orphanage?'

Jack suggests. 'The sooner we see what we're up against, the closer we'll get to solving this … if there's anything to solve, that is.' And Jack prays that they can help somehow. Coming from a big, close-knit family himself, he understands what Riley must be going through. Jack thinks of his siblings. The twins, Matthew and Oliver, are roughly Riley and Bill's age. Then there's Katie, a couple of years younger, and finally, little Meara. If anything were to happen to any one of them, Jack wouldn't know how he'd cope.

7

The Derelict Orphanage

MAX

The car rolls to a creaking stop. Heavy clouds creep soundlessly overhead, darkened fingers blanketing the greying sky. The sun disappears from view, and the temperature plunges. Max shivers and takes a moment to draw breath. She leans forward but struggles to see anything, then peers through the gaps Ruby and Kenny allow her and glimpses the remnants of a tall gated entry to a long overgrown driveway of a tree-studded estate. Two once-majestic brick pillars, on either side, stand crumbling, their purpose futile. Tossed aside, dangling from broken hinges, lie the rusted barriers, now too frail to stand alone. The tall brick wall enclosing the property has seen its share of neglect too. Graffiti defaces its former magnificence, its fortification decaying, its resolve worn away by time. An official notice, also vandalised, warns of danger and risk of penalty to any trespassers. The once-formidable entry now stands rotting before them, sanctioning access to anyone daring to enter. Again, Max shivers, wondering who in their right mind would ever voluntarily cross its darkened threshold.

Ruby snatches Max's hand and crushes it in hers, her eyes wide. Max winces, but says nothing.

Jack turns in his seat and looks out the back window. He lets out a breath, then turns his attention to them, a look of apprehension in his eyes. 'Um, I vote we wait for Riley and Bill to rock up. What d'ya reckon?'

Peanut half laughs. 'Buddy, ya won't get any arguments from me!' He shakes his head. 'Will ya get a load of this place? I'm creeped out already, and we haven't seen the orphanage yet! Those kids are nuts! What were they thinking?'

Max lets out a shaky breath. She's not the only one spooked. Knowing this makes her feel less like a coward. You would think their experience with ghosts would make this a breeze, but it doesn't. Somehow, this feels different.

'Yeah, we'll wait for the guys,' Kenny agrees. 'It shouldn't take them too long to get here. With their bikes, I reckon they know a few short-cuts here.'

And just as Kenny says it, Riley and Billy skid to a halt in front of them, creating a cloud of dust. 'C'mon, let's go.' Riley looks up at the darkening sky. Wasting no time, he leads the way.

Peanut backs the car up a little, then carefully guides them through the entrance and down the driveway, navigating around the numerous deep potholes and overgrown bushes on the disused path. The ride's a bumpy one, and Max struggles to hold on, being flung against the door one second, then onto Ruby's lap the next. The food basket smacks her in the mouth more than once. When they finally come to a halt, she adjusts herself to look out the front window and catches a glimpse of the orphanage for the first time. Her jaw drops. She struggles to get a better look, but Kenny and Ruby again block her view.

'Bloody hell!' Peanut leans forward, hugging the steering wheel to get a better look.

Max needs to step out of the car. She reaches for the door handle, but Ruby promptly yanks her back.

Ruby's pupils, dilated to the point where the amber colour of her eyes can no longer be seen, startle

Max. 'Stop!' Ruby warns. Her grip tightens. 'I've got a bad feeling about this place.'

Max breaks from the hold. 'It's okay. I'm just getting out to have a better look.'

Once outside, Max takes a moment to study the orphanage, Ruby's warning aside. She frowns. There's an abundance of blue-and-white-chequered police tape criss-crossing the front-door entrance, barricading access. Then she realises that every ground level window is broken, missing or left gaping— without *any* tape, allowing unobstructed admission. She almost laughs. The first floor is much the same.

A large dilapidated sign in front of her, similar to the one at the entrance to the property, warns of structural instability and penalties for any persons caught trespassing, squatting or vandalising.

Riley and Billy approach the car. 'So what happens now?' Riley asks. 'Do you want to have a look around inside before it gets too dark?'

Jack looks at his watch, then up at the weighted clouds. 'I was thinking of pitching camp out here, but it looks like rain. What's it like inside? Is it safe enough for us to set up in there instead?'

'Sure,' Billy tells them. 'And there's a fireplace you can use. It's nothing flash, but it's good for a bit of lighting at least.' He looks skyward. 'And yeah, they've predicted a storm tonight.'

'I'm sleeping out here,' Ruby tells them. She points a shaky finger at the building. 'Rain, hail or storm, you're not gonna catch me spending the night in there.' She grabs onto Max's arm, her eyes pleading for backup.

A distant rumble has them all looking upward to the darkening sky. Max frowns. 'Are you sure? It won't be too bad if we stick together.'

'Too right!' Peanut waggles his eyebrows. 'Stick with me, Rubes. You'll be as safe as houses. Besides, if it's gonna storm like they say it is, you'll have Buckley's to no chance of keeping a fire going out here to fend off the wild animals.'

Ruby's eyes widen, but quickly reduce to slits. She crosses her arms and pouts. 'Then I'll sleep in the car.'

Jack rubs the back of his neck and sighs. 'Look, I'd rather we all stayed together. We can't all fit to sleep in the car, Ruby.'

Jack and Max exchange glances. From his look, Max realises it's up to her to help make things right. She acknowledges him with a nod and turns to Ruby. 'I think Jack's right. We need to stick together. Let's go in while there's enough light to set ourselves up. And maybe then, if you're okay with it, we can have a look around.'

Ruby groans. Her shoulders drop. 'Argh! I wish I

had my shield.'

Billy's eyes widen. He blinks a few times. 'Whoa! So all those stories we heard are true?' He nudges Riley. 'Wow! Straight out of Marvel comics! Our very own Fantastic Four's Sue Storm with her legendary forcefield!' Billy's eyes sparkle. He leans into Ruby. 'You know what? That's totally hot!'

Peanut steps between them, puffs out his chest and crosses his arms.

Riley quickly pulls his friend back in line and pushes forward. 'Anyway, there's a room at the back where you can set up. It might've been the kitchen at one stage. That fireplace I was talking about? It's there.'

Riley descends the slope of the land to the back of the huge derelict building, and they all follow. They enter an open courtyard overgrown with weeds and littered with bits of defiled plaster, broken glass and abandoned refuse from squatters of a more recent past. Max covers her nose to block the stench. A rusted metal frame from a period long gone hints at what might have been a child's swing, secured firmly in its place, weathering the odds.

From here they climb the stairs that lead to the back entrance, careful not to fall through the rotting floorboards. They stop at the doorway, now without a door, and peer inside at the long, dark, narrow corridor. After some hesitation, they enter and make their way down it. Off to the right lies a large room with a fireplace that's seen better days.

'This is where we left them,' Riley tells them.

Max looks at the blackened walls where a fire had once taken hold but had been extinguished in time to prevent the whole building from catching alight. The other walls appear sullied with layers of images and hidden messages scrawled in a flurry of colours. Victims of aerosol cans and reckless abandon.

Riley points at the smudged footprints on the dusty wooden floorboards. 'When we came back the next morning, Billy and I found the place like this … deserted, with only a few footprints that hinted they were here. The fireplace hadn't been lit, and the rest of the building seemed like no one had been in it for years. No footprints, no nothing. Of course, the place has had the cops and detectives go over it with a fine-toothed comb since, so a lot of the evidence may be too messed up for you guys to look at and have a clear idea on what you're searching for.'

Billy scratches his head. 'But what exactly *are* you looking for?'

'A portal,' Kenny tells them. 'A passageway into another dimension.' He rubs his brow. 'And they're not that easy to spot. In fact, portals are virtually impossible to see, and only become visible when they start oscillating with activity. And this only happens when someone's about to pass through them. One added advantage we have is that we've worked out that the gateways give off thermal energy, so we can use thermal-imaging goggles to detect them.' Kenny reaches into his backpack and retrieves a pair to show them.

Both boys stare open-mouthed at him.

Jack shrugs. 'I guess all this talk of portals and gateways is a bit weird when you first hear it. You'll get used to it.'

Max bites her lip to hide a smirk. To her friends, Kenny's extensive knowledge of most things doesn't surprise them … it's something they've come to expect. But for their new friends, Kenny's fountain of knowledge must seem strange, to say the least.

Billy opens and closes his mouth a few times— looking very much like a fish out of water. 'Kenny, mate, you lost me at *oscillating!*

Kenny's cheeks colour.

Max grins and shakes her head. His incurable shyness still blows her mind. 'You've got to understand,' she begins to explain to Billy, 'our Kenny's super smart. He knows stuff that your average kid doesn't. He often breaks out with wads of useful information, so you'll soon get used to him talking about stuff most of us just don't get.'

Kenny shrinks from the praise. His complexion reddens further. 'Yeah, so, um, I'll just go get us some wood for the fire.' He turns and makes his escape.

Riley nudges his friend—and not too subtly. Billy scowls. 'Hey! What did I say?'

'Go and apologise, you twit. You embarrassed him!'

Jack shakes his head. 'Look, you're better off letting it go. He hates fuss.'

Riley gawks. 'Far out! Smart *and* modest. What a legend!'

Max recalls Kenny telling them that Riley became a little starstruck when he first phoned him. And she's not surprised. Kenny's awesome. He's everyone's hero. They'd still be stuck in the ancient realm had it not been for Kenny and his brilliant mind.

While they wait for Kenny to return, they take steps to prepare the fireplace, Jack taking the lead with his knowhow. Once done, they arrange the sleeping bags to border it.

A short period passes before Kenny comes back. Without drawing attention to himself, he slips by them to dump a load of sticks he'd found outside.

After that, Riley suggests he shows them around. Together, they decide to inspect the lower level. Riley leads. Kenny, with the trusted thermal goggles firm on his face, follows close behind, with Billy, Peanut and Ruby.

Max shadows Jack at the rear, careful not to trip over the multitude of rubbish at their feet or drop into one of the many gaping holes in the floorboards.

With senses on high alert, her heart racing, she takes in each room and every darkened corner. Her gut sits heavy. She doesn't know what it is about this place, but there's definitely something wrong with what she's feeling. She tries to shake it off, reasoning that it's an overreaction to what she'd read while researching the place on the internet.

Suddenly, her skin crawls. A shiver runs down her spine. She looks over her shoulder, sensing a presence, but there's no one there. Her breathing accelerates. And then movement, caught from out of the corner of her eye, has her heart thumping at a gallop. She clutches her chest, praying her heart doesn't give up on her now. She looks ahead at the others. *Did anyone else see that?* Clearly, they hadn't. They move onward. She takes a moment to settle her nerves before following—staying a little closer to Jack.

Her friends stop to look into every dilapidated closet, cupboard and locker, searching for clues. As they delve deeper into the recesses of each room, Max can't help but feel more and more overwhelmed by the strange eeriness escalating with her every step. A surge of adrenaline courses through her veins. Her chest aches. She's had enough. She's ready to run. But on they go.

They exit one room to enter another. But this room feels worse. Air, thick with an unimaginable sense of despair and suffering. The wall's hidden secrets seep from the darkened corners to taunt her.

Something tugs her hair. Hard. Her breath hitches. The room starts to spin. Unable to utter a word, she grabs Jack's shirt.

He turns to steady her. 'Max?'

She can hear him, but is powerless to talk. Inwardly, she's screaming a warning for them to get out, to run. Something's not right about this place.

And then she feels herself being lifted and carried to the back room. Her eyes close. Soon, the sensation of suffocation wanes. Her breathing steadies. Jack lowers her to the floor and places something soft beneath her head. She feels his breath on her clammy skin. 'Max?'

Her eyes open. She blinks a few times.

Jack leans in closer, his eyes dark. 'Hey, are you okay?'

Ruby dives to Max's side. 'What happened? You kinda freaked us out.'

The others surround her.

She looks at them. What should she say? That she experienced a paranormal phenomenon? That a ghost just yanked her hair? Peanut would only laugh and remind her that some of their best friends were once ghosts.

But somehow, this is different. The energy she picked up wasn't a positive one.

Her eyes squeeze tight. Could she have imagined it? She rubs at the sting lingering at the back of her head. No, she most definitely hadn't.

She sits up and looks about them. They're safe. The sensation wanes.

She forces a smile. 'Pretty pathetic, huh?'

Jack frowns.

'I'm okay,' she tells him. 'I guess all this talk of the place being haunted caught up with me. Stupid, right?' Jack's expression doesn't alter. She takes his hand. 'Hey, I'm fine. Really. I must've held my breath too long. That's all. Stupid rookie error.'

Jack taps her cheek and grins.

Her lip curls. 'Note to self ... remember to *breathe*.'

Her self-reprimand alters the mood.

'Hey, you should eat something,' Peanut tells her. 'Get your blood sugars up.'

He shrugs at Kenny's look of surprise. 'I guess. Dunno. I saw it in a movie once.' He laughs. 'Maybe we should take a break. I'm feeling kinda peckish, myself. How about some of Annie's apple strudel?'

He looks about to locate one of the food baskets, sees none, then dives for Max's backpack.

Half-way through rummaging, he stops. 'Oi, what's this?' He turns to look at Max, holding up a large white drawstring bag with a red cross plastered on it, and a *please-explain* expression on his face.

Kenny laughs. 'Come on, Peanut! Have you ever known Max to go anywhere without her first-aid kit?'

Peanut pries it open and searches through the medical supplies, pulling out all sorts of heavy-duty items. 'Bloody hell! What were you expecting to do with this?' He holds up the compact leg splint Max had packed that morning.

Max feels her face flush.

Ruby laughs. 'Geez, Max, you've really got everything covered this time.' She winks at Jack, clearly recalling the time he'd broken his leg. 'Shame you can't do your *healing* thing here. It'd save you carrying around a whole medical supply shop.'

'Far out, Max!' Peanut cries out. 'Your so-called *kit* takes up most of the space in your backpack. There's hardly room for any of Annie's goodies!' His shoulders slump. 'Looks like I'll have to go back to the car for the food baskets.'

Max's lip curls. 'I've packed some cookies— they're in a container down the bottom. Knock yourself out.'

While Peanut busies himself with the task of locating the biscuit tin, Max takes a moment to think back to what just happened. Although being able to fool her friends, she can't pretend to ignore what her sixth sense screams about this place. Ghosts, spectres, spirits … whatever you choose to call them, something paranormal resides within its crumbling walls. And it's clear they're not very happy.

So, it would appear, the decaying, derelict orphanage isn't as abandoned as they were led to believe.

8
Delusion

JACK

The fire crackles, safely contained in the old hearth. Jack remains by Max's side as they bunk down for the night. After the scare she gave him earlier, flashbacks of her limp, unconscious body being dumped in the realm's ancient forest by Herodus' men returned to haunt him. He nearly lost her then, and it just about destroyed him. Now more than ever, he's determined to keep her in his sights.

He snuggles down into his sleeping bag, pulling the covers to his chin. It's a little draughty in the room, and the air has a bite to it. Max looks at him and smiles. Her eyes close but snap open again when he yanks her sleeping bag towards him. She's way too far from him. She needs to be closer. Again, she smiles. He takes her hand and squeezes it. Now satisfied, his lids grow heavy. He listens as Peanut, Ruby and Kenny toss and turn, trying to find comfort. Riley and Billy had left earlier with the promise to return first thing in the morning and take up the search again.

Outside, as predicted, a storm brews. Jack listens as a gale picks up, howling through the cavernous building. And if he lets himself believe it, he could swear the wind was trying to say something. Lightning suddenly cracks through the sound of the gale. The room lights up. He jolts. His imagination toys with his composure. He shakes it off and laughs. *Great! More atmosphere. That's all we need!*

Very quickly, the rain comes. Thankfully, the windows are boarded up, so there's no dilemma there. Although from the sounds of things, the wind's doing its best to create havoc … thrashing at the fortified openings.

Jack snuggles further under the cover of his sleeping bag. He loves listening to the sound of the rain. It soothes him. He looks across at Max, curled up at his side, her breathing shallow and even. He thinks about what happened earlier. He knows there's more to her fainting spell than what she's letting on. For some reason, she's holding back from opening up to him. He's learned that Max picks up on things way before most. Some kind of intuition. That time Ryker was in trouble in the Dark Forest and close to death, she saw it all in a dream.

Before the realm, Jack generally didn't believe in such things, but after what he's witnessed, he can't deny it—Max has a gift. Her premonitions have been bang on the money. He's tried talking to her about it, curious to know exactly what she sees and feels when it happens, but each time he approaches the topic, she clams up. He can tell it freaks her out, so he doesn't push the issue.

The fire, snapping and popping, comforts his troubled thoughts. The sound, so familiar, reminds him of the camping trips he's taken with his family, and it relaxes him somewhat. But still his mind races. Unable to find sleep, he goes over what happened earlier. Perhaps there was something he may have missed that Max had picked up on. Yes, the place reeks of history and hard times, but there's nothing spooky about it. The rooms are trashed, and there's clear evidence that squatters have used the place in the recent past, but there's nothing to suggest paranormal activity that he can tell. But that's not saying much—he's no expert. And even if there was, they've experienced ghosts before. Admittedly, it was a little hard to get their heads around in the beginning, but not triggering any drawn-out trauma.

Jack sits up, crosses his legs at the ankles and rests on his arms behind him. He looks about the spacious room. There's really nothing glaringly obvious to get suspicious about. Yes, some of the floorboards are missing—probably used for firewood. Smashed glass from the boarded-up windows litter the ground. The built-in cupboards and closets have been stripped of their doors and trashed. There's a large flattened cardboard box and a wooden packing crate in one corner—perhaps used as makeshift furniture. He thinks back to what he saw in the other rooms: a couple of mouldy mattresses strewn here and there; some abandoned bits of clothing, blankets, newspapers, and empty drink cans and beer bottles.

He closes his eyes to listen for anything out of the ordinary. There's the sound of the creaking window shutters outside as they dangle from their hinges, flapping and banging in the wind, and the whistling from the gale as it picks up speed and races through the hollow structure. But it's just what he'd expect from something so beaten and neglected. Jack can't find anything that screams 'haunted'. It's just a run-down, old building that's seen better days.

Jack thinks back to what Riley told them earlier. When he and Billy turned up the day after the prank, the whole place looked undisturbed apart from this back room. Jack frowns. *There has to be more to it.*

Jack yawns and settles back down, cradling his head in his hands. They'll have a better look in the morning, but now he needs some sleep. He rolls onto his side to face Max. She looks peaceful. He inches a little nearer and places his arm across her waist. He leans in towards her; their heads bump. His lids become heavy, and in moments he's asleep.

A sudden chill during the night stirs Jack awake. For a moment, he's disorientated, but the dying embers in the fireplace soon remind him where he is. The storm has passed. He snuggles closer to Max, seeking the warmth he needs, then settles to doze again. But, through hooded eyelids, he sees something that shocks him. He sits upright, completely awake, and rubs at his eyes, not truly believing what he's seeing. And then, just like that, it's gone. His heart pounds. He struggles to breathe.

His gasping causes Max to stir. She jerks upright. 'Jack! What is it?' She scans the room. 'Did you see something?'

'I … I'm not sure.' He questions whether he'd imagined it.

She grabs his hand, almost painfully. 'What do you mean?'

'I … I can't tell if it was real or a dream.' *Yeah, that must be it; it must've been a dream.*

'But what did you see?' Her gaze darts around the

room. She sits up on her knees, seizes Jack by the arms and shakes him. 'Jack!' Max's breathing accelerates.

Jack doesn't want to freak her out, but there's no other way of explaining it. 'Look, I can't be sure, but I think I might've seen a ghost.'

She gasps.

'But, like I said, it could've been a dream for all I know. I was half asleep when it happened.'

Their anxious whispering stirs Kenny and Peanut awake.

'What's happening?' Kenny asks with a yawn. He stretches and rubs at his neck.

'C'mon, guys! Some of us are trying to sleep here,' Peanut grumbles. He rolls over, adjusts his sleeping bag and prepares to settle.

'Jack just saw a ghost!' Max blurts out.

Kenny and Peanut sit up. 'A *what*?'

Ruby wakes. 'Huh? What's going on?'

Max dives to her side. 'Ruby! Jack just saw a ghost!'

Ruby gasps. She grabs Max's arm; her gaze darts around the room.

Jack jumps to his feet. 'Now hold on, Max, I said it could've been a dream. I wouldn't bet my life on it or anything. So stop freaking everyone out.'

Kenny lunges for his backpack, rummages through it and pulls out an electrical device. He switches it on. A small, round green LED glows briefly in the darkness before fading. 'Tell me where you saw it,' he tells Jack, his voice unstable.

Jack pauses to examine the device. 'Far out, Kenny! What's that?'

'Later.' Kenny cuts him short. 'Focus! Show me *exactly* where you saw it.'

Momentarily distracted by Kenny's assertiveness, Jack points to the spot where he saw the illusion. Clearly, Kenny is taking things seriously.

With unsteady hands, Kenny aims the device in the direction Jack indicates. A series of lights on the screen of the device flutters, fluctuating between green and a yellowy orange. He points it around the room as if chasing something. The lights on the screen fade. He quickly returns it to the spot Jack first indicated, and the lights on the screen become yellowy orange again. Kenny gasps.

Jack's senses heighten.

Max runs to his side and burrows into him.

'Kenny! What the heck's going on?' Peanut's outburst makes Kenny jump. He carelessly turns the gadget onto Peanut. The screen turns red.

'Everyone, switch off your phones! Quick!' Kenny instructs.

No one questions him. They dive into their pockets for their phones.

Kenny then directs the gadget back to where Jack saw the entity. 'Okay, if you're still here, talk to us.'

Peanut splutters. 'Come off it, Kenny. You're kidding me. Right?'

Ruby pounces onto Peanut, muzzling his mouth.

Kenny tries again. 'We're not going to hurt you. We're just looking for the three kids who went missing. We want to help,' Kenny explains to the darkness. 'So speak to us.'

Jack exchanges a worried look with Max. He doesn't know what to think. Has Kenny lost his marbles? Suddenly, his attention is diverted to the device in Kenny's hand—the screen again turns red.

Kenny jumps, almost dropping the device. He leaps to Jack's side, hands him the gadget and instructs him to keep it aimed in that direction. He then dives into his kit once more to retrieve what looks like a television remote control. His hands tremble as he activates it. He lets out a shaky breath. 'Okay, we're listening.'

Jack stares down at the screen on the device in his hand, beads of sweat forming on his brow. Incredulously, within moments of Kenny asking, the lights on the screen turn red, then orange, then red again, as though picking up on some kind of frequency beyond their hearing capability.

A cold shiver runs down Jack's spine.

9
EMF

MAX

Max's heart just about stops. She questions whether she'd imagined the colour change on the gadget in Jack's hand, but the look on his face tells her she hadn't. Peanut and Ruby spring to their side.

'We're listening,' Kenny repeats, slowly getting to his feet and inching his way back towards them, the remote-control thingy extended out in front of him.

But all eyes are on the device in Jack's hand. The screen remains red. No one breathes. Suddenly, something unseen whooshes past them, almost knocking them to the ground.

And then, the light on the screen turns green before fading.

Kenny drops the gadget he's holding and snatches the one back from Jack. He sweeps the room, pointing it in every direction. The indicator lights remain quiet.

Kenny drops to his haunches, visibly shaken. The device topples to the floor. He steadies himself and sits, draws his knees to his chest, buries his face in his lap and takes a moment to compose himself.

Max's chest aches from what just happened. So she was right. It wasn't her imagination. Something unnatural haunts this place. If ever she needed proof to believe it, she just got it.

Kenny sniffs and swipes his nose with his sleeve.

Max looks down at him and, despite her own shock, squats by his side and tries to console him, stroking his back. 'We … we're here for you, Kenny.' She gulps down mouthfuls of air and tries to calm her racing heart. 'Take … just take your time.'

Kenny clears his throat, removes his glasses and swipes the wetness from his eyes. 'I don't believe it. I mean, I *do* believe it, but it's surreal. Did you guys catch that?' He shakes his head. 'Tell me I didn't imagine what just happened.'

Jack, ashen-faced and speechless, struggles to put two words together. 'Mate! Far out. But what the hell?' He runs his fingers through his hair repeatedly, then turns to look at the others. 'Okay, so there's no denying it. Something just happened. But *what?*

'Yeah!' Peanut picks up the device with the coloured LEDs and studies it. 'What *is* this? We all saw the lights changing colour, and I guess we all kinda get what it does. But how?'

'And what's this thingamajig?' Ruby reaches for the discarded gadget at Kenny's feet. 'It looks like some kind of recorder.' She examines it a little closer, presses a few buttons and waits.

Kenny jumps to his feet and flies to Ruby's side.

Max leans in closer to have a better look. She holds her breath, not sure what to expect. In the deathly silence, she vaguely hears something that could only be described as static. She frowns. *Is that it?* Her gaze darts to the others. They must've heard the same thing. They look just as puzzled.

Ruby rewinds it, then adjusts the volume to maximum. They huddle in closer.

And then they hear it.

'Maaax! Heeelp meee!'

Max stumbles backwards. Jack catches her.

'Now!' the voice cries out from the recorder.

Ruby flings the gadget from her grasp. Peanut grabs it, mid-flight, and offers it to Kenny. But Kenny takes a few steps back with his hands up, his head shaking.

Peanut now has both devices, one in each hand.

His eyes darken. 'Hey! This ain't some kinda joke, is it? Because I'll tell ya right now, it ain't funny!'

Kenny recoils. 'No way! I promise.'

Jack rubs his chin. 'Are you sure, Kenny? You didn't plant that message yourself to spook us? 'Cause I'm with Peanut on this one. It's not funny.'

Kenny appears horrified that Jack would even think it. 'I swear, Jack! It's this place. It's haunted! The recording isn't a trick. It doesn't lie.'

Peanut shoves one of the devices under his arm, and with a free hand, yanks Ruby to his side. Ruby grabs the LED gadget from Peanut and sweeps the room with it. The LEDs remain quiet.

The five friends stare at each other in silence.

Jack frowns. 'But I don't get it! Did any of you hear anything? I know I didn't.'

Kenny adjusts his glasses; a tendency he has when he's agitated. He draws in a deep breath. 'At least I can explain that.' He takes a moment. 'We didn't hear anything, because these digital recording devices pick up on things we can't hear.' He frowns and shakes his head as if trying to process what's going on in his mind. 'When it comes to detecting paranormal activity, you're gonna be blown away with the stuff that's out there. It definitely has *my* head spinning.'

He scratches his head. 'So, okay,' he continues, 'there's this thing called EVP—*electronic voice phenomenon.* Our ears aren't capable of tuning into voices and sounds made by ghosts and the like. The sounds they make can only be detected on these kinds of recordings. It has something to do with the electromagnetic energy ghosts give off.' Kenny looks at their blank faces. 'Um …which is what this gizmo does … the one with the coloured lights.' He reaches for the device in Ruby's hand. 'This is called an EMF detector. An *electromagnetic field* detector. It's designed to locate spirits.' Kenny looks at the vague expression on their faces. 'Because spirits are made up of EMF and have been known to manipulate the EMF around them.'

'Un-be-lievable!' Peanut's eyes go round. 'Kenny, where's all this verbal vomit coming from? Have we fallen through a portal and don't know it or somethin'? Mate! Really?' Peanut clicks his tongue. 'And to think they actually make stuff for this kinda thing!'

Kenny laughs. 'Hunting the paranormal is big business. I told you you'd be surprised.'

Max studies the darkened room, a little spooked, but at the same time, a little relieved. Kenny has provided them with proof—this place is haunted. It's unmistakable. He said it earlier—the gadgets don't lie. Yet, still, she struggles to get her head around it all.

She looks at Kenny in awe. The depth of Kenny's

knowledge on these things astounds her just as much as it does Peanut. She takes a moment to digest everything that just happened.

She frowns. 'So why did you ask us to turn off our mobiles?'

Again, Kenny adjusts his glasses. 'That? Well, I didn't want the energy coming from the phones to confuse what the detector was picking up on. What we saw on the EMF device was true. It was picking up on the ghost.'

Kenny stops suddenly and dives for his backpack. He pulls out the laptop and hits a few buttons, but ceases when he realises it's not working. He groans. 'I should've known. It's flat.'

'Flat?' Jack asks in surprise. 'I thought you charged it before we left this morning.'

Kenny shrugs. 'I did.'

Jack frowns. 'Then that should've lasted the whole weekend. Shouldn't it? It's not like we've been using it.'

Kenny smiles a crooked smile. 'No, Jack, *we* haven't been using it ... but *they* have!'

Max gulps. '*They* ... as in *plural?* Don't tell me there's more than *one!*

Kenny shrugs. 'I can't tell you how many there are, Max. All I know is these gadgets wouldn't be doing this kinda thing on their own. Ghosts absorb energy in whatever form they can.' He looks at his mobile. 'Hey, I'm nearly flat. How's everyone else?'

Max pulls out her phone, switches it on and sees she has only ten percent of her battery left. 'But this was fully charged …'

'My point exactly,' Kenny tells her. 'Luckily, I thought to bring battery back-up.' He pulls out two power banks and a few packets of AA batteries. 'Jack and I will recharge our phones, but the rest of you, keep yours switched off. Save whatever charge you've got.' He pats the AA batteries. 'And these are spares for the devices.'

Max does as Kenny instructs them to do.

Again, she looks about the room and groans. *Ghosts!* It's almost too much. Should they just call it quits and leave? She looks at the others. Is she the only one thinking of piking out? She rubs her temples, feeling a whopper of a headache coming on. She'll take some paracetamol before it takes hold.

It's then that she notices her first-aid kit isn't where she had left it. She frowns, then shrugs. It probably got kicked to the side in all the madness. She'll look for it later. More importantly, she thinks back to the message on the recording. There's no mistaking what they all heard. It clearly singled *her* out. But why her? And how did it even know her name? *Weird!* A shiver runs down her spine.

She rubs her arms at the chill. Clearly, her experience with ghosts hasn't prepared her for what's happening right now.

Jack tugs her into a side hug. His warmth instantly makes her feel safe.

'Hey, I think we need to build up the fire before doing anything,' Jack says to them. He turns to Kenny. 'We could use what's left of the stack you brought in earlier.'

Kenny looks at the dwindling pile and frowns. 'We're running low.' He looks elsewhere. 'Hey, maybe we can use that,' he suggests, pointing to a broken wooden packing crate. 'Might keep it going for a bit.'

'Yeah, but for how long?' Jack looks about the room with a frown. 'We can't use what's left of the cupboards. Chances are they're coated with paint that's most likely toxic.'

He grins at Max's questioning look. 'Hey, I'm no *Master Google*. It's just that I've helped Dad with some reno stuff before. There could be lead in the paint. It's something they did before, not knowing how harmful it can be.'

Oh! Useful. Max had no idea. But enough of that. They need more firewood to see them through till the morning. She notices again the gaping holes in the floor. 'What about the floorboards?'

He shrugs. 'I guess we won't be the first ones to do

it.' He turns to the boys, 'Hey, guys, give us a hand?'

Before letting her go, Jack pulls her into a hug and smiles down at her. 'Are you okay?'

She smiles at his thoughtfulness and nods. With Jack by her side, how could she *not* be?

He strokes her cheek with the back of his hand, then stops. His brow furrows. He reaches for something around her neck. She'd completely forgotten about it—her new silver locket. She hadn't shown it to him yet.

He leans in to have a closer look. 'Hey, when did you get this?'

Max smiles. Her father had given it to her that morning. 'It's from Dad—an early birthday present.'

He turns it over in his hand. 'Really? Your birthday isn't for another three weeks.'

She laughs. 'I guess he couldn't wait.' She takes it from him to look. Although calling it a locket, strictly speaking, it isn't one. She had hoped she could place a photo of her mother in there, but the simple, heart-shaped pendant didn't allow it. It's sealed. All the same, she loves it. 'Pretty, huh?'

Jack smiles. 'Almost as pretty as you.'

In the background, they both hear Peanut groan and click his tongue in disapproval.

Jack laughs. 'Come on, let's help the others with the boards.'

Jack hands her a torch and squats by one of the openings in the floor. He yanks at the floorboards. A few come away easily, but some are nailed down securely.

Max gets to her knees and angles the light to help Jack with what he's doing. She peers a little closer, curious to see what lies below. Beneath one of the lifted boards and between the timber beams supporting the floor sits a rusted metal box. 'Hey, look at that!' Max reaches down and lifts it from its hiding place.

The others gather to look over her shoulder.

'Cool, a hidden treasure!' Peanut's enthusiasm has Max eager to see what's inside. It could be something valuable, like money or jewels.

Ruby claps her hands. 'Ooh, this is exciting!'

The front latch screeches and groans in protest as Max struggles to unclasp it. So do the rust-encrusted hinges of the lid when she finally manages to force it open. Once done, she shines the torch in to reveal its contents. She frowns. A few small rocks, some shells and what appears to be a collection of bones. Not the kind of treasure she was hoping for. But, given its hiding spot, interesting nonetheless.

'Someone's treasure all right,' Kenny says excitedly. 'This is so cool! I wonder how long it's been here?'

Max regards the way every piece has been carefully

packed. 'I wonder if they belonged to one of the kids from the orphanage? Cherished finds, hidden with care.' She smiles as she picks up each piece, imagining the stories behind them.

Ruby points to something in the box. 'That can't be a tooth, can it?'

Max sees what Ruby is referring to. Something long and white, wedged at the bottom of the box. It's about twenty centimetres in length with a pointed end. Max carefully clears a path to get to it. Once she has it, she stops a moment to admire it, then holds it up for everyone to look at.

'Whoa, it's huge!' Peanut takes it from her to examine it closer. 'Will you get a load of this! What the heck did this come from? It must've been massive!'

'Hey, what's that? Can I have a look?' Kenny reaches for something that Max had pulled out earlier while rummaging to get to the tooth. He studies it for a while, turning it over in his hand a few times, and frowns. 'Hmm …'

Max shines the light on the object of Kenny's distraction. It really is quite odd-looking. Something she's never seen before.

Suddenly, Kenny's eyes go wide. 'No!' He mumbles something unintelligible under his breath and shakes his head. 'It can't be.' He snatches the torch from Max to examine it better. Everyone's interest is piqued. Kenny turns the object around so many times, it has Max dying to hear what Kenny thinks they've found.

He stops, looks up and gulps. 'Do you guys know what this is?' His voice is barely a whisper.

Jack takes it from him to have a closer look. 'I've seen pictures of this. Is it a nautilus shell? We learnt about them in maths—something to do with logarithms.'

'Close,' Kenny tells him, his eyes suddenly alive with mischief. 'But you're about *seventy million years* off the mark.'

Jack stops short. 'Say what?'

Peanut splutters and laughs. 'Come on, Kenny! That's a bit of a stretch.'

Colour rises up Kenny's neck to taint his cheeks. 'I'm telling you, I'm nearly one hundred percent positive …'

'Look, we all know you've been blessed with a healthier dose of grey matter than most,' Peanut interrupts, 'but I reckon this time you're way off. As if!'

Kenny shrinks back.

Jack gives Peanut a sharp nudge.

'Come on, Jack. Don't tell me you believe him?' Peanut sniggers. 'Man, you're so gullible. Kenny's just pulling your leg. Of course, it's a … a whatchamacallit shell. Tell 'em, Kenny.'

Kenny looks down at his sneakers.

Peanut persists. 'Come on, Kenny, admit it. *Seventy million years?* You're kidding, right?'

Kenny shrugs.

Peanut grabs Kenny in a head lock and messes up his hair. 'I knew it! You tricker. But I'll tell ya somethin', you nearly had me going there.' He laughs. 'Nice try, kiddo.'

Max inwardly groans. Kenny was clearly on to something there. Something important. And instead of standing up for himself, Kenny clammed up. She bites back from saying something. Pulling Peanut up on it would only create a scene and embarrass Kenny further. She makes a mental note to talk to him about it later.

10
HOLY SPRITZ

JACK

Jack lets slide what Peanut just did to Kenny … for now, anyway. He'll pull him up on it later. He could see that Kenny had discovered something interesting about that weird coiled shell thingy and was keen to tell everyone. But Peanut had to open his big mouth and say something without thinking, and so put a stop to it. Jack sighs and looks at his impulsive friend. He rubs the nape of his neck. No, now's definitely not the time. There are other, more pressing issues. The fire, for one, needs building. They'll be in total darkness soon if they don't do something about it. Jack considers pulling up some more floorboards, but feels uneasy defacing the old building further, especially now, after finding the rusted box. There's a story to why the box was hidden there. Treasures from the past, stashed for safe keeping. Somehow, knowing this makes it feel wrong. Without a word, he goes about replacing the boards they pulled up earlier. He shrugs at the questioning look he gets from his friends.

'I remember seeing some wooden crates in the room down the hall,' Kenny says thoughtfully. 'Maybe they'll do.' He looks at Jack. 'Give us a hand?'

Jack smiles.

They bring back the crates and begin to split them for the fire. Thankfully, while they're doing this, Kenny's EMF detector remains quiet. A shiver runs down Jack's spine as he remembers the eerie voice on the recording—or, more to the point, its message. He looks across to where Max is sitting, exchanging whispers with Ruby. *So why did the ghost single her out? And how did it know her name?* With a sudden unsettled thought, he stiffens. He scans the room. *Are we being watched now?* He looks to the EMF detector for confirmation. But nothing. It lies quiet.

Jack looks at the time on his watch. Having to wait in near darkness, at 4:00 am, is unravelling his composure. He wishes the sun would hurry and rise.

'Hey, has anyone seen my first-aid kit?' Max asks, rummaging through their belongings on the floor.

She lifts the backpacks, looks under the sleeping bags, then goes through her own kit again. 'Peanut, any idea where you put it?'

Peanut walks up to her, scratching his head and looking around. 'I left it, um … right here, I think.'

The friends join in the search. It's then that Jack spots something. Where there were random footprints on the dusty floor previously, now there's an obvious drag mark. He shines the torchlight on it to get a better look. 'Hey guys, check this out.' The mark leads out the door and into the long corridor just off the room. He estimates that it'd be the same size as Max's first-aid kit. He goes to investigate, but stalls at the doorway. Behind him, his friends almost bowl him over. They crane their necks to look over his shoulder.

'You're kidding me! They've gone and nicked Max's first-aid kit?'

Ruby turns to Peanut. 'Who has?'

He shrugs. 'The ghosts, of course!'

Ruby scowls. 'Yeah, right, Peanut! Because first-aid kits are highly sought after. Especially when you're *dead!*' She clicks her tongue. 'Stop trying to freak us out! This place is spooky enough!'

'Oh my God! GUYS …'

Peanut, Ruby, Max and Jack whip around to see Kenny pointing at the EMF detector on the floor, his finger shaking. It's red. Suddenly, a whoosh of air rushes past them. The light fades from orange to green before going blank.

Jack gulps. 'It might sound completely bonkers, Ruby, but I think Peanut might somehow be right.'

Peanut blinks several times. 'What the hell's going on?'

'Charlie, I wish you wouldn't use that word.'

'What word?'

'*Hell!*' Ruby gets out from between gritted teeth. 'Because, like it or not, you might not be that far from the truth.'

Jack swallows hard. 'What do we do? Do we try to track it down?' Secretly, he hopes they all agree to wait until daybreak, but Peanut pushes past him, grabs the torch and inches into the hallway.

'Wait!' Kenny calls out in a loud whisper.

Peanut jumps and throws himself hard up against the wall. 'What! What d'ya see?'

'Nothing,' Kenny says, hiding a smirk. 'I'll just grab the EMF detector.'

Peanut clutches at his chest. 'Far out, Kenny! You scared the crap out of me!'

Kenny darts into the room and returns seconds later with the device. Before going further, he points the gadget past Peanut, down the long dark hallway.

Max peers around Jack and lets out a ragged breath.

Her grip on him tightens. 'Good, it looks clear.'

Peanut takes a moment to regroup.

'Um, guys,' Ruby steps back with her hands up. 'I … I can't do this. I vote we don't go. Call me a chicken, but there's no way I'm going to chase after a stolen first-aid kit without a shield to protect me. Sorry, Max, but if the ghosts want your stuff so bad, let them have it.'

'Ruby, we stick together,' Jack reminds her. 'There's no splitting up the team. Okay?'

All eyes are on Ruby. She gulps loudly, then nods. They turn back to the corridor.

'Wait!' Max calls out suddenly.

Again, Peanut throws himself against the wall.

'Oh, sorry.' Max covers her mouth to hide a nervous snort, then reaches into the back pocket of her jeans to retrieve a tiny clear glass spray bottle.

Peanut just about growls. 'Will you lot quit it? You're giving me a heart attack here! What's the problem now?'

Max inches out into the corridor towards Peanut and squirts some fluid from the bottle into his face.

Peanut splutters. 'What the hell, Max!'

'*Peanut!*' Ruby snarls.

He flinches. 'Oops, sorry, Rubes.'

One by one, with bottle in hand, Max squirts them all, each getting a spritz of the clear liquid.

Lastly, she closes her eyes and does herself. 'Just a little holy water. I had Father John from the parish bless it for us.' She then stands ready, armed with the consecrated water in the tiny glass vial, poised, waiting. 'Okay, let's do this!'

Her friends stare at her in silence.

'What?' she cries out, wounded. 'You asked for protection; well, I figured we'd need all the help we can get.'

Still, they stare.

She shrugs her shoulders, then giggles. 'Well, it can't hurt, can it?'

Jack chuckles. 'No, Max, it definitely can't.'

They laugh.

With a smirk on his face, Jack takes the lead. The whole *blessing* enactment disperses his jitters and gives him the confidence he needs to follow this through. 'Come on, we've a thieving ghost to catch.' He looks at Max and gives her a wink. 'Nobody steals from my girl and gets away with it!' So, with the torch firmly clasped in his hand, Jack follows the trail of the missing first-aid kit. He stops when they reach the landing of the outdoor staircase. The drag marks end there.

Kenny dives in front of Jack, the EMF detector hovering unsteadily in front of him. For a moment the screen remains quiet. But then, to Jack's astonishment, it starts to flick intermittently to orange. Kenny races down the stairs. 'It's out there! Come on. Follow me.'

Without pausing to think, they take chase. The five friends race through the courtyard and out to an open field, thick with long grass. Jack watches the screen flicker from orange to red, as if they're closing in on it. The path becomes difficult to navigate. The overgrown vegetation, drenched from the rain, hinders their progress. Jack glances over his shoulder to make sure everyone is keeping up and suddenly smacks into Kenny, almost knocking him over. Jack takes a moment to steady him. He then looks at the screen. It's quiet.

In a frenzy, Kenny redirects the device, pointing it with purpose, sweeping it from left to right in twenty-degree increments. But no matter what direction he aims it, the screen remains inactive.

Kenny's shoulders slump. He lowers the scanner. 'We've lost it.'

Jack takes a moment to catch his breath. He stoops to rest his hands on his knees, then takes a minute to go over what just happened.

Max rubs his back. 'Hey, are you okay?'

He straightens. 'Yeah. You?'

'Maybe it was for the best we lost the signal,' she tells him.

'I agree,' Ruby says. 'What the heck were we

thinking? Running into the black of night, not being able to see one step in front of us? We could've fallen into a ditch or something.' She rubs her arms to stir up some heat. 'And now I'm cold and wet.' She huffs. 'And I can't believe I'm saying this, but how about we get back inside?'

Peanut places his arm across Ruby's shoulders and gives her a squeeze. 'I'm with you, Rubes. Let's get out of here.' He turns to go. 'We can take this up again in the morning.'

II
The Writing's On The Floor

MAX

Later that morning, they relay to Riley and Billy what happened during the night. Max still can't believe it. A ghost stole her first-aid kit! What's more, like idiots, they took off after it! And then, once dawn broke, directly after this noteworthy twilight escapade, they went out again, too eager to do nothing and incurably curious to follow up where they left off. Jack had led the way, retracing their steps down through the courtyard and into the tangled overgrowth of the field where the chase ended. Here, they advanced some twenty metres further and came to a rambling creek at the rear of the property. Almost a river.

Now, back at the orphanage, sitting with Riley and Billy by the waning fire, they debate what their next step should be.

Jack shifts in his seat. 'I hate asking this, but did the cops check the creek? You know, just in case …'

Max grimaces. She was wondering how they were going to broach a topic so delicate. With the creek so close, the chance that the kids strayed there and met their demise shouldn't be ruled out.

Riley looks down at his feet and nods. 'Yeah, they did. They got police divers in and everything.' He clears his throat. 'But they didn't find anything. Not that they were expecting to, mind you, because there weren't any signs of anyone going to the creek. But they had to check anyway. A clue could've got washed away with all the rain we've had recently.'

'So,' Billy asks hurriedly, 'you didn't end up finding the first-aid kit this morning?'

'No. At least not out there,' Ruby says. 'And we haven't plucked up the nerve yet to check out the rest of the building.'

'I can't imagine it'll be back in here,' Kenny says. 'All evidence points to it being taken outside.'

Billy jumps up and offers Ruby his hand. 'Come on, I'll show you around. I know this place pretty well now.'

Peanut leaps up, stands between them and frowns. 'If there's any *showing around* to be done, *mate*, you can take us all!' He bumps Billy's hand aside and offers Ruby his hand instead. 'You ready, babe?'

Ruby pauses, studying Peanut with a frown. 'Um, don't you want to eat something first?' She gestures to the sandwiches Max had laid out for them to share. 'I don't know. You're kinda looking a little *hangry*.'

Peanut flicks a glance at the food, appears to consider it for a split second, then turns his back on it. 'Nope, I'm good. Come on, you lot, let's go.'

Max repacks the food with a smirk on her face. She's loving this new-and-improved version of Peanut. There's nothing like a good dose of the green-eyed monster to remind someone of their priorities.

So, hand in hand, Peanut and Ruby follow Riley and Billy as they navigate the empty rooms of the orphanage.

Kenny follows, carrying all sorts of gadgets. He's so overladen with gizmos, Max offers to take the heat-detecting goggles, and Jack takes the voice recorder.

Kenny begins reciting interesting facts about the old building's past. 'Did you know this place is over one hundred and ten years old and had over two hundred kids living here at one stage? Imagine that many kids crammed in this place! No wonder so many kids died here. And you know what? A lot of them were buried on the grounds, especially the ones that died in 1919 from the Spanish flu pandemic. Back then, they were considered a health risk to the community, so they were prohibited from being buried in the local cemetery.'

Riley's eyes go wide. 'Wow, Kenny, you sure as heck know a lot about stuff. In fact, you know more about our town than *we* do.'

'And that's not all,' Kenny continues, 'the kids were buried in shallow graves only a few metres from the creek, so when the floods in 1925 hit, a lot of their remains were washed down to the river. Their resting place gone forever!'

'Far out!' Billy cries out.

Kenny shakes his head. 'I know, right? Those poor kids! Can you imagine?'

Billy laughs at Kenny's misunderstanding. 'No, I wasn't talking about the kids.' He pauses. 'Don't get me wrong, I feel sorry for them and all, but wow, you're pretty clued-up on things. First the electromagnetic field thingy and now this. Beats me how you know so much about everything!'

Max smiles. 'Pretty impressive, huh? Oh, that reminds me, there's something we need to show you later. We found something under the floorboards last night. Someone's hidden treasure. Kenny reckons we've come across something prehistoric!'

Billy's eyes go wide. '*What?* No way!'

'Yes way!' She laughs.

'Come off it, Max,' Peanut groans. 'You're not gonna go there again, are you? Kenny was pulling our leg. He even admitted it.'

Max's brow puckers. 'You listen here, Peanut! Kenny admitted to no such thing. He found something, and you railroaded him into …'

Suddenly, something whooshes past her, spinning her around and nearly knocking her to the floor. Thankfully, Jack is quick to break her fall.

'What the hell was that?' He looks down at her with concern. 'Hey, are you okay?'

It takes a moment for Max to recover. 'Did you feel that?'

Jack's eyes dart about the room. 'How could I not? It near sent us both flying!'

Ruby clings to Peanut, her eyes searching the room. 'What's going on? What's in here with us?'

Kenny scans the room with the EMF detector. At first the screen shows no presence, but in one corner of the room the light turns red.

Max gasps; her heart pounds.

The group huddle together in the centre of the room, looking in every direction.

'I want to go home,' Ruby whispers. 'Please, let's

just get out of here!'

Suddenly, Peanut cries out, his finger pointing at something on the floor in the corner of the room. 'What … what the hell's happening?'

Right before their eyes, letters start to appear on the dusty floor. First an *M*, then an *A*, followed by an *X*.

Max gasps.

The first three letters are written slowly, but the next few are scribbled with urgency.

H—E—L—P!

Ruby yelps. 'That's it. I'm done! I'm outta here!'

The next thing they know, the spectre whooshes past them and out of the room, slamming doors as it makes its escape down the corridor and out into the courtyard.

They take chase.

Max doesn't hesitate to follow. Anywhere out of there is better than staying. She has totally had enough too.

They pause at the top of the stairs, look out to the field, and watch the long grass part seemingly of its own accord. The only sound heard is that of a disturbed, rusted swing, screeching inexplicably as it sways back and forth.

Max gawks at the empty rusted frame. *How is that even possible?*

'It's getting away!' Peanut breaks her moment of distraction and takes off after it.

Jack calls out for him to stop. But Peanut vanishes from view within seconds, swallowed by the tall grass.

Kenny exchanges a look with Jack before rushing after him. 'Let's go,' he calls over his shoulder. 'He needs the scanner!'

They race to follow. Max has trouble keeping up with the rest of them, but when she finally catches up, she sees Peanut enter the creek, dive beneath its surface, then disappear.

On the bank, the others stand motionless, their breaths held, waiting for Peanut to resurface.

But Peanut doesn't.

12

FACETIME

RYKER

From the depths of his subconscious, Ryker hears the vibration of his cell phone on his bedside table. It stops. He rolls over. Seconds later, it starts again. Its persistent humming stirs him awake. He reaches out, groping in the dark to find it. He has it. But before he can answer it, it stops again. He curses. But then a thought comes to him. It could be an emergency. It's 2:11 am here in South Africa, but mid-morning in Sydney. Aelianna, at his side, sighs in her sleep and rolls over. Ryker dives out of bed and into the hallway before closing the door, so he doesn't disturb her further. As he fumbles to access information on the recent caller ID, the phone vibrates in his hand. It's Kenny.

'Kenny?'

The voice on the other end hesitates. 'Um, hi. Is this Ryker?'

Ryker doesn't recognise the caller. He frowns. 'Who's this?'

'Riley. You don't know me. But something's gone wrong. We need your help. Kenny's not here, but I've been given instructions to contact you if things go wrong. And they have. Big time!'

Ryker curses under his breath. He runs his hand over his bristly hair, pacing the corridor. 'What happened to Kenny? Look, never mind, how about you put Jack on the phone?'

The voice hesitates again. 'Um, Jack's not here. He … ah …. went through the portal too.'

Ryker stops. '*The portal?*' Again, he curses. 'Then get me one of the others. Get me Max.'

The boy, Riley, lets out a shaky breath. 'They've all gone. Peanut, Max, Ruby … everyone! They chased a … a … ghost into the creek and never came back. It's been half an hour already. Man, you've gotta do something, we're shitting bricks here, and I don't think I can handle any more of this.'

The boy starts to cry. 'First my brother, and now the rest of them. They're all gone! Do ya hear me? GONE!'

Ryker's pulse races. The boy sounds young. Perhaps a teenager … about fourteen or fifteen years old. He can only imagine what this boy is going through.

He then hears a muffled exchange of words on the other end of the line. Then there's a new voice. 'Hey, this is Billy. Ryker, is it? Hey, man, we need your help. Kenny said you'd help. You're part of this *Triple C* thing. Right?'

Ryker rubs his face. 'Yeah. Look, listen to me, tell me exactly what's happened. Where are you?'

Billy fills him in. Ryker listens without interrupting, pacing back and forth, taking it all in. Ryker can picture, clear as day, what happened. He thinks of Peanut and his impulsive ways. *Bloody idiot!* He then thinks of Max and the rest of them. His teeth clench. *What the hell made them ALL go?*

'Hey, are you still there?' Billy asks, his voice tentative.

Ryker's mind races. He needs to think. He moves to the kitchen, puts the phone on speaker, rests it on the counter, and paces.

In the background, he hears Billy's muffled voice. 'Riley, I think I've lost him.' Then a lot clearer. '*Oi,* Ryker! Can you hear me?'

Ryker sits by the phone and rubs his temples. 'Um, yeah. Yeah, I'm here. I caught everything you said. Just give me a sec to think things through.'

'So, can you help, or what? We're kinda desperate here. Should we call the cops?'

Ryker picks up the phone and holds it closer. 'Billy, listen carefully. Tell me again *exactly* what happened just before the ghost made itself known to you. And I mean everything. Paint me a picture. I want location, dialogue, sight, sound, smell, taste … anything that might give me a clue.'

Billy describes the room they were in, and what the conversation was at the time. 'Max was about to tear strips off Peanut for something he did … something to do with a box of treasure they found.'

'A prehistoric treasure,' Ryker hears Riley call out in the background. 'Tell him that Max called it *a prehistoric treasure.*'

'Oh, yeah, a prehistoric treasure,' Billy continues. 'They found something hidden under the floorboards. Anyhow, Max was crowing about Kenny and how he knows so much, and that's when the ghost showed up and scribbled the words *Max* and *HELP* on the dusty floor.'

'So them talking about the find stirred the ghost to react,' Ryker says to himself. 'Hmm … could be something.' He stops to consider this.

Billy laughs without humour. 'Mate, you're talking like it's nothing that we've encountered a *ghost.* We're crapping ourselves here!'

Ryker chuckles. 'Yeah, you could say I've had some experience with this kind of thing. Anyway, you said something about Max's missing first-aid kit. Perhaps the ghost was angry with them for messing with its stuff, so it stole something of theirs as payback.'

There's silence on the line. 'Nah, I could've sworn the kit went missing before they found the treasure. But I could be wrong.'

'Billy, it might be pivotal, so try to remember.' Ryker can't imagine these young boys trying to deal with all this mess. 'Look, how about you let it go for the moment? Just get back to me once it comes to you. What might shed some light, in the meantime, is the contents of this treasure box. Have you guys had a chance to look at the find?'

Billy hesitates. 'Um, no, we haven't. Hang on a sec.'

Ryker hears them scrambling on the other side of the line. He figures they're going to get the box. He lets out a drawn-out breath. His thoughts begin to take shape from the information given so far. He's anxious to see where this new material will lead him. He paces and waits.

Moments later. 'Okay, we're back in the room where their stuff is. Riley's looking for it now,' Billy tells him.

In the background, Riley calls out that he found it. Ryker hears him run to the phone and take it. 'Ryker, I've got it.'

Ryker stops to listen as they rummage through the box.

'Man! What the hell is that?'

Riley's outburst has Ryker's immediate attention. He then hears Billy cry out. 'Whoa! Get a load of that!'

Ryker holds his breath. 'Guys, what is it?'

But the boys don't answer. They talk excitedly among themselves about the find. It's killing him that they're not filling him in. 'Hey, fellas! An account would be great right about now.'

But nothing; the boys are obviously engrossed in what they're looking at.

'GUYS!'

And then the call ends.

Ryker jerks back and stares at the phone. 'What the hell?'

And just as he goes to press to reconnect, his phone vibrates with an incoming FaceTime call from them. He breathes out a sigh and takes the call. A young boy's face fills the screen. He figures it's Riley. 'Hey! Riley, is it?'

'Yeah, hi, I'm Riley.' He swings the phone to show Billy. Billy grins and waves. Two seconds of blur later, Riley's face is back on the screen. 'Sorry about that, but there's no way in heck we could've described this. We figured we'd show you instead. Just look at this stuff!' Riley turns the phone to show Ryker the contents of the treasure box.

Ryker's eyes widen. 'Hey, show me that white thing. Is that a tooth?'

'Yeah, we thought so too,' Riley tells him. 'But look at the size of it!'

Riley holds up a sharp, whitish-coloured tooth in front of the screen for him to see. By Ryker's estimation, it's approximately fifteen to twenty centimetres long, but it's hard to tell. He leans in closer to have a better look.

'Maybe this is what they were talking about,' Riley says as he swings the phone around to face Ryker. 'You know, the prehistoric thing?'

Before Ryker has a chance to refocus, Riley flicks the phone back onto the find.

All this flicking back and forth is making Ryker dizzy. He blinks repeatedly, trying to focus on the tooth. Once he's had a good look, he shakes his head. 'Nah, it can't be, it's almost white,' he tells them. 'And if it was prehistoric, it'd be yellow or brown. Right? What about that coiled shell-looking thing? What's that?'

Riley picks up the crimpled, spiralled tubular

shell and holds it close to the screen. Ryker vaguely remembers seeing something like that before but thinks nothing more about it. He shrugs and asks Riley to show him the other items instead. The boys fumble, trying to show him.

Ryker groans. 'Look, it's pretty hard to tell by looking at the things like this. Send me photos. I'll have a better look that way. In the meantime, I need you guys to stay put. Don't do anything. I'll get something happening from my end. But I need you to report back to me if you think of anything or if the guys come back. Okay?'

Back face to face, Riley nods. 'Just hurry.' He swipes his eyes. His voice breaks. 'They were here helping me find my brother and his friends, and now they're gone.'

Billy takes the phone from him. 'Mate, it's killing him. We need your help.'

Ryker sighs. 'Hang in there, guys. I'll do what I can and get back to you ASAP.'

He ends the call, his head in a spin.

His eyes squeeze shut, and he groans.

What a bloody mess!

13
RESOLUTION

EDRA

Snuggled in a cosy corner of their local café, Edra and Jaeger sit side by side having breakfast. Her vegetarian frittata tastes divine, but Jaeger's big breakfast looks a little too enticing. Perhaps he won't miss one small rasher of bacon. She sneaks one and peeks at him, smiling. She can't help but smile. Life is good. Having Jaeger back fills her heart with insurmountable happiness.

Jaeger's eyes widen. 'Hey! You thieving little minx!' He grins and nudges her under the table with his leg.

Edra laughs and stuffs the bacon into her mouth whole.

He gives a wink.

'So I wonder why Ryker was so keen to meet up with me,' he says with a frown. 'If I didn't know better, I'd say he was up to something.'

And like a flick of a switch, Edra's euphoric bubble pops. Her appetite disappears. The pilfered contraband suddenly tastes like cardboard. Her back stiffens. She sits taller. Her teeth gnash. *Oh, he's up to something, all right!*

And that's exactly why I'm here!

Earlier that morning, and only by chance, Jaeger had mentioned he was meeting up with Ryker for breakfast. After hearing this, Edra had a sudden desire to catch up with Ryker for breakfast too.

Edra knows this casual tête-à-tête isn't as innocent a catch up as Ryker would have you believe. Ryker doesn't do innocent. And where Ryker is concerned, to be forewarned is to be forearmed.

Oblivious to her sudden unease, Jaeger goes on. 'The funny thing is, he rang me at 6:00 am on the dot, as if he'd planned it that way. Before six is too early, after six is acceptable. I guess all that military training is hard to shake off.' He shrugs and laughs.

But Edra isn't so easily fooled. She knows that whatever Ryker is up to can't be good. She keeps her face lowered.

Again, Jaeger nudges her. She looks up. He

frowns and reaches to caress away the crease on her brow. 'Hey, what's up?'

Edra looks away briefly, debating whether or not to voice her concern. She decides she should. She turns side on to face him and draws in a deep breath. 'Jae, when you've spent as much time with Ryker as I have, you get to know the guy.' She pauses. 'And you're right, he *is* up to something.'

His frown deepens.

Edra leans forward and cups his face in her hands. 'Promise me something?'

Jaeger takes her hands in his. 'What's going on?'

'Just promise me. Please.'

His eyes narrow, but his smile is warm. 'Edra, for you, anything.'

She blinks a few times and stops to refocus. His twinkling amber eyes have that effect on her. She draws another breath and looks at his lips instead.

Big mistake!

She shakes her head.

His nose will have to do. 'Okay'—she sits taller— 'so when Ryker gets here, don't agree to whatever he asks you to do. Just think about it first. Okay?'

'What makes you think he's going to ask me to do anything?' He chuckles and sits back in his seat. 'Edra, we haven't seen each other for a while. The guy just rang so we could catch up for a coffee. That's all.'

Edra snorts. 'Yeah, the guy rings you at the break of dawn just to meet you for coffee.'

Jaeger chuckles. He shakes his head and rests his arm across her shoulders. Her hand, he holds firmly in his grasp.

There's a total innocence about him that Edra adores. This is the guy she fell in love with all those years ago and loves deeper now. Someone honest and trusting, who sees the good in everyone. She looks down at her hand in his and smiles.

'Hey, look who it is!' he says suddenly. 'It's Lanny and Banj.' He waves. 'What a coincidence. I wonder what brings them here?' Jaeger stands as they approach. He greets Banji with a shake of his hand and gives Ulan a kiss on the cheek. 'Now, this is a surprise. I didn't expect to bump into you two.'

Ulan gives Edra a sideways look, her brow raised. 'Is that so?'

The twins slip into the booth across from them.

'So Ryker's up to something, is he?' Banji laughs.

Jaeger draws back and turns to face Edra. 'Hon, what's going on?'

Banji splutters. 'You mean you *honestly* didn't tell him?'

Edra shifts in her seat, colour flushes her cheeks. She peeks at Jaeger. 'Okay, so I might've called in the twins for backup.' She sits a little taller. 'Look, Jae, we all know Ryker, and I'll guarantee you that he's up to something … specifically something *realm* related.'

Jaeger looks from Edra to the twins.

Ulan reaches across the table to squeeze Jaeger's hand. 'Guaranteed!' she repeats with a nod.

Just then the bell on the front door to the café tingles. They look up to see Ryker, stone-faced, at the entrance. He hesitates a moment before coming towards them, then laughs awkwardly when he reaches their table. 'Had I known we were all going to be here, I would've brought Aelianna. She was only saying the other day that we should get together. So what's new?'

Edra's eyes narrow. 'Quit with the small talk, Ryker. What's *new* with you?'

Ryker throws himself down next to Banji and looks from Jaeger to Edra, then lets out a drawn breath. He smiles a crooked smile and throws his hands in the air. 'Okay, you got me.'

Jaeger's eyes widen.

Edra squeezes his arm. Her subtle reminder to him of his promise. She says nothing.

Ryker runs his hand over the top of his head a few times, a sure sign that the news won't be good.

Edra braces herself.

'Look, it's no secret the Aussies have plans to set up the CCC in Sydney,' he begins, 'and to a degree here in South Africa with us.' He pauses for the longest time.

Edra waits.

'Well,' he continues, 'it appears that they've already taken on more than they can handle.'

Too quickly, Ryker's hand shoots up to fend off any reprisal. He looks hard at Edra, then fills them in on what's happened in regional New South Wales.

'But weren't they supposed to act as a source of information for the authorities and not get actively involved?' Edra asks, her blood on the verge of boiling. 'I don't get it! How did this happen?'

Ulan frowns. 'I think I've got a pretty good idea *how*. It's got *Peanut's* name all over it.'

Ryker rubs his head again.

Edra groans. 'So now we're all supposed to get him out of a scrape? Un-be-lievable!'

Jaeger frowns. 'But I thought Peanut is our friend.'

Ulan moans. 'Well, he is. It's just that he's such a loose cannon. This is classic *Peanut*. A situation develops, and his knee-jerk reaction is to act on it without thinking. Am I right?'

Ryker looks at Ulan and sighs. 'Unfortunately, you are.'

He directs his attention to Jaeger. 'Look, don't get me wrong, Jae, he's a top guy and all, and he'd do anything for you. He saved my hide heaps of times.

And it was because of him that Aelianna was able to escape that godawful place. He really stuck his neck out for me.'

He turns to the others. 'But, guys, it's not only Peanut we're talking about here. It's all our Aussie friends. They've found another portal and have fallen through it.'

Edra turns to Jaeger. Her heart races. She's freaking out inside, her old demons taunting her. She prays that Jaeger keeps his promise to think about what Ryker is about to ask before committing to anything.

'So, for whatever reason,' Ryker continues, 'they've all re-entered the realm and haven't returned. I, for one, feel we owe it to them to do something about it.' He draws in a breath. 'Look, I was going to run this by Jae first before dropping this bombshell on the rest of you, but now that you're all here, I'll ask now. We've got to help them. Agreed?'

He looks at each of his friends. 'So … who's with me?'

Edra looks at Jaeger. His eager expression makes her stomach do a flip … and not in a good way. She looks away and curses under her breath, then pauses to consider her own decision.

She despises the realm and can't bear the thought of going through all that torment again. Her wounds from the past have yet to heal. But her friends need their help.

She groans. How can she *not* help? She looks at the twins, trying to gauge what they're thinking. Banji and Ulan exchange glances. Edra senses that Ulan has reservations. Their involvement last time was restricted to helping from the fringes, and Edra can see the same hesitant look in Ulan's eyes now.

There's an uncomfortable silence.

The twins take a moment to answer. 'Um, we'll do what we can, Ryker,' Banji finally offers. 'But just like before, we'll hang around the portal in case you need us. And that's as far as we'll go. We're not going back in.'

Ulan lets out a heavy sigh.

Banji frowns and shrugs, clearly not entirely happy with the decision.

All eyes are suddenly on Edra. A flush of heat tracks up her neck to taint her pale cheeks. She stops to take everything into consideration. The twins are all but out. And Jae, with his eyes twinkling, is clearly keen to commit. She draws a deep breath, crosses her arms and directs her gaze at Ryker. 'So … I guess my decision rests on whether you're including Aelianna in all of this or not.' She says this pointedly. Ryker's caveman mentality regarding Aelianna's return to the realm to visit her family is a known sore point. Now, since she's sitting on the fence with her verdict,

Ryker's answer will determine which way she leans.

Ryker takes a good while to say anything. He looks away and rubs the back of his neck before releasing his breath, then he turns to Edra, his eyes softening. 'Okay, if that's what you want, I'll ask her.'

With that said, Edra makes the only decision she can.

14

WHAT THE...?

JACK

Jack can't believe what's just happened. Moments ago, Peanut plunged into the creek and hasn't yet resurfaced. Jack waits on the bank, his breath held, willing him to reappear. The seconds tick away slowly … it's almost painful. Jack tries to calm his thinking. Does he go after him or does he stay put? He runs his hand through his hair—he's racked with indecision. But Peanut's been under too long. For sure, it's been over two minutes. The look of alarm on everyone's faces confirms he isn't imagining it. He makes his decision.

No more!

Jack rushes into the creek and wades through

the water to where he saw Peanut vanish. It surprises him; the water isn't as deep as he expected it to be … only reaching below Jack's waist, so he wonders how it's possible that Peanut has disappeared like that.

Jack suddenly loses his footing and finds himself suspended in a deep body of water. Shocked, he almost gasps at the unexpected change but quickly realises the consequences of doing that. He looks in every direction. It's so deep he can't see the bottom, and somehow, he's no longer anywhere near the surface. In fact, he's impossibly several metres from it.

In a panic, he kicks and claws at the water in an effort to propel himself towards daylight. But it's so far. Will he make it? His chest hurts—it feels like it's going to explode. His lungs burn—he's on fire. Almost there. But he can't hold his breath much longer. He's going to drown. He digs deeper, and after a few more desperate thrusts, he breaks the surface.

Never so grateful to fill his lungs with oxygen, he gulps down huge mouthfuls of air. He remains on guard, his gaze darting about, taking in the situation. But what he sees knocks him for six. He stops. His eyes widen; his mouth falls open. He spins in a circle, not quite believing what's surrounding him.

What the …?

Where the hell am I?

15
Not Again!

MAX

Max gasps. *What just happened?* She can barely believe her eyes. One second, she sees Jack wade in the shallow creek, tailing Peanut, who only two minutes earlier vanished mysteriously; the next, he's swallowed whole and doesn't resurface. Gone in the blink of an eye.

'Max, give me the goggles!'

Max jumps, startled by the urgency in Kenny's voice. It takes her a moment to register what he's asking for and then a few more seconds to realise she has what he wants dangling from her neck. She fumbles to get them to him, becoming entangled in the process.

Ruby appears from nowhere and smacks Max's hands away. 'Here, let me do it!' Once they're free, Ruby tosses the goggles to Kenny.

Kenny drops the EMF detector he's been carrying and adjusts the goggles over his own spectacles. He hands Ruby his phone before running into the water.

'Kenny, no!' Both girls cry out.

But Kenny doesn't stop.

'What's he doing?' Riley asks, fisting his hair.

They watch Kenny go deeper into the creek and dunk his head beneath the water's surface. He comes up spluttering seconds later, then races nearer to where they saw Jack and Peanut vanish. Again, he immerses his head and stops.

Everything goes quiet. Max holds her breath. He's been motionless for a while.

Come on, Kenny ...

And then he's up, gulping mouthfuls of air. He yanks off the goggles, along with his glasses, swipes the water from his eyes and readjusts his glasses. 'It's a portal! They've fallen through a portal!'

Max gasps. *A portal? In there?*

Kenny trips over in his rush to get back to them.

Riley's eyes widen. 'Far out! But how ...?'

'Hey! You know what that means ...' Billy laughs. 'We've found them!'

In his excitement, Billy dives onto Riley, knocking

him to the ground. The two rumble in excitement, hooting and hollering.

Riley stops when he realises that they're the only ones revelling in the find. 'Hey, Billy, quit it!' He shoves Billy aside. 'Something's not right.' He scrambles to his feet. 'What's wrong?'

Billy sits up. He frowns. 'But finding the portal is a good thing. Right?'

Kenny looks away, and then down. A puddle forms at his feet. He swipes the trail of water running down his face and takes a moment to answer. 'Um, how much do you know of what happened to us in the realm?'

Both boys look at each other. Riley shrugs. 'Just that you went into another dimension, found some missing kids and brought them home. You're heroes!'

Max groans. She exchanges a look with Kenny and Ruby.

Riley's smile vanishes. 'Hey, what's with the look?'

Max draws a breath. 'Riley, I don't know what you're imagining the realm to be like, but it's not a good place,' she tells them. 'It's dead-set dangerous. We were lucky to escape with our lives.' In a sudden panic, she thinks of Jack and Peanut. Her gaze darts back to the creek. They could be in danger! Time is wasting. They need to act now!

She glances back at Riley and Billy; both boys

look horrified. Again, Max groans. *That's all we need—a complete meltdown!* 'Look, what happened to us might not have happened to your brother and friends, Riley,' she adds hastily. 'They could've got away.'

'Absolutely!' Ruby adds. 'And you know what? I bet they've run into the forest and are safe with our new friends there. Molan and Medwin will look out for them. For sure.'

Kenny nudges Ruby. 'Hey, good point. I forgot. Medwin would've seen them coming. That's his thing … he gets visions of the future.'

Hearing this relaxes Max somewhat. Jack and Peanut would be safe too.

Billy scratches his head. 'So everyone's got freaky powers in this other dimension, then?' He thinks on it for a moment, and his eyes widen. He grins. 'Sick!'

Max can see where this conversation is heading, and she needs to stop it. She jumps to redirect their focus back to the matter at hand, and that is, to what they need to do next. She turns to Kenny. 'So what happens now? Do we call for help? I could ring Dad, and he can get the ball rolling and have the taskforce here in no time.'

After a few moments, Kenny shakes his head. 'Nah. Calling them will only hold us up.' Again, he pauses.

Max stops to think.

'Look,' Kenny says, suddenly decisive, 'while there's a chance they're still on the other side of the portal, I think I should go in after them.' He holds up the goggles. 'I've got these. And what with this new portal being submerged, chances are Jack and Peanut have ended up in another body of water, so they might have trouble seeing it to get back.'

'I don't get it. What's with these freakin' goggles?' Riley asks.

As he secures the goggles over his glasses, Kenny explains that the goggles pick up the thermal energy the portal radiates. 'Ryker's discovery of this has saved us heaps of times.' He turns to leave. 'Look, I'll be back with the boys in no time. After that, we can work out what we need to do to find the others.'

'I'm coming with you,' Ruby says. 'There's a chance you'll run into guards. My shield will come in handy.'

Max's mind races. What if they need her help? No! She's not about to be left behind. They're a team. 'I'm coming too!'

Billy jumps to his feet. 'What? You're not *all* going? What about us? What are we s'posed to do?'

Riley frowns and crosses his arms. 'Yeah, I don't know about that. What if you don't come back?'

Ryker comes to mind. Max dives for the phone

in her back pocket, switches it on, only to find the battery has near zero power. 'We need Ryker, but my phone's just about flat.'

Kenny snatches his phone back from Ruby. 'Good thinking, Max. But take mine, it's charged.' He takes a moment to retrieve Ryker's number, then holds it out for Riley. 'Here, take this. If we're not back within thirty minutes, call Ryker. He's part of the CCC. He was in the realm with us. He'll know what to do.'

Both boys glare at the phone like it's a bomb about to go off.

'Don't worry, you won't need to call him. We'll be back before you know it,' Ruby tells them. 'Because there's no way in hell I'm staying in there a minute longer than I have to.' She says this through clenched teeth. 'And because he's making me do this again, once I get my hands on him, Peanut won't know which way to run.'

Again, Kenny offers Riley the phone. 'Just in case. Okay?'

Riley hesitates. 'Are you sure about this?'

Max smiles. 'Absolutely!' She tries to sound convincing, although right now, she's feeling anything but sure.

Kenny hands Ruby the goggles. 'You'd better go up front. You'll need to activate your shield as soon as we enter.' He stops to take a breath. He looks at her. 'Ready?'

Ruby inhales sharply and nods, then adjusts the goggles. She reaches out for Max's hand. 'Don't let go, no matter what. Okay?'

Max squeezes Ruby's hand, then turns to grab Kenny's. 'You too.'

Kenny gestures to go ahead.

The three friends enter the water. Ruby edges towards the spot where they last saw Jack and Peanut vanish. She pauses to tie back her hair into a tight ponytail, then dunks her head. She stops briefly before bobbing back up. 'Okay, I see it.'

Max secures Ruby's hand in hers again and gives it another squeeze. She thinks of Jack, and this gives her the courage she needs to do this. 'Think of Peanut, Rubes. The boys need us.'

Ruby nods. She takes in a few deep breaths. Max and Kenny do the same—there's no turning back.

As one, they take a step forward towards the unknown.

16
WHAT DO I THINK?!

JACK

Treading water, taking in what he's seeing, Jack's attention homes in on movement in the distance. It's Peanut. He's at the edge of the bank, hauling himself out of the water. Jack calls out to him and waves, but he's too far away to be heard. Although thoroughly spent following his near-death experience, Jack summons what little strength he has to swim the distance to him.

He finally reaches the water's edge, exhausted, and finds Peanut sprawled on his back, breathing heavily. Jack drags himself out, puffing and panting, and falls at Peanut's side. Neither one says a word.

Jack sits up to look around. He nudges Peanut

with his foot. 'Hey, are you okay?'

Peanut remains silent. His arm draped over his eyes.

'Peanut?'

Peanut groans. 'I've gone and done it again, haven't I?'

Jack says nothing.

Peanut raises his head and looks about. 'Where the hell are we?'

Jack studies the area closer. He shakes his head in disbelief. 'Will ya get a load of this place!'

Peanut falls back and buries his face in his hands. 'I seriously can't look anymore.'

But Jack can. How can he not? He can hardly believe his eyes. Again, he shakes his head. 'I reckon we've found ourselves a new portal.' He clicks his tongue. 'It'd definitely explain the missing kids. What d'ya think?'

Peanut curses. '*What do I think*? I *think* I've had enough! Mate, I can't do this again.'

Jack gets to his feet—he needs to look some more. He draws a breath, taking it all in. The creek and the overgrown grassland at the back of the orphanage are now a huge lake in the middle of a tropical rainforest. And not just *any* tropical rainforest either, it's a rainforest on steroids. Ferns the size of houses, vines as thick as elephant trunks, trees reaching up to the heavens … Everything is gargantuan in comparison to anything he's ever seen.

Peanut peeks through the gaps in his fingers and groans again. He sits up. 'Somethin' tells me we won't be hassled by portal guards or forest ferals in this place. And we sure as heck won't be getting any help from the likes of Molan and Medwin.' He looks around, then rubs the back of his neck. 'It's not the same realm, is it?'

Jack squats on his haunches. He considers what he's seeing, what he's smelling and what he's sensing. He releases a troubled breath. 'No, mate, it's definitely not the same realm.'

Peanut gets to his feet, shields his eyes and peers at the lake. 'D'ya reckon we can get back?'

Jack's head drops. In the past, locating portals to the ancient realm was hard enough, given their translucent nature. Finding *this* one will be near impossible. They'll drown trying.

Peanut takes one look at Jack's face and groans. His shoulders slump. 'No, I didn't think so either.'

17
WAIT, WHAT?!

MAX

The moment the water soaks her sneakers, Max questions what they're about to do. Ruby must sense her hesitation because she tightens her grip on her. They inch forward. Her heart thumps so hard, it's painful. Without warning, the ground beneath them falls away, plunging them into an unexpected depth of water.

Max gasps without thinking. Her lungs fill with liquid. Her eyes widen—she's going to drown.

In a flash, Ruby produces her shield, encircling them within a bubble of air. They're safe.

For now.

Coughing and spluttering, Max struggles to draw

breath. At her side, Kenny slaps her back, then stops suddenly, eyes widening. He dives at Ruby, yanks the goggles from her, secures them over his glasses and peers into the depths of the murky water. He points with a shaky finger. Max sees it. Her eyes bulge. Something's coming towards them. Something dark and formidable. Something *huge*. But before she has a chance to see what that something is, they're propelled upward at an alarming speed. And then with a blop, the sphere, still intact, breaks surface level.

Tumbled and shaken, the three friends await stability as the orb bobbles on top of the water. They stare at one other, wide-eyed and ashen faced, neither one capable of stringing two words together to make sense of what just happened … or what they just saw.

Kenny, the first to react, wrestles to disentangle himself. He dives onto all fours, adjusts the goggles and peers through the floor of the transparent barrier, his hands cupped, framing his eyes to get a better look. He freezes and falls back with unmistakable terror on his face.

'It's coming again! We've gotta get out of here!'

Max can't breathe. She's frozen on the spot, unable to move.

Ruby sucks in a breath and lunges forward to get a better look—her nose pressed hard against the barrier.

Kenny whips off the goggles and shoves them on his head. 'Not now, Ruby! *Run!*

Run?

Max snaps out of her catatonic state and does her best to *run* in an enclosed ball. She throws herself into a chaotic, frenzied scurry in an attempt to propel the orb forward.

Clambering over one another, the three quickly realise that running within the pliable sphere is virtually impossible. They trip and fall in a tangle, accomplishing nothing. So they resort to crawling. Now on all fours, like mice in a mouse wheel, they find a rhythm to inch them closer to a distant bank.

Max steels herself to stare forward. Her sole focus is to maintain a pace to stay the course. She doesn't allow thoughts of what she saw to distract her. If she did, she'd crumble into a mass of hysteria.

And then she spots Jack and Peanut in the distance, egging them on. She just about cries, but chokes back the tears and pushes harder.

After a mammoth effort, they reach the muddy bank. Ruby retracts the shield, and Max scurries up the slope as fast as her legs can carry her. She whips around to scan the lake. There's no sign of the beast. They're safe. She collapses in a heap.

Jack falls to her side. 'Hey, are you okay? What just happened? You look like you'd been chased by a ghost.'

Max shakes her head. She's having a hard enough time trying to catch her breath, let alone explain what just happened. Or more to the point, *what* they'd just escaped.

Anxious to know, Jack turns to Kenny instead. 'Mate?'

Kenny holds up his hand, gesturing for Jack to wait. Between gasps, he tells them. 'There's something in there.' He points towards the lake. 'Something I'm struggling to get my head around.'

Jack and Peanut exchange an apprehensive look. They wait to hear more.

But Kenny struggles, mumbling to himself—his words incoherent. Nothing he says makes sense. They hear him mutter and groan as though he were at odds with his thinking. And then he stops. He sits for a long while, stone-faced and silent, hugging his knees and staring vacantly across the body of water.

Jack and Peanut scan the lake too. Rattled.

Peanut squats at Ruby's side. 'Rubes, what's going on? What's in there?'

It all becomes too much for Ruby. She cups her face in her hands and falls to pieces, inconsolable.

Peanut strokes her back. 'Hey, it's all good. You're okay now.' He turns to Jack, shaking his head. 'Bloody hell, Jack! We were *in* that lake!'

Max shudders, realising the truth in that. At least she, Ruby and Kenny had the protection of the shield. The boys had nothing. She reaches for Jack's hand and crushes it in hers. 'You're alive, and that's all that matters.'

Jack's eyes widen.

Peanut flinches. '*Alive?* Wow! That bad, huh?' He lets out a troubled breath. 'Man, I don't know what it is that you saw in there, but I sure reckon we've bitten off more than we can chew with this one.'

Distractedly, Jack toys with the ground with a stick. He says nothing.

Peanut gets to his feet and shoves his hands in his jeans' pockets. 'This is *way* too big for us to handle on our own. I vote we go back and let the taskforce take it from here. What d'ya reckon? We've got Ruby's shield; we've got the goggles … nothing's holding us back … let's get outta here.'

'What! Go back? *In there?*' Ruby jumps up. The colour drains from her face. 'There's *no way* I'm going back in there! That … that *thing* in there'—she points to the water, her voice shaky—'is massive … it's humungous! And I, for one, am staying clear of it!'

Peanut frowns and shrugs. 'But, Rubes … your shield.'

Ruby whips around and glares at him. She fists her hands on her hips. 'Charlie, you're not listening!

I'm *not* going back in there! I *can't* … and I *won't!*

Peanut clicks his tongue. ''Course you can. You're awesome … you can do anything.' His smile turns into a lopsided grin. 'Remember the dogs?'

Her eyes like daggers, her face flushed, Ruby all but growls. 'Don't you dare put that kind of pressure on me!'

If Peanut knew what was good for him, he'd have the sense to back off.

But Peanut doesn't.

'Come on, Rubes!'

And Ruby won't have any more of it. She stomps away, cursing under her breath.

Max hasn't seen Ruby so rattled. Not since they first met—when Max discovered Ruby's ugly past. Ruby had been assaulted at her previous school. She'd very nearly died from the attack, and it had left her broken. It took a lot of patience and a great deal of time to build back her confidence.

But Max knows they don't have the luxury of time now. She needs to turn this around *ASAP!* She takes off after her.

After a short distance, Ruby stops. She turns and grips Max's hands. Her eyes fill with tears. They probe the depths of Max's eyes as if begging her to understand.

Max waits, giving her the time she needs.

The others approach but remain silent. For that, Max is grateful.

Ruby sighs. Her shoulders slump. 'Can't you see, Max? With the dogs, it was different. It was *them* against *me*. That I could handle. And I'd still be able to handle. But *this*? This is totally another level. No way could I let anything happen to you'—she turns to take Peanut's hand, then looks at Jack and Kenny—'to any of you.' Ruby clears her throat, choked with tears. 'I've seen what's in there. And I don't think I can trust myself to not freak out. I'll lose it. I know it. And then what? We'll be *done for*, that's what.'

Jack turns to Kenny and frowns. 'Mate, you saw it. What the hell are we talking about?'

Kenny squats on his haunches, still visibly shaken. 'Jack, you wouldn't believe me if I told you.'

Max still can't believe it. And she saw it!

She pauses a moment to look about to take it all in. The gigantic tropical forest, the strange plants and, of course, the sanctuary that harbours the massive water-living monster. There's no denying it. It's real.

Perhaps *too* real.

She considers what she's learned of the past—a past, long, long gone. And although reluctant to have it confirmed, she needs to hear it. She needs to know for sure. 'Kenny, *where* exactly are we?'

Kenny takes a long, hard look around. Every

tree, every fern, every ripple on the water. He shakes his head.

Peanut shifts uneasily. 'Mate, are you shaking your head because you don't know or because you can't believe it?'

'Oh, I know where we are, Peanut,' Kenny says with a humourless laugh. 'And you're right, knowing it has floored me. But it's the not knowing how we're going to get back that's got me stumped.' He glances at Ruby. 'With or without the shield.'

Ruby looks away.

Max holds her breath.

Jack remains silent.

Peanut rubs the back of his neck. 'Okay. So it's not ideal, but we'll work it out. Somehow.' But then he stops. 'Wait, you said you've figured it out. So where are we? The Daintree? The Amazon? The Congo? Where?'

Max holds her breath, waiting. Kenny takes his time answering, and it's killing her.

Again, his gaze skims across the lake, then into the forest. He draws in a deep breath, then gradually lets it out. 'From what I can gather,' he says after some deliberation, 'we've travelled back in time again.' He turns to face them. His lip lifts at the corner. 'Maybe a *little* further back in the past than what we've already seen.'

Jack looks at him side on. 'Kenny, *how* far back?'

Kenny shrugs. 'Well, that creature that lives in there'—he jabs his finger towards the lake, his voice somewhat unsteady—'if my guess is right, is a *live* freshwater *Mosasaur*.'

His vague explanation is met with blank expressions. There's silence.

Kenny frowns. 'Um … as opposed to a fossilised one.'

More silence.

Kenny throws his hands up in the air. 'Guys, come on!' He slaps his forehead. 'That *thing* we just escaped from … you know that thing in the water … it's an aquatic predator of the *dinosaur* age!'

He pauses for a reaction. But there's nothing. Not a peep. Not a gasp. Not a flinch. Nothing. They all stare at him, their eyes wide.

'The fact is,' he continues, as though more clarity is needed, 'they've been extinct for sixty-six million years!' He looks at Jack and shrugs. 'How far back in time, you ask? Seriously? Approximately *seventy million* years.' He shrugs. His lip curls into a grin. 'Give or take a few thousand years.'

Max just about passes out.

18
Good Cretaceous!

JACK

Seventy million years! Hearing Kenny confirm his hunch suddenly has Jack light-headed. And then he remembers to breathe. He squats on his haunches, steadies himself, and waits a spell for it to pass. Ruby conjures her shield, grabs Max and clings to her. Peanut does a good impersonation of a fish out of water. Kenny surveys the area a little closer.

Jack wonders if there's a chance Kenny could be wrong. But he knows the answer without asking it. Kenny's superhuman database is never wrong. 'Mate, how sure are you?'

Kenny points to the huge trees. 'See those trees? They're ribbonwood or idiot fruit trees. More specifically, *Idiospermum australiense*. They've been around for over a hundred and twenty million years and today only exist in the Daintree Forest in north-east Queensland. Although typically huge—growing to the height of forty metres—they're nowhere near the size of these monsters. These are massive!' Kenny points to the tall ferns. 'And those ferns? They're *Dicksonia antarctica*, or man fern. They're still around today too, native to eastern Australia. They're known to grow up to fifteen metres in height and up to six metres in diameter. Far from these, which are two to three times that size. They date back as far as the Jurassic period and were a staple diet for plant-eating dinosaurs. And those sago cycads'—he points to several spikey-leaf plants—'are also still around and are known to have existed two hundred and seventy million years ago. You know, it takes up to a hundred years for their trunks to grow a few metres, and going by the size of these ones, they've been here a heck of a long time. They're the size of a house!'

Jack stops to look around. Every living thing around him looks like they're on super-charged growth hormones. There's no doubting Kenny's measure of things.

Peanut frowns. 'Yeah, okay, we get it—these plants are huge. Great history lesson and everything, but that doesn't prove anything. They're just massive!

You said it yourself—they're still around today. So what makes you think we've gone back a zillion years?'

Kenny smirks. 'Fair call, Peanut. But there's more. What I was going to flag were these other plants.' He points to a group of weird-looking trees, their massive, barbarous trunks studded with long, sharp, spine-like needles, their branches barren of leaves but heavy with enormous bunches of yellow-coloured seeds. And then he points to some spindly, mangrove-looking trees on the other side of the lake, their trunks covered with a carpet of green, their roots exposed several metres, elevating them high to the heavens.

'The thing is,' he tells them, 'my inner Google search isn't even registering them.' He shrugs. 'I draw a blank. I've got no idea what they are. They're a total unknown. It's as if they've never been found or documented to have ever existed.' He scratches his head. 'It's so weird. In all the time spent in the realm, this has never happened to me.'

And that in itself is enough to put a stop to Peanut's argument. The facts are undeniable. The portal unearthed at the back of the orphanage unlocks a passage to this prehistoric world.

'And I know what I saw in there,' Kenny continues, pointing to the lake. 'That was definitely a *Mosasaur*. Well, to be specific, it's a *Pannoniasaurus*, a genus of the *Mosasaur* … because it lives in freshwater.'

Peanut shakes his head, then slaps his hand on Kenny's back. 'There's no doubting you, mate. And sorry I grilled you earlier. But'—he steps away, motions for Jack and Kenny to follow him and lowers his voice—'it's not gonna help us get the hell out of here, is it? You both saw it … Ruby completely lost it. And I reckon there's no talking her around.'

Jack saw it, and he agrees the situation isn't looking great. He stops to think hard about how to move forward. 'Mate, she just needs time. She's rattled, that's all. You know how hard she can be on herself. She'll get her confidence back …'

And then, like a sledgehammer to the back of his head, Jack remembers *he* can fix this. He has superpowers. He can give Ruby the self-assurance she needs.

He doesn't waste time hauling his butt over the coals for being such an idiot, he'll do that later. Now, he's got to fix things. Without a second to lose, he gets to it. His eyes close to concentrate. He wills the fire within his gut to stir. He waits. Once at a level he's confident he can turn things around, he radiates the power of it to blanket Ruby, then extends it to cover the others … for safe measure.

In moments, its effects are unmistakable. The tension on Ruby's brow softens. Her death-like grip on Max weakens. Soon, Peanut and Kenny have the girls relaxed and smiling at their shenanigans. Once again, Jack gives himself a mental kick. The panic could've been averted if he'd intervened sooner.

But time is wasting. They need direction. Peanut is right. This is way too big for them to tackle. They've done what they set out to do, and that was to locate an undiscovered portal. Now it's time for Gerard Thompson to take over.

The sooner they get back, the quicker they'll have Riley's brother and friends home.

That's *if* they can get back. Remembering Kenny's earlier trepidation in their returning the way they came, he groans.

But there's no other way!

Or is there?

Again, Jack takes a moment to study the rainforest and the lake. But Max's sudden outcry diverts his focus.

'Oh God! What's that?'

He whips around to see Max pointing to a spot in the forest.

Ruby produces her shield in an instant. Within the bubble, they're safe.

Max presses against the clear barrier, squinting to get a better look. 'Over there … I saw something move from behind that giant fern.'

'I'll go,' Peanut says. 'Rubes, let me out.'

Ruby is ready to protest, but Jack indicates she should let him.

Her eyes widen. 'What? No way! We don't know what's out there! Didn't you watch *Jurassic Park*?'

Jack fortifies calm over Ruby, then reminds her that Peanut will be safe while he's invisible. 'He'll just check it out and come back.' He turns to Peanut. 'Right?'

Peanut nods.

Ruby softens to Jack's magic. The tension on her brow melts away. She blinks a few times, then lowers the barrier for Peanut to exit before reinforcing it shut. Peanut vanishes. They watch the foliage magically part before him as he begins his search.

Jack remains alert, his senses firing, ready for anything. He jumps suddenly. There's an outcry, followed by a scuffle.

'Oi! What d'ya reckon you're playing at?'

It's Peanut. But it doesn't sound like he's in danger. Just peeved.

Then a voice unfamiliar to him cries out for help. Jack prepares to run. He instructs Ruby to let him out. But Ruby grabs him by the arm and motions for him to wait. They stop and listen.

'Help! Help! What, what's going on?' The person—a young boy, it seems—sounds petrified.

'*What's goin' on?*' They hear Peanut cry out cynically. '*I'll* tell ya what! You're sprung! That's what!'

The tussle continues. The boy again screams for help. And then it stops. For a moment, there's silence. 'Oi! What's this? You sneaky little brat!' They hear Peanut cry out. 'You've got a hide! So ya thought you could nick our stuff and get away with it, did ya? Well think again, *buddy*! You, *my friend,* have got a hell of a lot of explaining to do! Come on!'

The disturbance beyond the shrubs surfaces. A young boy stumbles into the clearing, seemingly alone, his arm yanked upwards.

Peanut materialises, the missing first-aid kit held up high.

The boy turns, sees Peanut for the first time and starts hollering.

Ruby retracts the shield. Jack dives onto the stranger, knocking him to the ground, and slaps his hand to his mouth. He scours the forest. The ruckus may have attracted unwanted attention. But all is silent.

Jack studies the small boy. 'Shut your trap, you twit! D'ya want to get us killed?'

The boy's eyes widen. He stops.

Jack loosens his hold. This scrap of a kid, scrawny and dishevelled, doesn't look like he's any real threat.

Jack takes a moment to examine him. The boy

looks as though he's come straight from a history book. His clothes, although threadbare, appear outdated. His pants, held up by rusted metal braces, come to his knees. Short scuffed-up chestnut-coloured leather boots, missing their laces, cover his sockless feet. His tattered, grimy button-up collarless shirt, and the lopsided brown checked cap on his head, look like something his great-grandfather would've worn as a boy. He'd swear the boy has come from another era entirely.

'So here's your ghost!' Peanut announces triumphantly. 'And I use the term loosely because, as you can see, he's not one!' He glares at the boy. 'I don't know how you did it, but you sure fooled us! You thieving little rat! So you thought you could scam *and* steal from us, did ya?'

The boy pushes against Jack and manages to shake him off. He scrambles to get to his feet. 'I had to,' he says, gasping heavily. 'It was the only way to get you to follow me!' He looks at Max. 'Max, I need your help.'

Stunned, Jack looks from the boy to Max and then to the first-aid kit. Peanut's assumption is right. 'So it *was* you? But how?'

The look on the boy's face turns smug. His eyes sparkle with mischief. 'So where are *Riley* and *Billy*?'

Peanut splutters. 'What the hell! Okay, Houdini,

time to come clean! How d'ya do it?'

Max clicks her tongue and frowns. She approaches the boy, her hands extended in a friendly manner. 'So you're the ghost from the orphanage.'

Again, Peanut splutters. '*Ghost?* Max, will ya look at him? He's real—he's alive. And I've got the bruises ta prove it! It's all a trick—sleight of hands, smoke and mirrors. You know … that kinda thing. All of that weird stuff back at the orphanage is this kid's idea of a sick joke.'

Kenny rubs his chin and studies the boy. 'Max is right, you know,' he says after a closer inspection. 'Look at what we know about ghosts. Take our friends, Jae, Seb and Eddie. They died in the ancient realm and became ghosts. And then the portal brought them back to life when they returned home.' He runs his hand over the top of his head. 'So I figure that's what's happened here, but in reverse.' He turns to face the boy. 'Am I right?'

The boy's face screws up. 'Um, I'm not sure what you mean. All I know is when I died, I became a ghost. And when I enter the creek at the orphanage, I end up here, alive.' He shrugs. 'Dunno. I can't explain it. It just happens.'

Jack blinks. This boy, alive and sitting in front of them, is a ghost come back to life. Somehow, it all makes sense.

The boy sighs. 'I guess it's okay being a ghost. But to be honest, it has its limits. Haunting grows old really quick. Plus, no one visits the orphanage anymore. I get bored. I'd rather be here where I can breathe in the air and feel the sun on my skin.'

A sudden thought comes to Jack. This kid may be their ticket out of here. 'So you just go back and forth between the two dimensions when you feel like it?'

The boy frowns. '*Dimensions?*'

Peanut scowls. 'Yeah. You know, one minute you've carked it and you're a poltergeist in the twenty-first century, the next, you're doing your own *Walking with Dinosaurs* doco.'

The lines on the boy's forehead furrow deeper. 'What d'ya mean, twenty-first century? Boy! How long have I been dead?'

Jack rubs his brow. They need to get out of there. 'Look, mate, we'll fill you in later. Right now, you need to help us find the way back to the orphanage before we *all* end up dead.'

Kenny approaches the boy. He frowns and scratches his head. 'So how do you get past the *Mosasaur?*'

The boy looks at him, his expression vacant. He frowns. 'Buddy, you've got me again. I've got no idea what you're talking about.'

Kenny points to the lake. 'What? You've never

come across it? Are you kidding me? It's only an eighteen-metre, prehistoric, carnivorous beast of a reptile. And it lives in there. How have you missed it?"

Again, the boy frowns. And then his eyes light up. 'Who? Nellie?' He chuckles. 'Nellie wouldn't hurt a fly. She's my best friend!' He looks at their stunned expressions and laughs. And keeps on laughing … a bent-over, full-blown belly laugh.

He takes a moment to catch his breath, wiping the tears from his eyes. 'I should fill you in,' he tells them with a smirk. 'Years ago, I found Nellie, washed up on the shore of *The Big River*—on the other side of the mountain. At first, I didn't think she was alive, but she was. Only just. I brought her here and looked after her until she got better. I fed her whatever I could scavenge from the lake. You know, fish, crabs, that kinda thing. She was only a little 'un back then. Didn't know she was going to grow up to be so big now, did I?' He looks across the surface of the lake and scratches his chin. 'You know, at first, I thought she was some kind of seal. Turns out she isn't.' He grins and finds a spot on the ground to sit. 'A *Mosasaur*, you say. Well, I'll be!' He shakes his head. 'Lucky for Nellie, the lake's so big, then. She might need to grow some.'

Max sits at his side. She wraps her arms around her knees and smiles. 'So what's your name?'

The boy lowers his gaze. Colour rises to flush his cheeks. 'Um … Albert.'

She grins. 'How old are you, Albert?'

'I'm … I'm fourteen,' he says, his chin tucked into his chest.

This surprises Jack. He figured, by his size, he was a lot younger. He then recalls Kenny telling them about the hard times kids like Albert lived through back then. 'So you were an orphan at St Hubert's?'

Albert looks up at him and nods.

Kenny sits on the other side of him, cross-legged, doodling in the dirt with a stick. 'Albert, tell me something. When were you there? I mean, what year?'

Albert shifts, his posture a little less rigid now. He looks at Kenny. 'Um, I guess from when it first opened. St Hubert's was new then. Well, it smelled new, anyway. Fresh lick of paint on the walls. Linseed oil and beeswax scrubbed into the floorboards. You know the kind of thing. Nothing like it is now … trashed.'

He sighs. 'It was after my pa died,' he continues, 'back in the war. And my ma, well, she died of a broken heart, they say. That's when St Hubert's took me in.'

Kenny rubs his chin, deep in thought for a moment. He stops. 'Albert, am I right in guessing you were born sometime in 1905 and were eight years old when they took you in at the orphanage?'

Albert's eyes pop. 'Wow! How d'ya work that out?'

Kenny shrugs and smiles. 'Just from what you've told us and knowing a little history.'

He turns to the others. 'Albert must've died during the pandemic—after the Spanish flu hit Australia in 1919,' Kenny tells them. 'Remember, I mentioned the shallow graves near the creek at the back of the orphanage? Well, a lot of them were washed away in the floods of 1925. That's probably when Albert discovered the portal.'

Albert scratches his head. 'I don't quite follow you, mate. But you seem to me to be a pretty smart bloke, so I guess what you're saying is right.'

Although all this small talk is interesting, they need to get going. Jack exchanges a look with Peanut. He cocks his head towards the lake, indicating he should make the first move.

Peanut nods in silent agreement. He clears his throat. 'Um, so, Albert, since you're so cosy with *Loch Ness Nellie*,' he starts with a grin, 'I reckon you could show us how to bypass her so's we can get the heck out of here. What d'ya reckon?'

Albert jumps up. 'What? No!' He turns to Max. 'You're a healer, right? We need your help!'

Healer? Jack folds his arms and studies Albert a little closer. 'How come you called her that?'

Max being referred to as a *healer* isn't something he's heard since the ancient realm. Hearing it again, and here of all places, floors him.

The younger boy cowers at Jack's intimidating stare.

Max jumps up and steps between them. She presses her hand on Jack's chest and motions for him to back off, then turns to Albert. 'Hey, so, um, Albert, where did you hear that?'

Albert looks from Max to Jack to Max again. 'What did I say wrong? That's what the forest people call you, ain't it? And … and so did Ryker.'

Forest people? Ryker? Jack almost falls over. 'What the hell! You'd better start explaining yourself. And talk fast!'

Max tugs Jack's shirt and gives him another warning look.

Her eyes soften when she looks at Albert. 'You're not in trouble. We're just trying to understand what's happening here.' She shrugs. 'How do you know so much about Ryker and me?'

Again, Albert's gaze flits to Jack. He shrinks from his glare. 'I … I was in the forest that day when Max fixed that man's broken arm. That's all. I swear I didn't do anything bad.'

Max raises her hands in a gesture of sincerity, trying to calm him. 'It's okay. We believe you.'

She smiles.

There's nothing forced or fake in Max's approach, just mindfulness. Jack respects that. It's clear his hard-nose approach isn't getting them anywhere. He steps back.

Max gives Albert a moment. 'Go on.'

Albert shoves his hands in his pockets, lowers his gaze, and scuffs the dirt with his well-worn boot. 'I think they call him Alger. You know the one …' He peeks at Max; his lip curls. 'And boy, it was like magic! You sure are amazing. I've never seen anything like it.'

Kenny scratches his head. 'Hold on, I'm confused. How is it that you were there—in a completely different dimension to this?' He pauses, then his eyes light up. 'No way … you've found another portal! And there's a way to travel between all *three* dimensions. Right?' In his excitement, Kenny doesn't pause to give Albert a chance to speak. 'So if returning home through the lake isn't an option, we can at least go back via the ancient realm.' His brow furrows as he considers it further. 'Hmm. Not ideal, but I guess it's doable. Beats the current situation we're in. So … tell us. How do you do it?'

Albert frowns. He looks from Kenny to Max and shrugs.

Kenny's blathering appears to have stumped the

boy. Jack figures the kid, most likely, didn't understand the half of it. He gestures for Kenny to try again.

Kenny's cheeks colour. 'Um, so, let me put it another way. How do you go to the place where the forest people live? The place where there aren't any dinosaurs?'

'Oh! That!' Albert chuckles, but before he has a chance to answer, the ground beneath their feet shakes for the briefest of moments. Everyone freezes. Seconds later, they feel it again. And then again.

Albert's wide eyes and ghostly complexion tell Jack that something's coming. And that *something* isn't exactly a good thing. And in light of their situation, and how exposed they are, they need to find cover. Fast.

The ground trembles again. In the distance, massive trees quiver, then part, paving the way for the unseen giant approaching. Huge winged animals nesting in the trees take flight, screeching their objection.

Albert snatches the first-aid kit from Peanut and takes off at a sprint, disappearing into the forest before anyone realises they should be keeping up.

'Quick! After him!' Jack yanks Max by the hand and takes chase. She flaps behind him like a rag doll, struggling to keep up. He glances over his shoulder to make sure the others are following. Peanut and Ruby are hot on his tail. Kenny trails a little at the rear.

A tremendous roar nearby sets them off. They scramble in terror, tripping over themselves in an attempt to get away.

But where are they heading? Albert is nowhere to be seen.

'Stop!' Jack calls out. 'Albert's gone, and we'll never find him. Ruby, activate your shield. We'll be safe as long as we're under it.'

But in her panic, Ruby doesn't stop.

They hear another earth-shaking roar. This time, the sound is a little nearer. Jack needs to reach Ruby to calm her. He takes chase, and the others follow. But she's frantic in her escape, and before he knows it, she's gone.

He stops to catch his breath, swallows hard and searches the forest. And then he catches a glimpse of her strawberry-blond ponytail, and he's off again.

Ruby charges ahead blindly and becomes entangled in the vines and brush. She fights to free herself. Hysterical. Jack catches up to her and pulls her from the forest's web. At once, he radiates his blanket of calm to settle her. The effect is instant. She softens in his arms, and her erratic breathing settles.

The others catch up.

Ruby reactivates the protective barrier, and they squat low behind the giant ferns, taking a moment to catch their breath and listen. They hear the beast drinking from the lake in the distance. For a moment, there's composure; Jack works hard to maintain it.

Max takes the opportunity, in the quiet madness, to heal Ruby's gashes. Ruby smiles her thanks.

And then, without warning, the vegetation before them parts. Jack gasps. They're face to face with the meanest-looking reptile he's ever seen.

For the briefest moment, no one moves. Jack dares not breathe. The one-metre-tall, three-metre-long dinosaur leans in closer, angles its face to study them, then snorts. Its steaming breath fogs the shield.

And then there's pandemonium.

All five scream and scramble to escape, smashing up against the barrier. Jack is quick to rationalise they're in no better place than under the shield. They're safe as long as Ruby keeps it together. If she loses it, so will their chances of staying alive. She quickly becomes his sole focus.

The creature releases a high-pitched squeal and strikes at them. They all dive to avoid the attack, but the barrier remains intact.

Jack puts everything he has in keeping Ruby calm and in control. And she does, magnificently. The beast is no match for her. After repeated attempts, the reinforcement doesn't waver. She smiles. Her confidence skyrockets.

With its dagger-like teeth bared, dripping with saliva, the dinosaur continues to lash at them to no avail. The commotion it creates, though, rouses another to investigate. With two of them now clawing and mauling at the shield, Jack prays Ruby can maintain her composure long enough to keep them safe.

And then a shadow, cast from above, eclipses sunlight. Jack looks up and freezes. He knows enough about dinosaurs to recognise this one. Hovering over them, standing at four metres tall, the almighty *Tyrannosaurus rex*. Jack watches the majestic giant raise its enormous head, its intention focused, set for the kill.

Distracted by the obstacle to its meal, one of the smaller reptiles fails to see the threat coming. And then it's too late. A squeal, so deafening, so tortured, breaks the silence, the victim caught and locked in the merciless jaws of the dominant beast.

The *T. rex* slams its victim against a nearby rocky outcrop with a sickening crunch, silencing it forever. Its limp body, now flung high in the air, is again caught with a snap of a jaw, and is made a meal of in two gulps.

The second dinosaur, previously oblivious to its mate's demise, suddenly becomes aware of the towering beast now with its sights set on *it*. It shrieks a high-pitched screech and prepares to run. Again, too late. The fatal strike, instant.

All they see is the splattering of blood over the shield.

Jack throws himself over his friends, reinforcing his blanket of calm. After what they just witnessed, he can't afford any one of them losing their nerve. Especially Ruby.

Concealed beneath the cloak of blood, Jack scarcely allows himself to breathe, let alone move.

The earth beneath them trembles once again as the giant withdraws.

Somehow, they've evaded death. No one speaks. The whole experience is almost too much.

Jack wills himself to think. They need to get out of there.

But how?

19

MASTER GOOGLE

MAX

Max's body is a mass of quivering jelly, her breathing erratic. She clenches her teeth to stop them from chattering. Jack pulls them all into an embrace, and in an instant, she feels the blanket of calm melt away the shock. Her eyelids grow heavy; her pulse settles. Never in a million years would she have imagined she'd have such a horrifying experience. She looks across at Ruby, takes her hand in hers and squeezes it, forever thankful for her unyielding endurance. Ruby smiles. She cocks her head towards Jack. They both know that if it wasn't for Jack's resolve, they'd be goners. His ability to calm everyone in the past has saved their necks so many times already.

Max studies the crimson shield above. The rivulets of blood trickling down the dome thin to allow a stippled view of the forest once again. The image of the brutal attack on the first dinosaur being slammed against a large rock formation comes to mind. Max peers through the murky barrier to get a better look. She notices that they're at the foot of a huge rocky outcrop. She cranks her neck to see it and wonders about the likelihood of there being a cave or hollow inside. They need to find shelter while they work out a plan to escape this place.

Kenny draws adjacent to her and angles his head against the shield. He gives Max a thumbs-up signal and nods his agreement as if reading her thoughts. 'We've gotta find somewhere safer,' he whispers. 'More predators will come once they've caught a whiff of all this blood. We're too exposed.'

'I'm with you,' Ruby says in a lowered voice. 'Let's get out of here. I don't know if I can keep the shield reinforced against a stronger attack—even with Jack's support. Those two smaller ones were hard enough.'

'*Deinonychus,* singular form; *Deinonychuses,* plural,' Kenny randomly tells them suddenly. 'They're pack hunters. They existed during the early Cretaceous period—about one hundred and fifteen to one hundred and eight million years ago. They—'

Peanut slaps his hand over Kenny's mouth to silence him and frowns. 'Not now, Kenny!'

Kenny's cheeks colour.

Max arcs up. She's done with Peanut's repeated jibes on Kenny. 'Back off, Peanut! You know he can't help it.'

Kenny chuckles quietly. 'Hey, Max, don't worry. It's cool. I would've muzzled myself if I was quick enough.'

Peanut grabs Kenny in a headlock and messes his hair.

'Come on,' Jack prompts, 'let's find somewhere safe.'

They move as one. Jack leads.

But they struggle to see where they're going, the view hampered by the blood. Jack suggests to Ruby to deactivate the barrier, then reboot it to give them a fresh shield.

Ruby takes a moment to inspect the area. And then, with a pop, the shield is no more. Blood from the massacred dinosaur splatters over them. Max gasps; Kenny splutters; Jack cries out.

Peanut swipes at his face and flicks away the offensive fluid. 'Argh, Ruby! Gross!'

Suddenly, they hear movement in the near distance. The rustling of disturbed foliage indicates something's fast approaching. Ruby reactivates her shield. They run.

Coordinating the escape proves tricky. Peanut races ahead, his long legs carrying him at a speed that Max's short legs can't keep up with. Jack yanks him by the shirt to slow him down. Eventually, they fall into a rhythm and sprint to find somewhere to shelter.

They soon realise that whatever had picked up on the scent of blood hasn't followed. Jack's idea of refreshing the shield may just have saved them.

Up ahead, they notice an opening in the huge rockface big enough for them to squeeze through, and within, a darkened hollow. Peanut volunteers to investigate. Ruby grabs Peanut's hand, her eyes pleading. He gives her a crooked smile. She swallows hard and releases him from the safety of the shield. He disappears.

They wait.

They hear Peanut tripping and cursing—no care taken to be silent. Max cringes with every sound he makes. She turns to Ruby. The look on Ruby's face says she's going to strangle him the second she gets her hands on him. Max bites her lip to hide a smirk.

Again, they wait. Now there's silence. Too quiet for Max's liking. Peanut has been gone too long. And just as she thinks to follow, Jack asks Ruby to release him from the sphere.

Max tugs him back by the shirt. 'We'll all go.'

His expression shows his apprehension, and knowing Jack, his concern is more for Peanut's safety rather than his own. But Max won't let Jack put himself at risk. They need to stick together.

She smiles to reassure him and then makes light of the situation. 'I figure if there was a problem, we would've heard something by now. Right?'

Jack's tense look softens. He nods.

He prepares to lead the way when Ruby grabs his arm. 'Me first. I've got the shield. Remember? Plus, I want to get to him first!' She laughs at his stunned expression. 'Relax, I won't kill the twit, *this* time.'

Jack grins.

Ruby moves forward. One by one, the others follow, squeezing through the tight opening.

Once inside, the light dims considerably, and they struggle to avoid the boulders blocking their path. Max bumps and trips several times, then smiles to herself, knowing now why Peanut was making such a racket.

'Hey, what's going on?'

Max jumps, her hand clutching her chest. 'Peanut! How about a little warning next time?'

Peanut materialises. 'But I haven't had a chance to check it out yet.'

'We didn't hear you scream blue murder,' Kenny says with a chuckle, 'so figured it must be safe to enter. And I reckon being in here is way safer than being out there.'

Max peers into the darkness. They're in a cave of some sort. How deep it goes is too hard to tell, and what lurks in its depths is anyone's guess.

'Hey, get a load of this!' Peanut says excitedly. 'A firepit.'

It takes a moment for Max's eyes to adjust and see what Peanut is referring to. She notices the remains of a campfire, small rocks arranged in a circle around a sunken pit, fragments of charred wood and what appear to be animal bones.

'I reckon we've got ourselves some cavemen here.' Peanut squats lower to have a better look. 'Cool!'

Kenny attempts to hide a grin. Peanut sees it, jumps up and calls him out on it. 'Oi! What's with the smirk?'

Kenny stuffs his hands in his pockets. 'Um, your comment about cavemen …'

Peanut waits, his arms crossed, chin jutted forward. 'Yeah? What about it?'

'Well,' Kenny continues, 'I don't think that's right.' He clears his throat and straightens his shoulders. 'To be perfectly honest, it's impossible.'

Peanut snorts. '*Impossible*? How d'ya work that out? Just look at the evidence.'

Kenny tries to hide a grin. 'Peanut, I don't have

to look at it to know. Just take it from me, you're way off on this one.'

Peanut pouts. 'So you're telling me, just by looking at it, that I'm wrong? That a caveman hasn't left it?'

Kenny grins. 'Um, yep.'

Peanut clicks his tongue. 'Come off it, Kenny! How?'

Jack nudges Peanut, a smile twitching at the corner of his lips. 'Seriously? D'ya really want to go up against Master Google on this one?'

Max grins. She can see this ending up with someone having egg on their face.

Again, Kenny clears his throat. 'Okay, you want me to prove it? I'll prove it. And I can tell you now, I won't need any help from a superpower for this one.' He looks at Jack and gives him a wink.

'So,' he begins, 'without getting into the nitty-gritty of things, based on the fact that this place is overrun with dinosaurs, it's safe to say we're in the *Mesozoic* Era; a period of time which extended from approximately two hundred and twenty-five to sixty-five million years ago.' Kenny stops and smiles, clearly confident that bit of information should suffice.

Peanut frowns. 'And? ...' He gestures for Kenny to get to the part where he proves him wrong.

Kenny blinks. 'Peanut, dinosaurs died out *sixty-*

five million years before man came into existence. Man and dinosaur never existed at the same time. So unless there's a scaly critter in here capable of starting a fire, then I'm pretty sure I'm right.'

'Ha! Nice one, Master Google!' Ruby laughs and hi-fives Kenny.

Peanut groans and smacks his forehead.

Kenny chuckles and gives Peanut a friendly nudge. 'Don't beat yourself up, mate. It's all good.'

Jack shakes his head at his reckless friend. 'You really should learn to pick your battles, mate.'

'And that's not all,' Kenny tells them. 'The firepit was made by someone of more recent times.' He bends to unearth a small box, half obscured in the dirt. They all lean in to have a closer look. It looks like a box of matches. He brushes away the dirt. 'Check out the branding. Bryant & May.' He opens the box to find half a dozen white-tipped matchsticks.

He frowns for a moment, then smiles as a fact comes to him. 'Oh, now I get it!' And then, like a dam release, the information keeps coming. Mechanically, he proceeds to jabber on about them. 'These safety matches, originally manufactured in London by William Bryant and Francis May in 1861, were in production in Melbourne, Australia, from 1909 until early 1987. Initially, the striking sticks were tipped with white phosphorous, but in 1946 they started using red phosphorous, which is how we know them today, as *Red Heads*. So whoever lit the fire must've come from a period before 1946.' He stops and chuckles to himself. 'I reckon our little friend Albert kinda fits the bill. What do you think?'

Max smiles, impressed by Kenny's logic. 'Well, based on all that info, Kenny, I think you might just be right. Hey, I wonder what happened …' She stops suddenly, frozen on the spot, hardly able to breathe. Through the narrow opening of the cave, she sees a huge, gleaming yellowish-brown eye staring at them. The beast blinks, and then its slit-like pupil dilates. The giant snorts, its hot breath sending debris flying. Max shields her eyes and cops a mouthful of dust. She splutters and chokes, fighting to catch her breath, and scrambles further back in the cave with the others. The dinosaur cries out, its roar deafening. It then begins to claw at the opening.

'Ruby, your shield!' Jack cries out, and at once they're encompassed by the barrier and protected. But for how long?

The beast continues, repeatedly lashing at the opening, its bloodied talons penetrating the space. Bit by bit, the darkness of the shadow that protected them earlier is no more. And there before them, angling its head to view them better, stands a four-metre-tall *Tyrannosaurus rex*—quite possibly the one they encountered earlier—impatient and ready to attack.

Max clings to Jack. This might just be their very last moments together alive.

Jack looks down at her. His eyes darken. He turns to Ruby. 'Ruby, let me out!'

Before Max knows what's happening, Jack breaks from her hold and steps out to approach the monster.

With his hands raised, and a daring she can hardly believe, Jack goes forth in an attempt to tame the beast.

20
MISTAKE

RYKER

Ryker's stomach churns. Aelianna's face is aglow. Her eyes sparkle, her smile radiant. She's excited, and he can't believe it. There wasn't even a pause to consider it, not even a moment's hesitation. The instant he mentioned the idea of returning to the realm, Aelianna was totally committed. Her decision to go with them was made even before he finished telling her the plan. He groans. There's no way he *can't* take her now. She'll join the team whether he likes it or not.

He runs his hand back and forth over the top of his head. But he can't risk losing her—not again. *What if she chooses to remain with her family?* Just thinking about what it would mean to leave her behind, after they've been through so much together, sickens him to the stomach.

He shakes it off. The fear of that happening is irrational, and he knows it. Her love for him, he reminds himself, is without a doubt solid.

And then there's the risk of something happening to her! True, it's a gamble. The realm holds many enemies. Whether it's Wulf and his goons from the Dark Forest or the Ancients and their henchmen— Aelianna will always be an easy target. A perfect opportunity for them to take their revenge on him.

He softens a little, looking into her chocolate-coloured eyes. He can't help but smile. His own warrior princess … she shies away from nothing. Whether she's defending herself from the likes of the savage Wulf or his sidekick Titus, Aelianna has proven, time and time again, to be capable of holding her own.

He draws in a deep breath and shakes his head. These insecurities that plague him constantly are issues he needs to deal with. Something *he* needs to get over.

Determined to have everything go to plan, Ryker prepares for the mission, cramming his backpack with useful gadgets, ones that've come in handy in the past. Apart from necessities, such as a torch, a box of matches, his thermal-imaging goggles, the walkie-talkies, a compass and a flare gun, he packs a taser, two cans of pepper spray and, of course, his trusted hunting knife.

He watches Aelianna prepare a kit of her own. First and foremost, she stashes the backpack's side-pocket with the two Swiss army pocketknives he bought her the other day. He smiles, remembering it. Her eyes lit up when she first saw them. She couldn't believe so many useful implements could be crammed into one tool. And then she couldn't decide between the one that had a miniature knife, scissors and a saw, or the one that had a sizeable blade. So he bought her both.

Among the portable folding hunting bow, some arrows, a slingshot, a rope and an axe, Aelianna packs a few modest gifts for her family.

He chuckles at the contrast of her choice of effects to his and hands her a can of pepper spray and another of wasp spray—for any just-in-case, out-of-reach situations.

'You realise we won't be needing any of this,' he tells her with a laugh.

She stops and looks up from her packing with a question on her lips.

'I'm planning for it to be a quick in-out situation,' he says hurriedly. 'It'll be over before we know it.'

He'd prefer that she didn't consider this an opportunity for an extended family visit. 'Look, I know that Jack and the gang have been gone two days now, but I'm sure they're just catching up with old friends. We, on the other hand, won't be getting sidetracked by anything. I have no intention of staying a moment longer than we need to. We go in, find them and get out.'

He watches the radiance of her smile vanish as he says this and silently curses himself for being so cruel.

Aelianna purses her lips. She says nothing and continues to pack her kit.

He's gone and ticked her off. And he can't blame anyone but himself if she despises him right now. And this time, he doesn't need Max's reprimand echoing in his head to make him feel like a dog. He reaches for her hand to apologise.

She raises her chin and looks him in the eye. "Tis fine for *others* to *catch up* with old friends, but clearly 'tis not for *me*. Why *is* that, Ryker?'

He flinches. He's never seen Aelianna angry, and it shocks him. He needs to fix this. His mouth opens and closes, but nothing comes out.

Aelianna takes back her hand and exits the room in a huff. As she leaves, he hears her utter the word *mistake* under her breath.

He groans. It *is* a mistake—there's no questioning

it. His ill-chosen words should never have been said. Aelianna doesn't deserve that. His demons are for him alone to put right. What he needs to stop doing is treating her like a crystal ornament wrapped in cotton wool. She's far stronger than that. She's lived her whole life in the forest and survived. She doesn't need him beating his chest and turning Neanderthal on her.

And then a thought hits him. His breath catches. Beads of sweat form on his upper lip. The word *mistake* echoes in his ears. Her choice of word.

Suddenly, he needs to know. Is the 'mistake' his use of thoughtless words, or is it in reference to the decision she made to upend her life to be with him?

Oh my God! What have I done?

He calls out after her in a panic. 'Aelianna, please! I'm sorry!'

21
MISTAKE TWO

AELIANNA

Aelianna bites her lower lip to hold back from crying. She doesn't understand Ryker's behaviour. What has brought about this reluctance to visit her family and friends—now also *his* family and friends? She reflects on the many hardships endured in the past. In times of need, they stood as one. When there was hunger, Ryker provided them with food. Where there was danger, Ryker fought for them. When Ryker sought guidance, her father led them. When freedom was their goal, they banded together and battled as one.

So when had the allegiance turned to dust? *They had parted as friends, had they not?* She tries to place what may have caused a rift. But she's at a loss. There's nothing.

She calls to mind that day her father dragged her through the forest in search of Ryker, who was preparing to leave them. Without a doubt, the most embarrassing moment in her life. He begged Ryker to take her with him … to keep her from harm's way. What possessed her father to believe he would do this for them? Such a bold and foolish notion. Why should he? Ryker owed them nothing. Her heart had raced as she awaited his reaction. Above anything, rejection was her greatest fear. At first it looked imminent. The colour drained from his face as he stared at her. He had no words. Mortified by what she'd understood it to mean, she took off into the forest. Ryker gave chase and was upon her in moments. It was then he declared his sentiments—there was nothing more he could have ever wished for. His words, heard a thousand times only in her dreams, were at last spoken openly, and more importantly, sincerely.

A moment of perfection cherished.

And not once since that day had she any cause to regret the decision to enter this new, wondrous, intangible world and begin a life with this most incredible man.

That is, until now.

Wounded, Aelianna dives for the bed and buries

her head beneath the pillow, trying to mute Ryker's persistent plea at the door. Not since the day Ryker had returned to the forest in search of The Forbidden Passage has her heart ached so much. Then, although secretly wishing she was the object for his return, she knew at once, as their eyes met, that she was not. In that fleeting glance, he had shattered her heart into a million pieces.

Tears stream down her cheeks, remembering this.

She's in a mess of emotions. If only she could talk to Max. Max would see the folly in her thinking and have her reassured in a matter of moments.

A thought comes to her. Aelianna sits up and swipes at the tears. *But why can I* not *speak with her? Ryker often does.* She dives for the small black contraption on the bedside table that Ryker calls a cell phone, eager to share her thoughts with her dearest friend.

She disconnects the cord attached, sits on the edge of the bed, her back facing the door, and studies it a moment, trying to recall the steps taken to have Max's voice speak from within the box. 'It cannot be too difficult,' she tells herself, turning the device over and over in her hand. She frowns, then presses the button on the front … the one she sees Ryker often presses to begin. The device lights up as it awakens. She grins and presses the button again. It vibrates, and a series of circles appear, each with numbers and symbols within.

Still unfamiliar with many of the symbols, she hesitates. But she has learned numbers. Her face brightens. She recalls Ryker pressing the numbers in a particular pattern, and in her eagerness, tries to mimic his movements. The buttons pip as she does so. Again, the cell phone vibrates. Her heart skips a beat. She rests it against her ear and waits. There's no sound, no Max, only silence. She takes it away and frowns at it before returning it to her ear. 'Max! Are you in there? I must speak with you.'

Again, no response. She looks down at the apparatus, confused. The lit screen fades to black. She huffs and sits a little taller. 'You shall not discourage me, for I am determined to do this.'

She pauses to re-evaluate her method, and gazes vacantly out the bedroom window, thinking. 'The secret to success lies in the pattern Ryker uses with the numbers. I'm certain of it.' She then remembers him telling her that to decipher the encryption, she must use the symbols that make up her name. She dives for the book and pencil Ryker keeps in his desk drawer and writes her name with painstaking accuracy. Once done, she awakens the device to reveal the numbers once again. With great care, she enters the necessary symbols.

As a result, several small coloured images appear in neat squares on the screen. She grins with giddiness, then pauses to consider which image to press. Her finger hovers. ''Tis a green one, of this I am certain. But which one?' Two bright green images sit side by side along the bottom of the screen. She wavers between the two. The hesitation costs her. The screen fades to black. She groans.

'No, no, no!' She wags her finger at the device. 'You shall not defy me.'

Aelianna stops, combs her fringe from her face, pulls at her sleeves to free her hands completely, then takes a breath and prepares to go again.

The numbers appear. She enters the symbols of her name. The options are again before her. She pounces on one of them; the one oddly shaped like a banana fruit. And then, to her relief, several words appear. Among them, she recognises Max's name. Without hesitation, she taps the name, then holds the device to her ear. Her heart skips a beat when she hears a familiar tone. And then …

'Hi, you've reached Max.'

'Oh, my dearest friend, I have found you! Max, you will be so proud—'

'I can't come to the phone right now, but if you leave a message, I'll get back to you as soon as possible.'

She then hears a high-pitched beep, followed

by silence.

Aelianna takes the cell phone from her ear and stares at it. She frowns. 'Max, are you in there? 'Tis I, Aelianna. Please, speak to me. I *need* someone to talk to.' She pauses to hear a reply but hears nothing. Her heart sinks.

'Then talk to *me*, Lia.'

The unexpected timbre of Ryker's voice behind her makes her jump and drop the phone. She whips around to face him.

He steps towards her with his hand extended. 'Please.'

The sadness reflected in his eyes cuts her. She cannot bear to look at it. She turns away.

'I get it. You're angry with me, and I don't blame you. I've said some hurtful things. And if you don't want to talk to me, Lia, then please listen.'

She glances at his hand—the offer of peace there if she so desires. And she does. Ryker would never willingly hurt her. She knows this. But why this sudden hostility towards her family? She cannot fathom it.

She sighs, turns to look him in the eye and takes his hand. She should at least hear what he has to say.

He lets out a worried sigh. The tension in the lines of his face soften. 'I've been a complete idiot. And I'm sorry.' He reaches for the phone on the floor and turns it over in his hand. 'Max warned me about this. I should've listened. She was right.' He gives her hand a gentle squeeze. They sit side by side on the edge of the bed. 'I know I can be overbearing, and for that I ask for your patience. I'm trying. But when it comes to you, Lia, I can't help myself. I feel like I need to protect you—keep you from harm's way.'

She frowns.

His hands shoot up to stop her from responding. 'I know you don't need a big idiot like me looking out for you. You can handle yourself.' He grins. 'And probably better than I can.' He chuckles, then sobers. 'But I promised your father I'd look after you. And somewhere in my Neanderthal thinking, that meant to wrap you in cotton wool so you can't break.' His gaze goes elsewhere. He pauses. 'And if I'm being perfectly honest … I'm scared.'

Aelianna blinks. *A big, strong warrior such as he, scared?*

Ryker chuckles. 'Yeah, hard to believe, right? Give me vicious dogs, ruthless guards and savages from the Dark Forest any day.' His look softens. 'But the thought of anything happening to you while we're in the realm, Lia, makes me come undone.'

He looks away, his fists curl into tight balls, his knuckles bleach to white and his breathing accelerates.

Aelianna watches the transformation and wonders

where his thoughts have gone. She takes his face in her hands and stares deeply into his eyes. 'We will be prepared. We shall remain vigilant and not allow any harm to come to us. And there is also the support of the village folk. Nothing untoward will befall us.'

He pauses and looks at her. His gaze flicking back and forth between her eyes, as if organising his thoughts. He then caresses her cheek with the back of his hand and sighs.

She smiles. With some hope he will see the determination and confidence within her and lay all uncertainty to rest.

'Forgive me?'

She lowers her gaze and nods.

He reaches for the phone on the bed and chuckles. 'And look at *you*. Tackling technology on your own. Girl, that's pretty amazing. I'm impressed—you got Max's voicemail.'

'But have I called at an inconvenient time? Why was I unable to reach her?'

'Honey, Max is in the realm, remember?'

She frowns, not quite understanding his meaning.

'Cell phones don't work in the realm. They're a modern invention.' He shrugs, then tugs her into a hug and kisses the top of her head. 'I know. It's all a bit too complicated. Just know that they can only be used in our world. Okay? Maybe I'll ask Kenny to explain it to you once this is all over.'

She claps her hands. 'So we shall continue with the plan?'

He chuckles. 'Yes, my warrior princess, we'll continue with the plan. We'll leave tomorrow.'

Aelianna's heart skips a beat. Just one more sleep, and she'll be a step closer to being with her family again. She presses the palms of her hands to her eyes to hold back the tears and rubs at the sting in her nose. For the briefest moment, she had lost all hope. Ryker, in his obstinance, had held no promise of her ever returning home.

22

AND IT BEGINS

EDRA

She vowed never to step foot in the realm again, but here she is, braced and ready to take on the beast that nearly destroyed her not that long ago. So why do it? Edra looks into the eyes of the man at her side, the man she wholeheartedly loves, and knows the answer. She lost him once and will never risk losing him again. Wherever Jaeger goes, she goes.

Edra finds the strength to do this by placing her faith in Jaeger and trusting his judgement. When Ryker first bared his plan to re-enter the realm to help find their Aussie friends, Jaeger didn't hesitate to volunteer. Not for one moment. And it's his fierce sense of loyalty to Ryker that made him commit so willingly. She's sure of it. Because diving headfirst into something isn't typical of him. If anything, he's over-cautious. His track record speaks for itself. It took him forever to approach Edra and make known his interest in her. If Edra hadn't been so in tune with his disposition, she would've missed it. It was his awkward shyness that made her fall in love with him in the first place.

And so she gets it. Although Jaeger may not feel directly indebted to their Aussie friends for his newfound freedom, he certainly does to Ryker. And once committed, Jaeger never strays.

In truth, the decision to help Ryker was never going to be a difficult one—not really. As much as she loathes everything realm-related, Edra owes her life to the Aussies. If it wasn't for their grit and determination to find freedom, she, Ryker and the twins would still be imprisoned in a mouse-infested cell beneath an ancient arena, fighting medieval challenges to save their lives. So if Jaeger is willing to risk it all to help save them, then who is she to resist? Because the reality is, so is she.

Face to face with the wispy veil, suspended enigmatically before them, the four friends prepare to enter. Ryker, his cargo pants' pockets filled with things he says will come in handy and a hunting blade stashed in his boot. Aelianna, with a sizeable knife in its holster strapped around her waist and a portable hunting bow and some arrows in a housing on her back. Jaeger, his pockets filled with comparable gadgets to Ryker. And Edra, clutching a solid hardwood baseball bat. All four are now ready to take on whatever threat presents itself.

As was determined earlier, Banji and Ulan will remain in the real world. The jeep, well stocked with supplies, stands hidden in the brush, equipped for a crisis. A first-aid kit, an up-to-date CB radio, ropes, tasers, pepper spray, hunting knives, a crowbar, an axe. Anything that might come in handy, within reach, should an unexpected situation arise.

The air around them looms thick and still. The sun, with its blistering heat, prompts them to make a move. Edra reaches for Jaeger's hand. His smile tells her he's ready. Her hold on him tightens. It's moments like these she wishes they had Ruby with them, her shield a coveted advantage.

Edra focuses on her own superhuman abilities— her lightning-fast speed and spring-vault agility. She psyches herself, ready to call upon them, and then she stops to remember Jaeger's superpower. It's been so long, and his use of it so brief, she hardly recalls what his superpower was. And then it comes to her: hyperawareness—the ability to boost each of his five senses exponentially. A great skill to have when you need to hear or see something beyond normal human parameters, but not so great when it's something you'd rather not smell, taste ... or feel.

The memory of the horrific pain Jaeger endured while battling for his life in the barbaric beast challenge haunts her. To this day, his screams of suffering still plague her sleep. She steps away to compose herself, shaking away the toxic thoughts.

She refocuses. There's no room for negativity.

Edra turns to Ryker and waits for him to make the first move. He stands with his blade at the ready and the thermal-imaging goggles secured on the top of his head. Poised at his side, Jaeger reinforces the taser in his hand. Aelianna stands at the rear. She adjusts the bow on her back and reaches for Edra's hand. Together, they brace themselves for what awaits them in The Forbidden Passage.

Ryker hurls himself forward and vanishes. Jaeger is quick to follow. Not one to be anywhere without Jaeger, Edra yanks Aelianna and dives through the barrier to the other side.

It takes a moment for her eyes to adjust to the sudden change in dimness. The time difference takes them either to the early hours of the morning or, alternatively, the close of day.

The first thing she sees is Ryker's impressive form and nothing more. She attempts to sidestep him to look for Jaeger, but his solid mass moves to block her at every turn. She grits her teeth. A growl resonates in her throat. She looks up at him and stops. The look of regret in his eyes confuses her.

And then there's panic.

Something's happened to Jaeger!

After the briefest pause, Ryker steps aside. What Edra sees shouldn't shock her, but it does. With his shoulders slumped, his head bowed, Jaeger, suspended mid-air, floats before her as transparent as the veil they passed through only moments earlier. She gasps. Aelianna moves to her side.

Jaeger struggles to look at her. He turns away.

Edra can't speak. If the exuberance of life could be sucked from a person, then that's exactly how she'd describe Jaeger now. Or should she say, Jaeger's *ghost!*

She bites down on her lower lip, battling to hold back tears, and turns to Ryker. 'How did we not prepare for this?'

Ryker runs his hand over his hair. 'Edra, I … I don't know.'

But it's so obvious now. This was always going to happen. The return has reverted Jaeger back to how he was before leaving the realm. Dead.

Edra swallows hard. She battles to keep her head. Her demons, forever lurking in the fringes of her resolve, gather, ready to drag her back into a deep, dark hole. That same hole she once crawled into and lost herself in, and later, the one she clawed out of to keep living.

But the blame for this bungle lies with her just as much as it does anyone. She reminds herself of this, then pauses to collect herself. She thinks of Jaeger. This kind of reaction isn't helping. She delves deep to find the strength to fix this. 'Jae, you're okay, right?' she asks hesitantly. 'I mean, you're not in any pain or anything, are you?'

Jaeger looks at her for the first time. The emptiness in his eyes just about snaps that thin thread of composure she's somehow managed to muster. Again, she bites her lip to stop it from trembling, this time tasting blood.

Jaeger shakes his head.

Aelianna steps towards him and grins. ''Tis as it was the time we first met, is it not, Jaeger?' She presses her hand to her mouth to hold back a giggle. 'I remember the look on Father's face when we first encountered you. The colour drained from his face so quickly, he almost passed out.'

Jaeger smiles, remembering the time.

Aelianna reaches out to Edra. ''Tis not all so bad. In truth, 'tis a blessing. A secret gift.'

A blessing! … A gift! Edra almost falls over. 'How can you say that, Aelianna?'

'Why, is it not clear?' Aelianna's nose scrunches. 'Jaeger's presence as a spirit will deter the threats. Be it Wulf, his henchmen or the palace guards. All will flee at the sight of him.'

Ryker chuckles. He tugs Aelianna to his side and plants a kiss on her brow. 'Ten out of ten for thinking, my little visionary.'

He turns to Edra. 'She's right, you know. Jae's the secret weapon we never thought of.' He nudges her and grins. 'Edra, it's not as though he'll stay this way forever. Once we go home, Jae will return to normal. We know this already.' He gives Aelianna a wink. 'My ingenious girl! You're right, we *have* been handed a gift. Now, let's go use it!'

23

A Spanner In The Works

RYKER

Once again, Ryker is reminded of Aelianna's astuteness. She's bailed him out of yet another sticky situation. The trend becoming embarrassingly too frequent. That many times, he's lost count.

He recalls the time he had the thorny task of telling his friends that he'd stumbled into The Valley of Lost Souls and found Jaeger—as a ghost. The day Jaeger was killed was a day that tore everyone's world apart, especially Edra's. So revealing him as a ghost wasn't going to be an easy feat, but Aelianna, with her gentle and softly spoken manner, found a way.

Another memory comes to mind. The time he had all but lost hope of ever finding The Forbidden Passage. Had it not been for Aelianna's quick and shrewd intervention, they would never have found it. Singlehandedly, she had altered the course of all their lives. They found the passage. His mother's life was spared. And their future was secured.

And there are so many more incidences just like these.

What more does she need to do to remind him how special she is? Ryker looks at her, silently blasting himself for not valuing her as he should. And to think he virtually forbade her from coming. To enter the ancient realm without her? What was he thinking? But when it comes to everything concerning Aelianna, Ryker's thinking turns to mush.

One way or another, he's determined to better himself.

And it starts now.

Time to focus!

The task? To find their Aussie friends and return home. Safely.

It troubles him that they haven't heard from them for two days now. Earlier, he played down the urgency to Aelianna, but deep in his gut, his senses are firing. Something's gone wrong. The three kids who went missing through the unknown portal raises so many flags.

'Vigilant at all times. Expect the unexpected.'

Edra looks at him and frowns.

Ryker adjusts his backpack. 'Come on, we need to get going. Guards will be swarming this place at any minute. Let's find the guys and get the hell out of here.' He looks at Aelianna. 'Our stay will be brief—and only if it's safe.'

'I'll check things out,' Jaeger offers, his confidence restored. 'Give me a sec.' He whooshes down the passage ahead of them and returns moments later. 'All clear. We're good to go.'

They make their move.

Single file, they inch closer to the mouth of the passage. As they do, visibility improves, making it easier to navigate. At the entrance, Ryker secures the thermal goggles in place and scans the forest. He detects no thermal activity. 'Jae, fly higher and suss out the perimeter.'

In moments, Jaeger returns, his expression alarmed. 'I've spotted a couple of guys hiding in the scrub.'

'Friend or foe?'

'I couldn't tell.'

'Then get to work. Flush them out.' Ryker chuckles. 'Let's see if you've still got it in you.'

Jaeger darts off. Ryker gives Edra a wink.

She smiles.

Moments later, they hear a cry of fear and then a commotion. Ryker stands protectively before the girls, ready. But then he hears laughter and excited chatter. Relieved, his guard drops.

Movement from within the brushes soon reveals Aelianna's father, Molan, followed closely by their friend, Medwin.

Aelianna flies past Ryker to embrace her father.

Molan swipes the moisture from his eyes. 'Daughter, my heart is whole once again at seeing you. You look well!' He releases his hold to take Ryker's hand in greeting. He pulls his son-in-law in for a hug. 'And Son, you too appear to be'—he pauses to look him up and down—'well fed.'

They laugh.

'It would seem my daughter is a dutiful wife.'

'Molan, Aelianna is well skilled in many things, as you already know, but in the kitchen, she's a wonder.' He gives Aelianna a wink.

Molan grins with pride. 'She and her mother are alike. Both exceptional women. I have been blessed.'

Ryker takes Aelianna by the hand. 'And so too have I.'

Medwin approaches, guarded. 'Friends, we must take cover. Although the morn has only just begun, your arrival is likely to summon fortress guards. That is, if they are not presently advancing as we speak.'

Ryker couldn't agree more. In the past, their presence somehow has set off alarms, alerting guards. They're bound to be swooped upon if they don't get going.

They move, Molan leading the way, and venture deeper into the forest to an area evidently prepared by their friends. A large canopy of dense foliage conceals their hideaway, thick ferns bordering on every side. There's enough space for them to sit without being on top of each other.

Without delay, Medwin begins the conversation he's clearly anxious to have. 'So our ghostly friend informs us that you are in search of your people.' He gestures to Jaeger, then scratches his head and frowns. 'Alas, my premonition prepared us for *your* coming, but I must inform you, as much as this may distress you, I have had no vision of any others.'

Ryker frowns. *How can that be?* 'Are you sure?' But Ryker knows the answer to this already. In the past, Medwin's ability to see into the future has proven to be quite accurate, not to mention invaluable.

Medwin shrugs. 'As I said … nothing.'

Ryker's mind races. A million thoughts bombard him at the same time. He shakes his head. 'But I don't get it …'

It's then that Ryker notices a half-hidden object

protruding from the top of the hessian cloth Medwin wears. He reaches for it and draws it out. Dangling on a thin, black braided rope, tied around his neck, is a twenty-centimetre long sharp white tooth. His breath catches. He's seen something like this before. And only recently.

'Medwin, where did you get this?'

Medwin looks down at the pendant and shrugs. ''Tis an oddity, for certain. It has me baffled as to where such a tooth has surfaced from. The sheer dimension of it allows me to believe that the beast it has come from was of considerable size. Does it not? Quite extraordinary.' He stops to appreciate it.

Anxious to hear more, Ryker gestures that he continues. But Medwin appears too distracted by his thoughts to answer.

Ryker runs his hand over the top of his head several times. He needs to know more. 'Yes, but Medwin, how is it that you have it? This could be crucial!'

Ryker's outburst alarms the smaller man. Medwin raises his hands. 'Calm yourself, and I shall tell you.' He shakes his head and clicks his tongue. 'Forever impatient.'

Medwin turns to Aelianna. 'My girl, I see you have not succeeded in taming his impetuous nature.'

Aelianna smiles tentatively and places her hand on Ryker. ''Tis clear the pendant has caused you much concern. But what does it mean?'

Ryker positions himself to face her. 'I've seen a tooth like this,' he says excitedly. 'In fact, I'd say it's almost exactly like the one found hidden under the floorboards at the orphanage. One of the treasures.' He turns to the others. 'I mentioned it to you before. Remember?'

Jaeger and Edra exchange a look. Jaeger frowns. 'Yeah, so they're the same. I don't get it. What's it got to do with anything?'

Ryker rubs the back of his neck. There's a connection; he knows it, but right now, he's struggling to find exactly what it is. 'Look, I don't know, but it can't be a coincidence. It's linked somehow. I'm sure of it.'

Molan takes the tooth to examine it. 'I have wondered myself where you came across such a distinctive neck ornament. The twine itself is one I have never seen the likes of.'

Ryker leans in closer. Medwin removes the necklet and offers it to him to look.

'This braid work isn't from this time—it's modern.' They crowd Ryker to have a better look. 'See the quality in the finish. Simple handmade methods couldn't have produced something like this. It's too consistent. A machine has made it.'

Aelianna takes the braid. She nods. 'I agree, 'tis

not of our time.' She turns to Medwin. 'Can you tell us how you acquired it?'

Medwin shrinks from their gaze. 'If truth be told, it does not belong to me. It belongs to a stranger.' He shifts in his seat. 'Allow me to explain.

'One day, I came across a young boy in the woods. He was oddly dressed—clothing made of a fabric foreign to me, frayed and well-worn, but of a style I had never seen. And on his head, he wore a headdress of some description. Again, in a fashion unfamiliar to me. I demanded he reveal who he was, but I suspect I must have frightened him, for he took off into the forest like a hare chased by a fox. Sometime later, I happened to come across him again, this time spying from the undergrowth. He was unaware of my presence until I was upon him. I acted swiftly and seized him. Startled by my sudden appearance, he fought against me and escaped. I managed only to pull from his neck this pendant. Concerned for his well-being, I took chase. The pursuit led me to The Deep Tarn.'

Aelianna gasps. She and her father exchange a look. His eyes widen.

Ryker looks from them to Medwin and frowns.

''Tis a body of water, well known to the people of the forest,' Medwin adds to Ryker's questioning look, 'small at first glance, but ill-reputed to having no end to its depth, with a giant beast residing beneath its surface.'

Ryker's attention spikes. *A giant beast?*

Medwin continues. 'The child entered the water without reservation and plunged into its depths. I waited by the water's edge for the longest time, but alas, he never resurfaced. I fear he may have drowned or may have been taken by the beast. Regretfully, I have not set eyes on the child since that day.'

Medwin takes back the necklace from Ryker and sighs. 'My only wish is that the boy survived somehow. And perhaps, someday, I can return it to him. For it must have been something he truly treasured.'

Medwin looks at Ryker and shrugs. 'Thus ends the tale.'

Ryker stares vacantly. Again, the word *treasure.* A thought hits him. 'Tell me, Medwin, was the boy real? Or could he have been a ghost, like our friend Jaeger here?'

Medwin shakes his head. 'For certain, he was real. As real as you or I. Why do you ask?'

Ryker gets up from his crouched position to think, his head grazing the canopy of the confined space. Some of the missing pieces of the puzzle fall into place. Somehow, the ghost from the orphanage and Medwin's boy are connected. In fact, Ryker would go as far as to say they're one and the same.

The treasure links them.

'And you said that the pool of water he disappeared into houses some kind of giant monster?' He scratches his head. 'But you mentioned that the lake is small. It doesn't make sense.'

'Small only at a glance,' Aelianna reminds him. 'Its depth is rumoured to be endless.' She shakes her head. 'But the beast is only of childhood legends.' She turns to her father, her hand on his. ''Tis just a tale, is it not? Such a creature does not truly exist. Does it?'

Molan shifts in his seat, clearly hesitant to answer. After a while, he draws a deep breath. 'Daughter, I have seen the beast with my very eyes. I can attest to its existence.'

Edra startles.

Aelianna frowns. 'But how can that be? 'Tis only a tale. A story passed on from father to child, many times over.'

Molan looks about them tentatively and lowers his voice. 'What I am about to tell you, Aelianna, must never reach your mother's ears.' He expels a deep breath. 'As you know, it falls to me to provide for our people, being the village hunter. One bitterly cold winter, food was scarce, and I was compelled to enter the tarn in search of anything of substance to fill our stomachs. My thinking at the time was if such a serpent exists, then perhaps it is I who is destined to capture it. At the time, I had no idea of its size other than from what had been said to me as a boy. Truth be told, I, myself, held no conviction of its existence until it happened one day that I witnessed it myself.' His breath catches as he relives the memory. 'Oh, and what a majestic sight it was!'

Ryker's curiosity deepens.

Molan continues. 'The story begs to be told. Therefore, I will begin at the onset.' He leans in closer, his eyes sparkling. 'Now, to access the lake, I used provisions offered to me by the forest floor and fashioned a crude vessel. Fallen branches, vines for tethering. Before long, it was done, and I was afloat. As I sat waiting with my spear at the ready, the water surrounding me began to stir. The raft rocked. I braced myself in preparation, and the spear even tighter. I observed a great shadowy form emerging from its depths. A greatness far beyond my imaginings. Suddenly, the water divided, and the mythical beast rose from the depth of the darkness and leaped high into the air.' His breath hitches as he remembers it. 'Such magnificence, such grace. The sight of it had me transfixed, and for a moment, inattentive to the foreseeable danger.'

Aelianna gasps. Molan reassures her with a crooked smile. 'As you see, daughter, I lived to tell the tale. So all is well.' He chuckles and leans in to continue. 'As the beast's sleek and fishlike form fell upon the water's surface, the momentum created a swell so strong, it at first thrust me up to the heavens and then far beyond, deep into the forest. Shocked but thankfully unharmed, once able, I raced back, hoping to catch sight of it once more. Alas, all that remained of its presence was the subtle rippling on the water's surface. The beast was gone.'

Ryker releases his breath, held while listening to the captivating tale.

'I needed to ask myself whether I had imagined it,' Molan continues. 'How can such a creature reside in such a confined space? And what depth lies beneath the surface that allows a force so grand as to propel the weighted beast out of the water?' Molan turns to Ryker. 'Son, the fabled monster exists. But how it has come to endure the test of time, I have no idea.'

Ryker thinks.

'Could the lake be a portal?' Edra puts to them. She turns to Medwin. 'You mentioned the boy never surfaced? Maybe he vanished into another dimension. Is that possible?'

Medwin frowns.

Ryker hadn't thought of that. And if Edra has guessed right, this could be huge! Another missing puzzle piece. His breathing deepens.

At his side, Jaeger's transparent form vibrates with excitement. 'I think Edra's got a good point. They're telling us that the animal living in the lake is huge, but a creature like that, no matter how deep the water is, couldn't survive unless it could somehow access a larger body of water.'

Ryker considers his previous hunch about Medwin's encounter with the mystery boy and the large white tooth, his thoughts centred on the conversation he had earlier with the boys in Mahlee. One of them said something about the treasure found under the floorboards being prehistoric— Kenny's words, not theirs. And in Ryker's experience, he's never known Kenny to be wrong. He turns to Medwin. 'And you said that you had no premonition of the others entering the realm, but you had one of us coming.'

Medwin nods. 'My gift of foresight, as you know, is second to none. It confuses me as to why my vision has failed me this time. Ryker, I have had no other forewarning. This, I can assure you.'

Ryker barks out a laugh. The final puzzle piece falls into place. Ryker now understands what this all means. 'Oh, man! Why didn't I think of it before?' He curses himself under his breath. It's so obvious to him now. 'Medwin, you didn't see them coming, because they're not here.'

This stumps them. Aelianna and Edra share a questioning look. Jaeger whooshes closer, looking worried, as if he'd missed something somehow.

'Don't you see?' Ryker says with a laugh. 'It *all* makes perfect sense.'

His friends wait to hear exactly what's making sense, because to them, it's not so clear.

Ryker grins. 'Guys, the Aussies have stumbled across another dimension. A *different* dimension. And if my hunch is right … a *prehistoric* dimension!'

'Prehistoric!' Edra and Jaeger both cry out, alarmed.

Meanwhile, Aelianna shares a questioning look with her father and Medwin.

'And what's more, the dimensions are linked,' Ryker says with a laugh. 'That boy, the one Medwin mentioned, he's the ghost Jack and the others chased into the creek, back at the orphanage.'

Ryker gives them a moment for this to sink in.

'Is that why you asked Medwin if the boy was real?' Jaeger asks. 'Because he's actually a ghost, but comes to life when he enters the realm? And you think it's him? He's responsible for all this mess?'

Ryker rubs the back of his neck, sighs and nods. 'Yeah, I do. Because knowing what we do about ghosts, it all makes sense. We've got portals leading to three different dimensions. And our mystery boy is the link to all three. He's got to be.'

'Then if that's the case,' Edra says in a panic, 'we need to find this portal to the prehistoric world and save our friends. They're in massive danger!'

Aelianna grabs her sheathed blade at her side. 'Edra, what you say alarms me. Please forgive my ignorance, but I have struggled to follow your conversation. What is the threat?'

Ryker should've realised Aelianna's confusion sooner. He places his hands on her shoulders to explain. 'The beast in the lake, well, we believe it to be from a time before man ever existed—a time when only giant animals roamed the earth.'

The furrow on her brow deepens. He rubs his face and grimaces. He's not doing a good job of explaining things. He tries again. 'Lia, let me put it this way, the beast in the tarn your father saw that time is miniscule to what lives on the land in this other world. These dinosaurs are the size of the fortress walls and taller. Most are brutally savage.'

Both Molan and Medwin gasp. The colour drains from Aelianna's face. Her eyes widen. 'Then there is no time. We must prepare to leave.'

A rustling sound in the forest alerts them that someone or something is approaching, and at speed. Ryker steps out from their hiding spot, his hunting blade in hand. The others follow. Aelianna unsheathes an arrow from the holster strapped on her back and prepares the bow. Jaeger whooshes high into the sky in search of the threat. Edra stands ready, her baseball bat positioned on her shoulder. Both Medwin and Molan join Ryker, blades at hand.

Ryker looks upward, prepared to act swiftly on Jaeger's instruction. Jaeger motions he'll take on the threat on his own before disappearing from view.

At the same moment, in the opposite direction, a fleeting movement catches Ryker's attention. He whips around to investigate, but a clear sight of what caught his interest escapes him. Had he imagined it?

Suddenly a chilling cry for help diverts his focus. And then, unexpectedly, a young boy stumbles from the undergrowth and into view.

When the new arrival sees what's before him, he lets out another terrifying scream and raises his hands in surrender. 'Please, don't hurt me! I need your help!'

The scruffy-looking kid at Ryker's feet looks up at him with fear. Ryker blinks a few times and drops his guard.

24
No, No, Nooooo!

MAX

Max gasps. *What the hell is he doing?* Bare and unprotected, with the safety of Ruby's shield abandoned, Jack stands before the giant *Tyrannosaurus rex*; his hands raise, his words enticing composure.

The beast, having clawed at the cave's narrow opening attempting to access its prey, stoops before them, eyeing them through the gap. Its intention is clear.

They're in deep trouble.

Engaged in the battle of his life, Jack fights to tame the beast.

Max watches on, powerless to do anything, unable to breathe.

The snorting dinosaur pauses and studies him. Its enormous head turns to one side, taking him in. Then, ever so slowly, its massive eyelid appears to grow heavy and half-closes. Its previously dilated pupil reverts to a slit.

Max can't believe it. Jack's winning. He's gaining control. A tear of joy trickles down her cheek.

But then, unbelievably, Jack moves in closer, and a misstep costs him. He stumbles. Max doesn't dare move or make a sound. With her heart in her throat, she prepares for the fallout, ready to run.

For the briefest moment, the *T. rex* appears dazed, staring vacantly ahead. But then, with a snap of its leathery head, it breaks from its trancelike state. Its pupil dilates; its eye darkens.

Max, petrified on the spot, knows what's coming but is incapable of coordinating any thought process to cry out a warning. And then a deep, guttural sound fills the cavity, and suddenly there's pandemonium. Shattered rock flies everywhere as the beast rams its massive frame against the opening. Its clawed forearm pushing through the space and lunging at Jack.

Max screams.

In his rush to save himself, Jack stumbles backwards and falls, just out of reach of the attack. He continues to scramble away on all fours as the dinosaur ravages the entrance. He turns, his eyes filled with terror, his voice choked with fear. 'Save yourselves! Go deeper into the cave!'

Suddenly, the ground beneath her feet trembles. Max shudders to think what it could mean. And then, to her horror, boulders of rock and fragments of debris fall from above. Max watches in disbelief as Jack attempts to evade the crush of rock being dumped upon him.

Strangled words of warning go unheard. And then he's gone.

She can't breathe. She can't think. She's numb.

'LET ME OUT!' Peanut cries for Ruby to drop her shield. The protective dome dissolves, and in a frantic rush, he races to get to Jack.

Max stares ahead, unblinking, frozen on the spot. Her mind in a fog.

Her friends sprint forward and battle to clear the debris burying Jack, their own safety aside. But Max can't move. She battles to snap out of her stupefied state to help.

The beast lashes at them through the opening, which is quickly becoming large enough for it to reach them. Still, she stares ahead, frozen.

And then, from somewhere distant, Jack's final words come to her.

Save yourselves!

As though being zapped by live electricity, Max

jolts back to reality. Adrenaline courses through her veins to kickstart her thinking. They're in danger. They need to go. 'STOP! We need to get out of here! NOW!'

The access into the cave continues to widen. Their protective barricade crumbles. The *T. rex* is now upon them.

'GO! I'll distract it.' Peanut vanishes.

Moments later, a barrage of airborne rocks hit their target. The diversion works, drawing the beast's attention. Here's their chance. They sprint to get away—the back of the cave their only option.

Stumbling into the near darkness, debris and dust obscuring visibility, Max, Ruby and Kenny scramble to find a safer place to lie low.

Without warning, Ruby turns to go back. Kenny grabs her by her T-shirt to stop her. He continues forward, dragging her behind him. 'No! Keep going! He'll be okay.'

Max won't let herself think otherwise. She needs to stay focused. Thankfully, Ruby listens, and they continue deeper into the cavern.

Now on hands and knees, they inch further and further into the shadows. Progress slows to a crawl. But Max doesn't stop. Jack's final words, on repeat in her head …

Save yourselves!

Save yourselves!
Save yourselves!

Where this path is taking them, she has no idea. What lurks in the darkness is not something she can think about.

Save yourselves!

She pushes on, determined to do just that. The journey, hampered by the many obstacles, is an arduous one. Finding a path over the many boulders and sharp rocks in complete darkness proves to be a challenge. Max gropes blindly, using the walls of the cave to guide her. Ruby's firm grip on her shirt from behind and the sound of Kenny's heavy breathing reassures her. She's not alone.

Suddenly, the earth quakes beneath them. They freeze. And then they hear it—a tremendous crack followed by the sound of a massive dump of rock. Somewhere from where they'd just come has caved in. Without warning, a whoosh of debris hurtles over them, chasing after them into the cavity, threatening to bowl them over. Max dives to the ground, shuts her eyes and covers her head to avoid it.

When the dust settles, Max shifts carefully and sits up. A layer of rubble falls from her. By her side, Ruby chokes and splutters. A little further back, she hears Kenny. But where's Peanut?

'Wait! What's that?'

Max stops to listen, but hears nothing. And then she realises what Ruby is referring to. Up ahead in the near distance, she spots a faint glow of light. 'Ruby, I see it.'

'Me too,' Kenny whispers, approaching them.

And then, from behind, they hear movement. Something's approaching.

'Oomph! Ouch! Oh, crap!'

Ruby squeals. '*Peanut!*'

Max's breath catches. Right now, she could cry.

'Hey, guys, where are you?'

'Keep coming,' Ruby tells him, her voice thick with tears.

They hear him stumbling to get closer, and soon he's with them. 'Is everyone okay?'

Max's thoughts race to Jack. Jack is gone. How can *anyone* be okay? How will anyone ever be okay again? She thinks of Jack's mother … Jack's father. She thinks of Jack's brothers and sisters. Tears sting her eyes. *Poor little Katie!* Max bites her lip, struggling to keep that thin thread of control from snapping.

But it's too much. Images of what just happened flash before her: Jack with his arms raised, striving to calm the beast; the attack on the cave entrance; the devastating cave-in; the mound of rubble crashing down on him.

Her breathing quickens. Her heart pounds.

No, no, NOOOOO!

What has she done?

She left him. She left him and ran. Abandoned him when he needed her the most.

How could she *do* that?

An overwhelming blanket of dread threatens to suffocate her. She battles to breathe and claws at the tightness strangling her. Tears burn a trail down her cheeks like acid. Sparks of light explode in the darkness. The air thickens around her.

Then suddenly, her world stops.

And there's nothing.

25
NEVER ALONE

MAX

There's total darkness. A gentle voice speaks to her from a faraway place. Almost too far … she can barely make out the words. Perhaps it's nothing. Max squeezes her eyelids tighter and relishes the respite. What she's hiding from, she can't recall. She doesn't try to remember.

Max? Sweetheart … wake!

Her ears prick.

Go to them, my love!

Smooth like honey, the words, now clearer, are like a linctus to her ailing soul. She curls tighter in her protective ball.

They need you. Be my brave girl. Fight!

Her breath catches. The voice, strangely familiar, sends tingles down her spine. She listens closer.

Find that strength within. You can do it!

Although wishing it with all her heart, Max dares not believe it's true. 'Mum?' The word is but a whisper on her lips.

Yes, my love. You're not alone. I'm here with you and always will be. Now, wake.

It's a dream. It has to be a dream. Max fights to remain sleeping. If this is a dream, she wants to stay here—here with her beloved mother. Subconsciously, she reaches for the pendant around her neck and clasps it securely in her hand. Surprisingly, she feels an immense warmth from within—almost too hot. Strangely, it comforts her like nothing else. She presses it to her lips and smiles.

No, I'm not alone.

26
AFTER THE SHOCK

MAX

Max rouses to the smell of burning wood and the sound of hushed chatter. Her eyelids, heavy from sleep disturbed by anguished visions, refuse to open. A lingering ache in her chest torments her. She questions whether it was all just a dream. But then she remembers. Her eyes pop open. The *T. rex*. The attack. The cave-in. The rocks. The mound of rubble … And the desolation of what lies beneath it. She jolts upright, gasping for air. Kenny dives to her side. He pulls her to him. Max struggles to free herself, but his hold remains vicelike. He shushes her and waits. Finally surrendering to her grief, she crumbles. It's too much. The unbearable heartache. The unfathomable certainty. She can no longer hold it in.

Kenny rocks her in his arms as she weeps. 'Let it out, Max. Let it *all* out.' He sniffs and clears his throat—his voice thick with heartache.

She looks at him. His wet puffy eyes make her heart cry for his loss too. Loss of a profound friendship, unconditional.

An unexpected movement in the shadows startles her. She peers closer and stops. A boy, unknown to her, sits cross-legged, staring at her. Somehow, he seems familiar, but at the moment she can't quite place why. His eyes, dark in colour; his hair, a dirty blond. At his side lies a curled-up figure, their head resting on what looks like a rolled-up sleeping bag. At a guess, Max would say the person was a girl. Longish, messed-up, curly blonde hair strewn across their scuffed-up face makes it hard to tell.

And then Max realises who they are. She breaks from Kenny's embrace. 'You're them! You're the missing kids from the orphanage, aren't you?' She scans the darkened cavity. 'But where's the other boy?'

Kenny wipes the wetness from his eyes, leaving dirty streaks, and sniffs. 'Yeah, Max, it's them.' He clears his throat. 'This is Shaun, Riley's brother, and that's Bec.' He points to the motionless form lying at Shaun's side. 'Liam, the other kid, has gone with Ruby and Peanut to …'

Kenny stops and draws in an unsteady breath. He looks away, battling to go on.

But Kenny needs not say more. Max knows where they've gone.

So why am I sitting here doing nothing?

She jumps to her feet. 'I should be with them. They'll need me. Jack could still be alive!' There's a sudden urgency for her to get back to the cave-in. She hurries to leave but stops in her tracks when she realises that she can't see anything beyond a few metres of the firepit. She searches frantically for something to light her way. A torch, a broken branch she can set fire to. Anything that'll take her to Jack.

From behind, Kenny grabs her by the shoulders and swings her around. 'Quit it, will you?' He stops to draw breath. His eyes soften. 'Look, they've been gone a while—you've been out of it for some time. There's no point taking off now. We wait. We'll know what to do when they come back.'

Wait? For real?

Max grits her teeth. 'How can you say that? We're wasting time! Jack needs help!' She tugs at her hair. 'What the hell was I thinking? Leaving him like that! I should've stayed. I could've done something!'

Kenny's eyes narrow. 'We had no choice, and you know it. That *T. rex* wasn't going to give us up for anything.' He stops. 'Look, the guys have gone to see if it's safe to return. If it is, then we can all go. But first we need to help Bec.'

Max whips around to look at Bec. She realises, even with all this commotion, the girl hasn't stirred.

'Max, she's in a really bad way,' Kenny tells her. 'She needs your help.'

Max moves in closer. 'What's wrong? What happened to her?'

Shaun gets to his knees. With care, he uncovers her motionless form and uses a flashlight to expose her injuries.

Max's hand flies to her mouth. There's so much blood. She leans in closer. A patch-work of carelessly placed Band-aids and bandages on her bare back masks the extent of her injuries.

It's then that Max spots a familiar first-aid kit by Bec's side. 'Hey, is that mine?'

Shaun's chin dips, his expression sheepish. 'Um, yeah. But I can explain,' he adds quickly, his hands raised in defence. 'After the attack on Bec, we were desperate to do somethin'. She was in agony … totally screaming the place down. Poor kid. That's kinda why we're wormed so deep in this damn hole. We weren't safe anymore.' He looks at Max and blinks a few times. 'It was Albert's idea to go back to the orphanage for help, and somehow he found you!' His eyes widen. 'Man, of all people! What are the chances? He couldn't believe his luck. You're a healer, right? Albert said you are. So cool!' He shakes his head. 'Anyhow, in order to get you to follow him, he nicked your kit.'

His smile fades, and his enthusiasm wanes. He shifts in his seat. 'But things didn't turn out right, did they? Yeah, he got you here, but then you guys were ambushed. Not just by one *Deinonychus*, but two! Holy Moly! Albert honestly thought you were goners!' He blows out a troubled breath. 'You know what? It freaked him out—big time! He dumped the kit and flew right back out to see if there was somethin' he could do. And we haven't seen him since.' He stops, his thoughts gone elsewhere. 'I hope the little guy's okay.' He shrugs and shakes it off. 'Nah, 'course he is! He's pretty canny … the Artful Dodger, himself!'

Shaun looks from Max to Kenny and scratches his head. 'To tell you the truth, it's a miracle *you're* still alive! Those blasted overgrown lizards … man, they're vicious! It was a *Deinonychus* that tore Bec to shreds.' He sighs. 'But thanks to the stuff in the kit, she's finally asleep. Those little red pills totally knocked her out.'

Max smiles, thankful that her over-the-top, first-aid-kit obsession has finally helped someone. *Poor Bec! What a nightmare it must've been!*

She shakes off the mental image. 'Um, so you

know your dinosaurs, huh? Impressive.'

Shaun smirks. 'Nah. I'm no genius. It was Kenny who told us what the blasted thing was when we described it to him.' He glances at Kenny before looking back at her. 'Freaky smart guy, your friend Kenny.'

She smiles. That, she knows.

Max looks over the space they're in. The glowing embers in the contained fireplace give off enough light to reveal the extent of their safe place. The cave ends here. Strewn haphazardly on the cave floor are what appear to be fishbones and shells of creatures unfamiliar to her. Unfamiliar bar one. She stoops down to pick it up. Shaun offers her a torch. She turns the coiled snail-like shell over in her hand several times and realises it's something like what was found under the floorboards at the orphanage—the one Kenny identified as being prehistoric. Her head snaps up, and she looks at him.

Kenny smiles a crooked smile and shrugs. 'I knew it was an *ammonite*.'

Max softens. Poor Kenny. He didn't deserve the attack on him then, nor the one from her just now. She touches his arm by way of apology. He shrugs and smiles.

But there's work to be done.

Max squats by Bec's side, ready to begin. She

looks at the torch in her hand, impressed with the light it gives. 'Whose is this? It looks like something Ryker would own.'

'It's Bec's. She borrowed it from her dad. He's military.'

Her hand shoots up to stop him. She grins. 'Say no more, I get it. I'm just thankful for it.'

'So … this gift of yours to heal,' Shaun starts hopefully. 'How good are you? Can you fix her?'

Max grins. 'I'll do my best.' Having assessed the damage, she knows what needs to be done. She switched the torch off to conserve the battery and prepares herself. Her eyes close as she powers up the strength within her core. Very quickly, warmth radiates to her fingertips. She runs her hands over Bec's mutilated back and allows the heat generated to start the healing process. Some of the wounds are extensive. It surprises her that Bec was able to survive the attack at all.

'How long does it take?' she hears Shaun whisper to Kenny.

'It varies on how bad it is,' Kenny explains. 'I think Max knows when it's done by a feeling she gets.' He sighs. 'Hopefully not long. Once Bec's better, we can meet up with the others and get out of here.'

'She *will* get better, won't she?' Shaun asks, a waver in his voice.

There's no questioning it. The gift Max has been given—her ability to heal—still baffles her, so she doesn't take offence at Liam's scepticism. 'Have a look,' she tells him, removing the bandages. 'I'm almost done.'

'Already?' Shaun's eyes widen. He leans over to see.

Several of the gashes have healed, and the deeper ones appear to be fusing nicely.

'Crikey! That was quick.' He chuckles, his voice thick with emotion.

Max's lip curls. 'I guess I've had a bit of practice.'

Her smile fades, remembering the time she was imprisoned in the ancient realm and forced to heal the victims of the elephant stampede from the final battle. A stampede she and her friends were responsible for in their effort to escape the brutality of the world on the other side of the portal. Victim after victim were brought to her until every one of them was healed. There were days and days of minimal food and water, and worse, no chance to recover. Time was spent on broken bones, internal bleeding, crushed skulls … repeat. The process was unrelenting. And in the end, it almost killed her. The overuse of her power depleted every ounce of her strength.

A soft moan from Bec signals the injured girl's return to consciousness. Max shakes away the disturbing memories and inspects her completed work with satisfaction. 'Bec, how are you feeling?'

Bec's eyes open. She blinks, then jumps back alarmed and scrambles to get away. 'Who are you?' She spots her friend Shaun from the corner of her eye. 'What's going on, Shaun? Who are these guys?'

Shaun moves to sit at her side. He smiles. 'Believe it or not, the cavalry!' He chuckles. 'So how's your back, kiddo?'

Bec straightens; her eyes widen. Gingerly, she reaches over her shoulder to feel her wounds and sucks in a breath. 'What happened? The gashes … they're gone!' She draws back. 'And there's no pain.'

Max sits back as Shaun explains.

'So … you've got freaky superpowers?' Bec shakes her head. 'Now that's just totally insane!'

Max grins. 'Yeah, we all do. I bet you've got one too.'

Her eyes light up. 'Cool!' But then she frowns. 'How will I know what superpower I've got?'

'I reckon, after seeing you take on that dinosaur,' says a voice from down the passageway, 'your superpower has gotta be *courage*.'

Peanut, Ruby and a boy Max can only presume is Liam enter the small space carrying a smouldering tree branch. 'Man, I couldn't believe how daring you were when that giant reptile went for us. I was literally crapping my pants while you were egging it on!' the boy says with a laugh. 'Our very own Supergirl, in the flesh!'

He plonks himself down beside Bec and gives her a nudge. 'Hey, buddy, I'm glad you're doing okay.' He smiles, then looks at Max. 'So Albert wasn't pulling our leg … you fix people!' He leans over to shake Max's hand. 'Hi, I'm Liam, by the way.' He chuckles. 'Man, you've got *no* idea what a relief it is to finally meet ya.'

Max forces a smile. Although glad to be of use, she's anxious to hear about Jack. She looks at Peanut. He's been unusually quiet, and that doesn't sit well with her. But good or bad, whatever the situation, Max needs to know what they've uncovered. She draws a breath. 'So, did you find anything?' She bites her lower lip, waiting. Suddenly, she doesn't feel so well.

Ruby crouches at her side and takes her hand in hers. Her eyes well up. Instantly, a tightness forms in Max's throat. Tears prickle like a thousand wasp stings.

Ruby squeezes her hand. 'Hon, we couldn't get to him. I'm sorry. The *T. rex* has done a total job on the place. We're completely caved in. We're trapped.'

Her eyes squeeze tight. She lets out a shaky breath, oddly relieved. No news is good news. Right? There's still a glimmer of hope that Jack is alive. Max turns to

Ruby. 'I need to go to him. We need to find a way.'

Peanut jumps up. 'So let's do something about it instead of just sitting here!'

He paces back and forth, waiting for them to hustle, his hands shoved in the pockets of his jeans. 'Come on! We've gotta get to Jack before …' He battles to continue. He turns away and swipes at the track of tears trailing down his cheeks. Ruby, at his side, offers whatever comfort she can. His hands curl into fists. 'The bloody idiot! He had to go and be a damn hero!'

Max swallows the lump in her throat—her sentiments, not far from his.

But that's not getting them anywhere. They need to move forward.

Max reaches out to Peanut, but he stomps away. Ruby goes after him. In the shadows, they embrace and share a moment of grief.

It pains Max to watch this.

Peanut breaks from Ruby, wipes his nose on his sleeve and clears his throat. 'There's no point hanging around here. No one's coming for us.'

And it's those definitive words that get them moving. In silence, the group prepare to abandon their safe place. Liam and Shaun hand out tied-up bundles of dry tree branches that Albert must've stashed away over time. There are several of them. As torches, they'll provide enough light to guide them.

Kenny stops to transfer a flame to two of the bundles before snuffing out the campfire. 'We'll use these for now and save the torch for later.'

Bec dives for a dusty white calico bag, presumably containing her personal things. Max reaches for her first-aid kit. There may still be something of use in there.

Peanut leads with Ruby close behind. Max stays close to Bec, ready to help her if needed. Kenny, Liam and Shaun trail at the rear.

As they navigate the rocky terrain, Max can't help but think of what lies ahead. If, by some miracle, Jack has survived the cave-in, she'll need every last ounce of what's left of her power to heal him. But will it be enough? Helping Bec has compromised her energy levels as it is.

And if Jack hasn't survived?

Well, that's something she won't let herself think about.

27
REFLECTION

PEANUT

Peanut forges ahead. His single focus: tearing down the wall of rubble blocking the passage to Jack. With Max and Bec now recovered, they begin the greatest challenge of Peanut's life so far. He finds strength in its magnitude to take it on—and win. There's no stopping him. He's going to make this happen. They'll make their way to Jack, no matter what it takes.

And there're no ifs or buts about it. They *are* going to find him. And when they do, Max will fix him. Just like she's done for so many others before. She's done it for them; she can do it for Jack. She has to. Because a world without his best mate, Jack, will never be the same. They've been inseparable since they were kids. Since their first day of kindy, in fact.

How could he ever forget that day? Their teacher, Miss Simmons, had had to pry them apart as they brawled on the mat at the front of the classroom over a toy action figure. Peanut grins, remembering. It was *Spiderman*. Unbeknown to him, they each had the identical toy. Jack had brought his to school for *Show and Tell*. And when Peanut spotted it, he suspected Jack had somehow taken his and so wrestled him to get it back.

Jack got a black eye for his efforts.

Peanut chuckles, recalling that black eye … and the dressing down he got from his father. His ears rang for days. But would he change anything about that first day? *Hell, no!* That run-in paved the way to their steadfast friendship today.

Peanut slows his approach and pauses. He squats on his haunches, eyes squeezed tight. Once again, tears surface.

Jack has to be alive. He's gotta be!

But what if it's too late? What if Max can't bring him back?

His chest tightens, the pain unbearable.

A gentle touch on his shoulder curbs it. It's Ruby. His rock. He reaches for her hand. No words said, but the exchange, real and comforting.

Peanut shakes off his sombre thoughts and strengthens his resolve. They need to keep moving. And with Jack not here to direct them, someone needs to take the lead. Peanut wants to be that *someone*. He wants to make Jack proud.

With a newfound conviction, Peanut pushes forward, piloting the way. His mission: to get Jack and return him and their friends safely back home.

28
PUZZLE COMPLETE

RYKER

So this is the boy everyone's talking about—the ghost that transitions back to life ... back to being a living boy. The troublemaker from the orphanage, and the boy Medwin couldn't pin down, being one and the same. Ryker studies the trembling child before him and wonders if it's a trick. Can the boy be believed? Ryker frowns. *Vigilant at all times! Time to interrogate!*

He moves towards him, his huge frame instantly dwarfing the young boy. The child flinches at his probing glare.

'Why do you need our help?' Ryker leans closer to study him. 'And I warn you, you'd better be upfront with me. Our friends are missing, and I know you've got something to do with it. So spill!'

The boy cowers and stumbles backwards. He struggles to reply, stuttering in his hurry to answer. Before long, tracks of tears trail down the frightened boy's cheeks.

Aelianna positions herself between Ryker and the boy and whips around to face him. Her eyes narrow. 'Have you lost your senses, Ryker? He is but a child!'

'A *child* who plays games!' He sidesteps her and points his finger. 'This had better not be a game to you, *boy*!'

The boy crumbles in a mess of tears. 'Please! I know it's my fault, and I'm sorry. Truly, I am. I just wanted to find someone to play with. I finally did, and now they're trapped! Help me! Please!'

Aelianna rests her hand on the boy's shoulder. 'Who is trapped? You can reveal it to me. I will do all that is in my power to help.' She steels Ryker with another look. 'We *all* will. I promise you that.'

The boy swipes his nose with his sleeve, smearing the wetness across his grimy face. His show of vulnerability sways Ryker's assessment of the boy's character. He regrets having to grill him as he did, but he needed assurance that the boy can be trusted. And now he feels he can.

And if it's all an act, then the kid deserves an Academy Award!

As for Aelianna's reprimand … he'll deal with that later. She needs to understand that this kind of questioning is necessary. They can't afford to fall into a trap. It could jeopardise their lives. She needs to trust his training. His time with the cadets back home has prepared him well for such situations.

Edra steps forward and stands at Aelianna's side. She too gives Ryker a stink-eye. She turns to the boy and smiles. 'Hey, what's your name? I'm Edra.'

The boy looks away. His cheeks colour. 'I … I'm Albert.'

'You've been pretty brave, tracking us down. And on your own too! How old are you, Albert?'

He smiles, stands taller, and puffs out his chest. 'Fourteen.'

Ryker studies Albert as the girls talk to him. What he sees is a scrawny young boy—his only crime a desperate need for a friend. Ryker softens a little and takes a closer look. He guesses, from what he's wearing, that the boy comes from a period somewhere around the turn of the twentieth century.

A long time being alone.

'So tell me, Albert,' Ryker asks, 'who's trapped? And how can we get to them?'

Again, Albert shrinks from Ryker's gaze.

Ryker forces a smile. 'Look, I don't bite.'

Just as he says this, the scuffle he had with Wulf's

dogs comes to mind, and he chuckles, knowing too well that at times he does.

'Well, not really,' he adds. 'And as for you needing help, you've got to trust us. Tell us all you know. We've worked out that you cross from one realm to another. But you need to show us how you do it. Where are the portals?'

Albert frowns. 'Jack and Kenny used the same kinda words.' He scratches his head and shrugs. 'But I still don't get what the words mean.'

Ryker stops at the unexpected breakthrough. Confirmation now given that Albert has had dealings with their friends. He takes a moment to steady his thoughts. He needs to handle this in a way that doesn't spook the boy and has him running off screaming before giving them some answers. He needs to slow things down.

Ryker tries to imagine going through the experiences this boy has been through over the years … seeing life through his eyes. He gets it—the kid is from another time. He wouldn't have the foggiest notion what they're talking about.

He tries again. 'Albert, you know how you travel from one period in time to another? Well, this is called *crossing over dimensions*. And the way you do it is by passing through a portal—a door of sorts. One minute you're a ghost at the orphanage in Mahlee in the twenty-first century, the next you've travelled here, back to ancient times. And I'm guessing you've found a way to travel to the era of the dinosaurs. Am I right? Through a lake in the forest?'

Albert's face lights up. He nods. 'But we've gotta hurry. Bec, Liam, Shaun … they're all there, but they're trapped. There's been a cave-in. A large *T. rex* destroyed the entrance to the cave trying to get 'em. There's no way out. And I can't get through the rubble on my own. Ryker, they need you. With your superhuman strength, you'll be able to save 'em.'

Ryker frowns. 'How do you know this about me?'

Albert draws back, suddenly reluctant again to answer.

'Come on, buddy. If your friends are trapped and in trouble, you need us on board. So let's have it. How do you know this?'

Albert shifts his weight from one foot to the other as if piecing together his thinking. And then he begins. He talks of the time when Ryker had built a treehouse in the forest. Albert had hidden and witnessed it all. He'd watched him cut down the trees and split the wood—all with his bare hands and a simple axe. Albert had never seen strength like it.

Ryker frowns. 'You were there?'

Albert lowers his chin and nods.

'So you would've seen what happened next,'

Ryker prompts, curious to have the story validated.

Albert lets out a breath. 'Yeah, I sure did. Oof! And it wasn't pretty. Those guards were brutal! And that guy, Herodus? Man, he sure is a piece of work!'

Ryker chuckles and rubs the back of his head. 'Tell me about it. I've still got the lump to prove it!'

'The thing is,' Albert continues, 'I've been around a lot, and I've seen stacks of things. You might not know me, but I sure as heck know you. And of course, Max!'

Again, Ryker stops. 'Max?'

'Yeah, Max. I was there when you and Max were rallying the forest people to escape with you,' he tells him. 'I saw Max's power to heal for the first time. She fixed Alger's broken arm. Remember?'

Ryker recalls it clearly. *And all that time, Albert was there ... lurking in the background!*

'But Ryker, we're wasting time! We've gotta hurry and do something!' Albert cries out with sudden gravity. He rushes to explain the situation, launching into a detailed account of what's happened. He tells of the dinosaur attack on his friend, Bec, and then reveals, to Ryker's horror, that apart from the three missing kids from the orphanage, *his* friends are trapped there too. Max, Jack, Peanut, Ruby and Kenny. And that it's *their* lives that are in danger as well.

Ryker groans. *Could the situation be any worse?*

Albert's gaze remains fixed on his tatty boots. 'All this mess is 'cause of me. I've got to make things right.' He looks up, hopeful. 'And Ryker, you're the only one who can help me do it.'

Ryker needs a moment to take it all in. His head spins from the flood of information. He paces back and forth, running his hand over his buzzcut several times. His friends, together with the three kids they were searching for, are in deep trouble. One of them, he knows, is critically injured. He prays no one else is. Having Max there is of some comfort. For this, he is grateful—he's got great faith in her power to heal. *She can fix anything.* And this he knows from firsthand experience, having been brought back from the brink of death himself.

He stops pacing. His shoulders straighten. Now to take action. First and foremost, they need to locate the portal to the prehistoric realm. And time is ticking. So what's he waiting for?

His nostrils flare; his eyes darken.

'Come on! Let's track down this portal!'

29

THE VOICE

AELIANNA

Aelianna shudders at Ryker's harshness, shocked at his attack on the poor young boy. *Who is this stranger before me?* The man she loves with her whole heart is so altered she hardly recognises him. She cannot fathom his behaviour of late. The child, clearly distressed, is in need of their assistance. *Why the unnecessary aggression?* His impetuous nature, as Medwin referred to earlier, certainly needs taming. She frowns. But now is not the time to take on such a task. From what she has been able to understand, their friends are in danger. They have fallen into a world of giant beasts—a world she has no concept of, but knows only that they will come to harm if they do not make haste.

'Albert, can you take us to this place—to this cave you have mentioned?'

Albert looks at Aelianna and smiles. He lets out a breath of relief. 'I thought you'd never ask. Come on! Follow me. If we hurry, we'll reach the lake before sundown.'

Aelianna recalls the conversation they had earlier regarding an unexplored gateway to another world—one that exists within The Deep Tarn. This, perhaps, is their destination. She places her faith in the young orphaned boy without question and follows as he leads the way.

And so the journey begins to the mythical bottomless tarn of childhood tales.

Molan shadows Albert. Aelianna trails her father. She smiles, secretly relishing this new adventure with her father at her side. How she has missed their time together.

She sighs. Once their quest is accomplished, she is determined to spend a little time with her family before returning home. Surely, Ryker will respect her need to do this.

As they make their way, Aelianna thinks of her father and dear mother, both now well and strong. Forever grateful for the gift of health bestowed upon them by Max's father's healings, she'll never take this unexpected blessing for granted, nor ever forget.

Max's father had entered their world in search of his daughter, then captured and imprisoned within the fortress walls. Aelianna's parents, both ill, had suffered too long; her father, an invalid, her mother, bedridden with an unknown ailment. Although grateful to have them in her life as they were, the burden of looking after her parents, as well as her younger siblings, weighed heavily on her shoulders. Her service as a servant at the fortress was her only means to provide for them. Times were difficult, with very little food and constant hunger adding to her hardship.

Having survived such adversity makes Aelianna appreciate what she has now.

She smiles, thinking of the gifts she brought for her siblings. For Felix, her brother next in age, and of a simple nature, a colourful squeezy toy. She is certain that it will bring him much pleasure and keep his fidgeting disposition passive. For her younger sister, Sigrun, she chose a beautiful book full of pictures of majestic castles, heroic princes and golden-haired princesses; something she, herself, dreamed of as a young girl. And for her baby brother, Afon, a brightly coloured toy that plays enchanting music when wound—something she instantly fell in love with and had to have for him.

Aelianna is so happy in her new life that she could sing, but she knows the repercussions of doing so. Well warned of its power to alter lives, she represses the urge.

She thinks again of her brothers and sister and wonders how they are faring without her. Afon, especially, she holds dear to her heart, for Aelianna was like a mother to that baby when their own mother was unable to be.

She sighs. If only they all could return with her once this undertaking has passed. The life she has with Ryker is truly magical. To share with them the happiness she has would be a dream come true. And she is certain that, with a little encouragement, Ryker would be supportive of this.

Aelianna turns her gaze to him. He trails at the rear of the procession. His head down, his brow furrowed. *Such intensity! What must he be thinking?* But knowing Ryker as she does, she realises the answer without having to ask it. His single focus would be to free their friends and help them find their way home. Yes, he is often intense, but that stems only from his passionate nature. Never has she met anyone with such a deep and caring heart. And for that, she will always defend and stand by him.

They continue in silence. The journey, an extensive one. The sun, previously high in the sky, wanes.

They enter a part of the forest Aelianna has never set foot in. Without warning, Albert stops, stoops low and peers with caution through the undergrowth. Aelianna prepares herself, standing guarded.

Molan reaches back to caution his daughter. 'We are nearing the tarn. What lies between us and our purpose is yet to be seen. Wait here while we search the surrounds.'

Suddenly, a cry of warning comes from behind. Aelianna grabs her bow and notches an arrow as she turns to take on the threat. She spots *Vyvian*, one of the Invincibles, hovering high in the sky at a distance. Aelianna braces herself, well aware of the imminent danger; if one of the realm's champions is here, the others will follow.

Vyvian darts towards them. Aelianna draws her bow, ready.

Now within range, Aelianna has a clearer view of her. She draws her bow tight, ready to fire, then pauses, horrified at the scars on Vyvian's face. The tension on the bow slackens as Aelianna remembers Vyvian's final combat with Ryker and the rescuing taskforce with their flame-spouting weapon. *Such a tragedy.*

Alas, the ill-timed distraction costs them. Vyvian releases a myriad of bows, her sole focus Ryker, and one of the arrows hits its target. Ryker cries out in pain and dives from view.

Aelianna gasps in horror, but is quick to understand the urgency of what must be done. They'll all die if she fails to collect herself. Hysteria must wait. She regroups, draws her bow and fires, but misses. She prepares to fire again but finds she cannot, overcome by an unexpected disorientation, her thoughts suddenly scrambled.

And then an unfamiliar voice echoes in her ears. *Aelianna, what are you doing with this traitor? He is not your equal! He is all-controlling and seeks only to gratify himself.*

Startled, Aelianna searches the forest for the offender. She sees nothing.

He does not truly care for you. You are a novelty to him—a plaything!

Alarmed, Aelianna abandons her weapons and presses her hands to her ears. 'What witchery is this?' she cries out. 'Who speaks such cruelty?'

And he tells you he loves you. He does NOT! He has love only for himself! Look at what his so-called professed love has done to Vyvian!

LOOK AT HER!

Behold her disfiguration! HE has done this to her! HE destroyed her! HE ravaged her beauty! His attempt to burn her alive failed! Beware, for you will meet a similar fate. HE will destroy you too!

Aelianna cannot bear it any more. The poisonous words bleed into her subconscious thoughts and distort her misgivings towards Ryker. She screams to block them out.

And keeps on screaming.

Ryker appears from the shadows of his protection and cries out to her. She hears nothing. The panic in his eyes goes unnoticed.

He thunders towards her, screaming words of warning. His arms flailing, his expression frantic. She sees him. Her pulse races; her breathing accelerates.

And then …

Her eyes darken. Her pupils dilate.

Suddenly, Ryker is the enemy.

Aelianna reaches for her bow and arrow, positions the arrow, rests the twine against her cheek, draws on the bow and releases.

And this time she makes certain …

She does not miss.

30
Sing!

RYKER

Ryker clutches his chest and falls to the ground, face first. He struggles to get to his knees and looks down at the blood gushing from his wound. He can't believe it—Aelianna has just tried to kill him! A few inches lower and he'd be a goner. He needs to stop this madness before Archimedes does any more harm. This mind control he has over her is only a taste of what he's capable of doing.

Ryker gets to his feet, grabs the protruding arrow, yanks it free and races towards Aelianna. But Vyvian is relentless in her attack. He battles to avoid being hit—sidestepping one arrow after another. The one that hit its mark earlier, although not life threatening, had pierced his forearm as he shielded himself with it. He'd yanked that one free too. And the blood keeps flowing. He presses his hand to the wound and inches his way towards Aelianna, diving from the protection of one boulder to another.

To his relief, Ryker spots Jaeger diverting Vyvian's focus. She screams at the sight of him and hightails it out of there. Now's his chance—Ryker runs to warn Aelianna of Archimedes' tricks.

But then, from the depths of the forest, the threat Ryker had anticipated appears. He recognises Titus— one of Wulf's thugs—Athos—the other Invincible— Archimedes, of course, and another he has yet to have the pleasure of meeting.

Ryker smiles. This new guy, being smaller in build and stature, should be no match for him. Before making his move, Ryker looks back to ensure Edra and Medwin are safe, then ahead to where Molan is tussling on the ground with his daughter, and finally at Albert, half-hidden behind a tree. Time to act. He calls out for them to block out Archimedes' influence by singing. (Jack's method of scrambling Archimedes' mind control by silently singing has saved his butt in the past and *may* just save them all now.)

With a song strong in his thoughts, Ryker steps forward to face the enemy.

Suddenly, Aelianna falls face down, writhing in

pain. Ryker's focus diverts, and instantly her pain becomes his. He collapses to his knees. The pain slices through him like cuts from a thousand daggers. He can barely breathe. He struggles to fight against it and gain back the advantage. And with words of empowerment sung through clenched teeth and a herculean effort, he does.

He catches his breath, then stands tall, arms crossed. He grins, knowing his revenge will be sweet. Edra and Medwin step forward to join him, together in a clear expression of defiance.

Archimedes' shocked expression reinforces Ryker's confidence.

Ryker looks to where Aelianna continues to thrash about in pain. 'Lia, use your voice! The pain will stop.'

Molan urges his daughter to listen, his throat thick with tears. 'Do as he says. Use your voice, my beloved lark. Sing!'

At once, and to Ryker's utter relief, fractured melodic notes reach his ears, and very soon the thrashing abates.

Ryker can breathe once again. He returns his focus to Archimedes. His eyes narrow.

It's payback time!

But before he knows what's happening, a force from behind knocks Ryker over, face down, and a heavy weight on top of him prevents him from getting up to fight. It's the unknown Invincible, and it shocks him that he didn't see him coming. One second, the brute is spectating from the fringes, the next, he's on top of him, relentlessly beating the back of his head. Momentarily stunned, Ryker battles to retaliate.

But he must.

He cries out an almighty roar and rolls over, throwing the unknown Invincible sideways, then he pounces on the man, straddles him and curls his fist, preparing to throw a punch. But incredibly, the attacker pinned beneath him vanishes.

Dumbstruck, Ryker looks about and sees his aggressor some distance away, laughing.

Ryker scrambles to his feet and charges towards him. But his tormentor is quick to vanish once again. Ryker swivels on the spot, disorientated, and turns to see a fist aimed straight at his face. Without thinking, Ryker blocks the attack with his injured arm. He gasps at the pain but shakes it off, then seizes the thug and throws a few weighted punches of his own.

'Take him out, Cadmael!' Athos cries out. 'You have the advantage.'

Advantage? Ryker almost laughs. Now that he has him, the smaller man doesn't stand a chance.

Ryker raises his fist once again, but in a blink of an eye, Cadmael is gone.

Ryker looks about to locate him. He sees him lingering at a distance, his face bloodied, fear in his eyes, and looking very much like he's ready to take off. Ryker growls and goes after him. But, once again, Cadmael vanishes. And this time, he doesn't return.

Athos curses and cries out. 'Titus, act now!'

Ryker turns to see the giant, muscle-clad, bald-headed bully stomping towards him. He reaches for the ready-to-go taser he has in his cargo pants' pocket, but the zipper catches. And a moment's hesitation costs him. Titus grabs Ryker in a chokehold. His grasp tightens. Ryker does everything he can to throw him. He jabs him in the gut with his elbow, stomps on his feet, kicks back, and claws at his hold, but the ogre is unwavering—nothing breaks the beast's vicelike grip.

Ryker sees stars. His vision darkens. He has nothing left to give.

Then suddenly, a melody, pure and sweet, sails to his ears to weaken the noose around his neck.

Titus falls to his knees.

And so does Ryker. Gasping for air, he battles to shake off the state of hypnosis brought on by Aelianna's mesmerising singing.

He must conquer this. He digs deeper and calls on Jack's jamming technique—a song of his own—for help. And he succeeds. Back in control, Ryker looks up to witness Aelianna in her glory. Titus,

Athos and Archimedes have fallen under her spell. All three goons wear bewitched expressions on their faces. Their eyes glazed over. Their focus clouded.

The friends band together and prepare for the fallout once the singing ends. Medwin and Molan stand ready with their blades. Edra flexes her hold on the baseball bat.

Aelianna races to Ryker's side, her eyes full of regret as she takes in his wounds.

Ryker staggers to his feet and squeezes her hand. 'Come on, we've got work to do.'

Within moments, their attackers break from the spell. They regroup and prepare to pounce.

Aelianna reaches for her bow and readies an arrow. Ryker tugs her to stand behind him, his impressive hunting blade unsheathed and ready. 'Let's finish this!'

But the unanticipated look of terror on the enemy's faces makes Ryker question what's put it there.

Athos points skyward with a shaky finger. 'Spirits from The Valley of Lost Souls have escaped! Run!'

Titus gulps. Archimedes cries out. They all turn tail and take off.

And thus, the attack is evaded.

Ryker chuckles. 'Who would've thought one measly ghost could do that?'

He shields his eyes from the sun to search for Jaeger, and the answer to the Invincibles' terror becomes all too clear. Hovering high above them are dozens of floating spirits, all wearing a smile on their faces and a glint in their eyes.

Jaeger breaks away and whooshes down to float before them. 'Looks like I missed all the fun!'

Edra races to embrace him but falls through him, ending up flat on her face on the ground.

Jaeger's face distorts in a grimace, and his already washed-out self becomes several shades paler. He clutches at his centre. Wisps of translucent broken pieces of his form float back together to fill the gaping hole made by Edra's attempt to contact him.

Edra holds her hand to her mouth and swallows hard as she looks at him. 'Eww, gross! That was just totally weird!'

Jaeger winces. 'It wasn't exactly fun for me either!' He shakes his head; his lip curls. 'Um, how about we make a pact not to do that again?'

Edra laughs. 'Agreed.'

Ryker points to the sky and chuckles. 'Jae, I'd say you and your, um, *collaborators* couldn't have timed it better. Thanks for that, buddy!'

He shrugs. 'Hey, no trouble. What are friends for?'

Movement from the corner of his eye has Ryker's guard up again. He relaxes when he sees Albert.

'Buddy, I nearly forgot about you. Are you okay?'

Albert remains at a distance. His head down, his hands buried in his pockets. He distractedly kicks at the dirt, then looks up at the spirits floating above. He frowns. 'I reckon we're not much liked. Are we?'

Aelianna moves towards him and rests her hands on his shoulders. ''Tis not that we dislike ghosts, Albert. The stories we are told as children rule our fear. Look how we have embraced Jaeger.' She smiles. 'He is no different in spirit from his living self—so we do not fear him. He is our friend. Is he not?'

Albert's eyes brighten. 'So you reckon *we* could be friends?'

Aelianna's smile widens. 'If it brings about an end to all your mischief, then most certainly we can.'

Albert lunges forward and embraces her. He looks up, his face aglow. 'I'll be good from now on. I promise!'

Ryker shakes his head. 'And all this madness could've been avoided. The poor kid just needed a friend.' He reaches out to mess his hair. 'We're here for you too, buddy.'

He looks at Aelianna in wonder. Never has he met anyone with so much calm and thoughtful logic. His respect for her skyrockets to the point where he could kiss her right now.

But now's not the time. There's work to be done.

He gestures towards the ghosts floating above them. 'Jae, what's gonna happen with these guys?'

Jaeger's face lights up. 'I figured they could come back with us. What do you think?'

Ryker takes a moment. There's a lot to consider. There are at least thirty spirits floating above them. Some young, some old, some male, some female. All victims of the portals. How's he going to do this? He looks up at their hopeful faces. Clearly, Jaeger had coerced them to coming to their aid with the promise of going home. And Ryker can't blame him. They deserve to return to their loved ones too, no matter the challenge to make it happen. He remembers the time he and Max planned a similar mass exodus. The fact that the ones needing their help to escape aren't exactly alive shouldn't really be an issue. Should it?

Jaeger flits back and forth before him, his expression hopeful. 'Ryker, they've been trapped here for God knows how long. Like me, they never found the way to cross over because they were never meant to be here. I was lucky; you found me and took me home. These guys deserve the same. Right?'

Of course, Ryker agrees, but there's the matter of their Aussie friends, trapped in the prehistoric world. That takes priority.

Could the ghosts come with them?

Chances are, once they leave the realm, they'll

no longer be ghosts. They've seen this phenomenon happen time and time again. And if that's the case, it'll mean there'll be more of them to look out for in this unknown world.

But could they be useful? More hands make light work …

He groans.

No, it's too risky.

Perhaps they should split up. Jaeger could take them back through the portal to South Africa while the rest of them go on.

But would Jaeger agree to this? Would he be happy to abort the mission at this stage?

He then considers Edra. He knows she'd never leave Jaeger's side.

She'll choose to go with him … no matter what.

And what about Aelianna?

It's too dangerous … she should stay with her father.

Ryker paces back and forth, mulling all this over and trying to find a solution.

The soft touch of Aelianna's hand on his arm has an instant effect on him. He looks down into her warm, deep-brown eyes, and his unease dissipates.

'Tell us your concerns, for it is clear there are many.'

She gestures to their friends. 'Ryker, we are here to help. The burden is not yours alone to bear.'

He lets out a troubled sigh. She's right. Why is he trying to come up with answers on his own? So Ryker voices his apprehensions.

Within minutes, a resolution is reached. The plan to evacuate the ghosts will need to take a back seat. For now, the Aussies are their priority, and time is wasting. It's decided that Jaeger, Molan and Medwin, together with the ghost brigade, will remain to watch over the girls while Ryker and Albert go to assess the situation. If all is safe, he'll return for them. Once they've freed their Aussie friends, then, and only then, will they make plans for the ghosts.

Content to leave his friends under the guard of Jaeger and this new faction of transparent helpers, Ryker follows Albert the short distance to the clearing surrounding the lake.

Once there, he stops to take it in. It's as Molan had described it—small and unassuming. No one would ever believe a monstrous beast lives beneath the calm surface. He wonders whether Albert has ever come across it. He frowns. He's better off not mentioning it. He'll accomplish nothing, only spook the kid. With that in mind, Ryker prays he has zero encounters with any leathery, meat-eating giants on the way.

He positions the thermal-imaging goggles firmly in place and prepares to go. With Albert at his side, ready to guide him through to the prehistoric realm, he turns to his friends, signals he's good to go with a thumbs-up gesture, draws a few deep breaths and takes the plunge.

31

BURNING

RYKER

The extreme chill deep beneath the water's surface threatens to divert Ryker's focus. His instinct is to gasp. But he doesn't. He can't risk jeopardising the mission. He steels himself to keep going. But something's not right. He adjusts the goggles and looks about. He can't see the glow of the portal anywhere. And by now he should. Albert swims ahead, propelling himself deeper and deeper into the darkness. Without question, Ryker follows.

The water surrounding him condenses the further he goes, compressing his form. His lungs burn, crying out for a reprieve. It's almost unbearable. But Albert continues, seemingly without effort. Ryker can't believe it. How is it that this scrap of a kid can endure this kind of pain as if it's nothing? Ryker digs deeper to reinforce his staying power. But he's struggling to find it, his chest in agony. His head feels like it's about to explode.

Albert doubles back and stops, poised before him, treading water, clearly not in any distress. He points excitedly and gestures for Ryker to keep coming. But Ryker hasn't got anything left to give. He desperately needs to breathe. His gaze darts skyward. Does he go back? But the surface of the water is now too far out of range. In a panic, he peers deeper, searching the dark, bottomless abyss for the elusive glow. And then he sees it. A faint glimmer in the distance. But it's impossibly far to get to in time. He'll drown trying. Again, he looks upwards, calculating frantically the risk of either decision. Does he continue towards the impossibly distant portal? Or does he use whatever he has left in him to go back?

He thinks of his friends. Friends who rescued him in the past, now buried in a stony tomb, destined to die without his help.

He thinks of Max—his buddy, his saviour, who now needs saving herself. He owes it to her to go forward.

But then he thinks of Aelianna. He can't abandon her—she needs protecting.

WHAT DO I DO?

It's agonising … utter torture!

He claws at his throat. He's burning—every inch of him ablaze.

But a decision needs to be made.

And that's when he realises how this will end.

He stops struggling.

32

QUANDARY

AELIANNA

The passing of such time should define that Ryker has succeeded. Aelianna paces at the water's edge, her logic failing to convince her that all has gone to plan. She suddenly considers Medwin. He could tell her. He should know. She rushes to his side. 'Please, Medwin, reassure me! All is well, is it not?'

Edra dives to his other side, clearly eager to hear news as well.

Medwin studies them both, frowns, then shifts in his seat. He looks away. For a long moment, he doesn't speak.

Edra's eyes widen; the colour drains from her face. Jaeger descends from the sky to be by her side, his concern for Ryker evident too.

Aelianna tries to quell their anxiety with a gesture of her hand for them to wait. She pauses to give Medwin the time he needs to delve into his reflections to seek a result. But his silence is fraying her fortitude. Every possible situation plays in her mind's eye. She draws a deep breath and reminds herself to focus only on the positive ones.

With eyes closed and concentration elsewhere, Medwin remains silent.

Aelianna struggles to be patient. Disparaging thoughts eat at her composure. She can wait no longer. 'Medwin, please!' She grips his arm. The older man flinches. She loosens her hold. 'Forgive me, but I must know ...'

'What do you see?' Edra says.

'Medwin, certainly you have, by now, some insight,' Molan says from afar, evidently anxious to hear.

Medwin reaches for Aelianna's hand. 'Child, I cannot betray to you, nor am I able to comfort you with any news.' He looks at each of his friends. 'What you all seek sits beyond my reach.' He shrugs. ''Tis a quandary for sure, but perhaps we can take from it that all is well.'

Edra settles back at hearing this. She looks at Jaeger and smiles. 'He's got a point. I guess no news is good news. Right?'

Jaeger frowns. 'I guess so. So now we wait.'

Jaeger darts back to the sky to resume his role as protector, but the moment he reaches the sky, he turns, points to the lake and cries out in horror.

Aelianna whips around to see what has befallen them. She races to the water's edge with the others.

Molan grabs hold of his daughter before she has a chance to get too close. She struggles to free herself but knows, before even catching sight of him, that some harm has come to Ryker.

Edra screams and falls to her knees, her face ashen. *No, no, NOOOO!*

Aelianna claws at her restraints, crying out to be released. 'Let me be! Father, I must see!' But Molan's hold only tightens.

Suddenly, the embrace weakens, and he steps aside.

Aelianna can hardly breathe. She cannot bear to move closer, but knows she must. Her feet are suddenly lead weights. She feels the support from her father as he walks her to the tarn's edge.

And there, dredged from its perilous depths by Medwin, lies Ryker's lifeless form.

33
CPR

EDRA

Edra, horror-struck, gapes at the body Medwin battles to retrieve from the water. Molan races to help him. She watches on numbly. A welcoming fog wafts across her consciousness and drapes over her … shielding her. Her eyes don't need to see this anymore. Somewhere in the distance, the fading hum of someone wailing drifts to her ears. The fog reinforces its protection. The distressing sound is no more.

Cocooned in this oblivion, Edra fails to hear Jaeger's plea for help. He frantically waves his hand in front of her face. 'Edra, you've got to do something! Snap out of it! You're the only one who can help here!'

'Jaeger, if there is anything at all Edra can do, please bring her back from whatever depths of despair she has gone to.'

'Medwin, I've tried! It's like she's checked out or something. The shock must've been too much.' Jaeger whooshes back and forth in a frenzy. 'We need her. There's a chance she might be able to save him. She knows CPR. We both do. But I'm useless to him like this.' He stops suddenly. 'Maybe …' But he doesn't wait to finish. He withdraws a few steps from them, then flies at Edra, charging straight through her.

Edra gasps. The shock breaks her daze. She sees Ryker's lifeless body before her. Her gut spasms. She doubles over and empties the contents of her stomach.

'Edra, you can bring him back! Do CPR!'

Her head spins. Edra senses the urgency surrounding her, but feels disorientated. Jaeger's words take a moment to sink in. She needs to breathe.

The grave expression on Jaeger's face brings her to her senses. She needs to act, and act fast. She hurries to Ryker's side, checks for a pulse, finds none, then tilts his head back, his chin up, and checks for any obstructions in his airways. She then pinches his nose, places her mouth over his, and prays that she's doing everything right before blowing a breath of air into his lungs. She watches his chest rise a little, then fall. She needs to do better. Again, she draws in a breath—this time deeper, places her mouth over his, and forces it into his lungs. Ryker's chest movement is decent. Encouraged, she repeats this a few more times. Edra then begins chest compressions. With both heels of her hands crossed on the middle of his chest, and her arms extended straight, she starts, throwing her whole weight behind each compression. *One, two, three. Four, five …*

Jaeger spurs her on. 'That's it, Edra! Keep going. You can do it!' He flits about, excitedly. 'Remember, you need to do thirty, then stop.'

Six, seven, eight, nine … Edra times the compressions with a song, soft on her lips … '*Staying alive, staying alive …*'

'I'll keep count,' he says. 'You concentrate on the timing.'

She reaches thirty, then stops. Without a moment to spare, she drags in a lungful of air, presses her mouth to Ryker's and blows. Again, his chest rises and falls. But her efforts aren't enough—there's no sign of life. She begins the round of compressions a second time, this time with everything she has. But she's burning. She won't be able to keep up this pace.

'Molan, she needs help,' Jaeger calls out. 'You've seen what Edra's doing. Take over!'

Molan steps in and mimics Edra's actions. Hesitant at first, but soon gathering momentum.

Edra falls back, breathless. She waits for Molan to finish before forcing another breath. Molan repeats the compressions a second time. Once done, she fills his lungs again, then stops.

There's no change.

Ryker's body lies lifeless before them.

Molan looks up to take further instruction. Jaeger's face dips—he shakes his head.

Aelianna cries out. She falls to Ryker's side and lays her head on his chest, sobbing.

Edra watches on, defeated. Hollow. Tears stream down her cheeks.

He's gone.

34
GLASS HALF FULL

MAX

They reach the wall of rubble created by the cave-in. It has completely blocked their passage. Ruby attempts to use her shield, pushing against it with everything she has, but makes no leeway. So Kenny takes the initiative to tear it down. With him in the lead, and sensitive to how this should be done, the seven friends form a human chain, working hand to hand to clear a path.

With the hope that Jack may have somehow survived the catastrophe, Max doesn't let up on the task—her thoughts consumed with finding him alive.

Look at it with a glass-half-full attitude, Jack would often tell her. Something she heard his father advocate.

She pushes on, reminding herself to stay positive. Although a monstrous struggle, she needs to. For Jack's sake. She grits her teeth. 'I'm not giving up on you, Jack. I'm coming!'

'Um … Yeah, I can see that.'

The comment, heard from behind, startles her. Max whips around and peers into the dimly lit passage. Someone's there. Or was it her imagination? She shakes her head. She's hearing things. She shrugs it off and throws herself back into the task.

'Whoa, steady on there, tiger! Where's the fire?'

Again, she stops. She's delirious—now she's hearing Jack's voice.

The voice chuckles.

She freezes. She couldn't have imagined that. That was Jack's laugh.

Ever so slowly, Max turns.

Sitting there in the near darkness, on the pile of rubble they've created, is the transparent form of her once-human boyfriend. Max cries out. Her hands fly to her mouth.

'Hi, Max.'

Behind her, Bec screams.

As one, the friends turn to see what the commotion is.

Jack rises and floats closer towards them, his hands held up in front of him in an apologetic manner. 'Oh, man! Hey, I didn't mean to startle you. You were just so caught up in what you were doing, I didn't have the heart to say something.'

Peanut grabs the torch wedged in the rocks and trips over everyone to get to him. He aims the beam directly at Jack. 'Man, is that really you?'

'Hey, Peanut!'

'But … but you're a ghost!'

Jack's lip curls. He shrugs. 'Yeah. I guess so.'

'Then you're …' Max struggles to say the word.

Jack smiles a crooked smile. 'Dead? Yeah, I imagine there's no other way of putting it.'

Ruby sidesteps Peanut to get a closer look, her hand extended to touch Jack's face. 'OMG! Now I've seen everything. Jack, are you okay? You look okay. I mean, for someone who's …'

Max slaps Ruby's hand away. Tears fill her eyes. 'Ruby! How the hell can he be *okay*? Just *look* at him!'

'But, Max, can't you see?' Kenny says with unexpected optimism. 'It's not all that bad.'

Max whips around so fast, Kenny ducks for cover.

'Okay, okay, I'll admit,' Kenny adds quickly with his hands raised. 'Jack dying isn't a good thing, Max, but Jack, as a *ghost*, could come in handy.' He turns to Jack with hope in his eyes. 'Am I right?'

Max can't believe what she's hearing. Heat treks up her neck to flush her face. She's ready to roast him.

Kenny's eyes widen. He stutters as he hurries to put across his point. 'And, and, and just think about it, once we return through the portal, from what we already know, Jack will come back to life.'

Max blinks a few times. She hadn't thought of that.

Kenny looks down at his feet and stuffs his hands in his jeans' pockets. His voice is soft. 'So, um, it's like I said, it's not all that bad.'

Kenny steals a look at Max from behind his fallen fringe, then glances back down. He scuffs the earth with his sneaker.

Max peeks at Jack.

Jack smiles. 'He's got a point there, Max.'

Max cringes. *Poor Kenny!*

She draws a breath. 'You're right. When you put it that way, it's not all that bad.' Max gives Kenny a tentative smile. 'Sorry.'

Kenny takes the few steps needed to reach Max and pulls her into a hug. 'We've gotta believe things will work out, Max, otherwise there's no hope.'

She rests her cheek against Kenny's chest and looks at Jack.

Jack shrugs and gives her a wink.

She nods. 'Glass half full, Kenny. Always.'

35
FEAST

JACK

Seeing Max this vulnerable tears Jack apart. It goes against his grain not to dive in and protect her. He watches as Kenny steps in to be the support she needs. But right now, he has to remain indifferent and not show his pain. Yes, he's dead, and although there's no guarantee he'll come back to life when they return through the portal, his decision to confront the attacking dinosaur is one he'd make again, and without any hesitation. His friends are alive because of it. That four-metre monster wasn't going to stop. And right at this minute, Jack needs to make light of the situation to help Max remain strong.

He smiles and gives her a wink. 'Oi, Kenny, I'm

still here, you know! Quit moving in on my girl!'

Max breaks from Kenny's embrace and smiles. 'A ghost for a boyfriend … now that's something I thought I'd never hear myself say.'

Jack chuckles. 'So let's see if being a ghost is all that it's cracked up to be.' He turns to Kenny. 'What can I do to help?'

'Buddy, we need you. We've been chipping away at this for ages.' Kenny gestures to the wall of rubble, his forehead dripping in sweat. He takes a moment to clean his glasses with his T-shirt. 'Can you tell how much further we've gotta go?'

'Give me a sec, and I'll check it out.' Jack braces himself for what he needs to do. In his short experience of doing this, passing through solid masses is quite unnerving. A creepy sensation he can't describe sweeps over him. It's like his insides turn to ice. His first encounter wasn't exactly fun, so doing it again makes him a little hesitant. He takes a few breaths to prepare himself, then flies towards the wall and vanishes through it. On the other side, he pauses to recover.

But there's no time for that. There's a job to be done.

He shakes it off and pauses to take in the damage. But his ears prick to the sound of something nearby. He's not alone. Guttural growls, snorts, tearing flesh and gnashing teeth on bones. Something hidden from view feasts nearby. He flies a little closer.

A high-pitched squeal followed by a yelp and a tussle alerts him that there's more than one. He flies higher and hovers over what appears to be a massacre. Half buried beneath a mound of rubble lies the body of the *T. rex* that attacked them earlier. And three smaller, dog-sized, feathered dinosaurs gorge hungrily, slashing and cleaving the remains of the bigger dinosaur; its insides already devoured. He draws back at the grisly sight. And then with sudden realisation he remembers that his body too is entombed somewhere in there.

He shakes his head. Now's not the time for weakness—he needs to find a way to save his friends.

He surveys the area. The entrance to the cave, once a sliver of an opening, is now a gaping cavity.

Movement outside has his undivided attention. He goes to investigate and spots a familiar three-metre-long, one-metre-tall dinosaur sniffing near the entrance, clearly tracking the scent of the *T. Rex* carcass.

Deinonychus!

Jack remembers Kenny saying these dinosaurs were pack hunters and realises that this solo oversized lizard won't be alone for long—soon there'll be more. He whips around to look at the smaller dinosaurs feasting, and is filled with sudden dread. The situation has unexpectedly taken a turn for the worse.

Where there's a kill, there'll soon be a bloodbath!

He looks back to the three-metre-thick wall of rubble.

Crap! They've gotta stop digging!

36
SAYING GOODBYE

EDRA

Time passes. All that could've been done for Ryker at the lakeside was done. And for reasons unknown, the one and only glimmer of hope Edra clung to at his time of death didn't eventuate—his spirit form never manifested itself as it should have. *But why?* Jaeger had no answers for this anomaly, nor did their newly formed spectre alliance. Ryker's lifeless body, dragged from the fatal waters, remained devoid of change. A total mystery, and one that Edra was compelled to come to terms with without explanation … or hope.

And so, regrettably, they put plans into place to depart, and laid Ryker to rest. Prayers for an eternal life, and words of farewell were said. No more to be done.

Edra tugs Aelianna into a tight embrace. This, their final farewell. Aelianna's announcement to remain with her family and not return with her is still a shock. Edra chokes back tears, struggling to find the strength to leave without her. Yes, Ryker is gone, but Aelianna belongs in *their* world now, not here in this barbaric place. Can't she see this? Doesn't she know that Ryker would've wanted this for her … that he would've insisted on it?

Knowing this makes it all the harder to bear. Edra bites her lip, battling to hold back from saying so. But if Edra were to be completely honest with herself, she'd realise her internal battle runs deeper than that. To leave now, without Aelianna, would mean she'd be severing a crucial tie to Ryker forever.

Forever!

Reality strikes, and it almost shatters her. Her hold on Aelianna tightens. It takes a long moment for the harshness of the truth to sink in. And yes, although the deep-rooted want for Aelianna to return with them is a selfish one, Edra can't bring herself to feel remorse in having such thoughts. It's all too overwhelming. How is she to manage the journey of grief without her? She had anticipated they'd tread this rocky, darkened path ahead together … side by side.

Edra's head spins. There's been little to no time to process any of it. Not Ryker's death. Not the unexpected bombshell. Not the abandonment. None of it! She can't grasp it. Aelianna's decision to remain makes no sense. *How can she think she'd be happy here?*

Tears prickle her senses. Her chest aches. Can anyone ever truly be happy after such a loss? Edra knows only too well the answer to that. Painful flashbacks of her own suffering cause a stir. She flinches, remembering the frigid and bitter emptiness that consumed her the day Jaeger was taken from her. In a panic, she releases Aelianna and searches the skies for him. With relief, she spots him, high above, waiting patiently for her.

Edra draws a breath. Her eyes close. She takes a moment to compose herself.

Aelianna takes Edra's hand and squeezes it. Her look sympathetic. Edra blinks. Such compassion and understanding in her own time of grief surprises her. She realises then, with sudden clarity, this isn't *her* decision to make, it's Aelianna's. And it's done. Aelianna needs family around her to help her heal.

Edra looks about the tiny mudbrick, thatched-roof village and knows, deep in her heart, that Aelianna's decision to remain is the right one. In time, and with this support, she'll find peace. One day.

Edra embraces Aelianna once more. With her trusted baseball bat at hand, Jaeger by her side, and a multitude of impatient spirits floating above them, Edra departs. She turns one last time and waves goodbye.

Surrounded by her family, Aelianna smiles a watery smile and swipes away her tears.

Edra's heart breaks a little.

'She's not alone,' Jaeger reminds her.

And he's right. She's not. She knows that now.

And more importantly, Edra realises, neither is she.

They move on.

Edra follows as Jaeger leads. Her guard up, her senses tuned, her mindset positive … well, mostly. She focuses harder to improve on that.

But after a while, her thoughts stray. Her teeth clench. This assignment has been a complete debacle from the beginning. They've achieved nothing. Not only have they lost Ryker, but their Aussie friends remain entombed somewhere in another dimension, with little to no hope of ever escaping. It's a situation beyond them now—it's time to get the authorities in.

As they should have from the beginning!

They soldier on. Jaeger remains close by her side. Their new friends hover high above them, on the lookout. Edra scans the dark recesses of the forest—

her guard up. She knows how vulnerable she is. Her only defence comes in the form of a well-worn baseball bat. The newly formed ghost brigade, although eager and willing to swoop in if trouble strikes, are limited in what they can do. She's under no delusion—she's making this journey on her own. A haunting can only do so much against a physical threat. Essentially, she's traversing a hostile forest, returning to a potentially guarded portal, solo.

Every rustle in the brush, every twitter in the trees, every flutter of a leaf is amplified. Her senses on overdrive, she's ready to run, but she counsels herself to remain calm.

Evidently picking up on her angst, Jaeger hovers closer. At times so close he occasionally brushes against her, the weird and objectionable sensation previously experienced clearly not an issue now. They continue.

The trek from Aelianna's home to the Aussie portal is a relatively short and undemanding one. Although not their journey's end, it's a necessary detour they need to make to locate the trail leading to the portal to South Africa, where she knows with certainty that help awaits them.

Edra uses her experience from her time spent in the forest with Ryker to pick up on clues of an identifiable pathway. Snapped branches, worn paths and telltale markings on boulders pave the way. Clues from the past, a gift from Ryker. She pauses for the briefest moment to be grateful, but doesn't allow herself to wallow in grief.

Soon, they enter a familiar area. Edra knows where they are. They're within reach of the Aussie portal. Edra motions for Jaeger to lie low. No doubt there'll be a guard presence, and they need to pass by unnoticed.

Jaeger swoops down to her. 'Stay put. I'll check things out.'

Edra waits within the shadows of the forest, hidden from view. The ghost contingent hang back, careful not to bring attention to themselves. She chews her bottom lip, anxious to move on. Jaeger needs only to locate the trail of moonstones left previously by Banji that links the two portals.

Time is ticking. She shifts restlessly. *Where is he?*

She squats on her haunches and reminds herself to remain calm. She listens and hears nothing but the tranquillity of the forest. This settles her somewhat. She searches the skies, ready to make a move as soon as Jaeger gives her the all-clear.

And then, to her relief, he's back, a penitent smirk on his face. He gives her a two-thumbs-up signal and motions for her to follow. They move on.

Soon they're back on track. The steady stream of stones paves the way. Up and down numerous steep inclines, through dense thickets and heavily wooded pathways, Edra doesn't let up. Her legs burn from exertion, her mouth parched, but she keeps at it.

Every now and then, Jaeger swoops down to check on her, a line etched on his brow. She hates being the reason for that frown. She smiles to mask her pain and pushes harder.

The sun, previously high in the sky, wanes. Light diminishes. Darkened clouds, thick with rain, threaten to hamper their journey. This spurs Edra to move faster.

Suddenly, their goal is within reach. High above the treetops, the impressive rock formation guides them to their way home. Edra's eyes squeeze tight, holding back tears of joy.

Jaeger motions he'll fly ahead to scout the area. Edra regroups, takes a deep breath and crouches low behind a boulder sheltered by large-leafed foliage. She waits. Moments later, he returns to her and reports information she half-expected to hear.

'We've got company,' he warns. 'The passage is protected. But by how many? I can't tell. I couldn't … I mean, I *didn't* get close enough to see.' He looks away, suddenly appearing troubled.

Odd. This news hardly surprises her. It was always going to be inevitable that protection around the portal would've heightened, given their presence.

She shrugs it off and looks to Jaeger to make the first move. But he hesitates. He turns away again, his expression worried.

Edra frowns. 'Okay, so it's not ideal, but, Jae, it's doable. Right? While you ghosts distract the guards, I'll slip past them. Too easy. Once I'm through, the rest of you follow. Okay?'

Jaeger says nothing.

His silence unsettles her. 'Jae?'

He shrugs. 'Hey, it's like you said … too easy.'

Edra's brow furrows. 'Jae, I'm sorry, but you couldn't lie to save yourself. What's wrong?'

He struggles to look at her.

This can't be good! She swallows hard.

He laughs unexpectedly. 'Look, quit stressing … you'll be fine. You'll zip past them in a flash, and they'll be none the wiser.'

'Oh, no, no, no! You're not getting off that easy!' She steps up and points a finger at him. She's so close, he's forced to look at her. 'Jaeger Friedrich Muller, you'd better talk. And talk fast!'

His eyes squeeze shut. He sighs, taking a moment to answer. 'Edra, as much as I want to, I can't come back with you.'

She draws back. This definitely wasn't something she was expecting to hear. Has she done something to annoy him? Is it something she said? But what?

And when? A million damning thoughts suddenly plague her. But it's ludicrous. She shakes them from her head.

The ghosts, having heard the conversation, swoop down closer to listen.

Edra frowns. 'I don't understand, Jae. What do you mean? It's not as if you *can't*. You've done it before …'

She stops. A sudden, alarming thought comes to her. *Oh my God! They're onto us—the guards have somehow come prepared. But how?*

Jaeger's chin dips. It just about destroys her to see him this way. 'Jae, what have they done?'

He shakes his head. 'I … I don't know. I can't figure it out.'

She waits.

'It's just so weird. Just then, when I tried getting close to the passage,' he says, 'I couldn't. I literally *couldn't*. Something stopped me. Something I couldn't see or feel, but real just the same.' He rakes his fingers through his hair and sighs. 'I couldn't get anywhere near it.' He looks skyward. 'And I can't image these guys can either.'

Edra stops. Could the news be any worse? They're so close to finishing this. Crossing the threshold home was meant to be the least of their problems.

She questions what may have changed. 'Jae,

think. What's different?'

He frowns, deep in thought. 'I don't know if it means anything, but there were a handful of small campfires lit at the entrance.' He shrugs. 'It just looked like they were settling in for the night. Nothing weird about it, but it's not something we've seen before. The guards seldom stay out after sunset because of the risk of being attacked.'

Edra agrees. She can't imagine there's more to it.

She then considers the likelihood of one of the guards being gifted with a shield, as Ruby is, and is about to say so when Jaeger interrupts.

'Oh, and there was this weird, painted hand on the rockface near the entrance. It was huge!' he tells her. 'And if I'm not wrong, there was an image of an eye on it. A blue eye.' He shrugs. 'I can't imagine it meaning anything.'

Edra's gut clenches. Now it makes sense. Clearly an oddity for him, but a revelation to her. She groans. 'A hamsa.'

Jaeger frowns. 'Um, you've got me.'

Edra grabs a stick and etches the image of what she's talking about on the dusty ground. She draws a hand, palm facing forward with an open eye in the centre.

'Yeah, that's it!' Jaeger confirms. But his enthusiasm changes at seeing Edra's bleak expression.

'Okay, clearly not a good thing. Why?'

She closes her eyes. Again, she groans. *Yeah, Edra! Why?* She rubs at her temples, not sure how to begin.

A self-professed authority on such things, she needs to come clean and explain, no matter the difficulty in exposing the pain of her past. While going through therapy, after their return from the realm, she'd bought all kinds of talismans and amulets, hoping something would help break her funk. She had stacks of them. Hamsa pendants, evil-eye charms, Corno good-luck earrings, horned hand charms, dragons, four-leaf clovers, horseshoes, dream catchers … every possible deterrent of evil and bringer of good luck from every corner of the globe. She can't say if any of them made a difference, but at the time, she depended on them heavily to help her get through each day.

Edra shakes away her disparaging thoughts. 'The hamsa is a symbol used for protection,' she tells him. 'In some cultures, people believe they ward off bad luck. Specifically, bad luck from spirits risen from the underworld. These amulets are pretty common. You've probably seen kids wearing them as charms. Burning incense or agarwood does the same thing. The scent is commonly thought to dispel evil spirits and attract good luck.'

And just as Edra speaks it, a faint scent of wood

burning wafts towards her on a slight breeze. At first, she thinks nothing of it, imagining it's from the fires Jaeger had mentioned, but then she recognises the smell of agarwood. Suddenly, it all makes sense. The random firepits, the painted hamsa. The Ancients are applying archaic methods to drive the spirits back to The Valley of Lost Souls. And it appears to be working.

They're in trouble.

Traces of smoke from the fire heighten. Without warning, and to Edra's horror, an invisible barrier drives Jaeger back; the force sends him and the other ghosts farther and farther from her. And then very quickly he's out of reach, soon to be gone from her.

But Edra won't let that happen. Her eyes darken.

Stop! Think! Do something!

And then she remembers. She has superpowers. Speed and agility. So why isn't she using them? She needs to act—and act fast.

The first things to tackle are the fires. She considers water, but there are no streams nearby. *But there's dirt!* Not wasting a second, she grabs a stick and starts digging.

Numerous broken sticks and a few bleeding blisters later, Edra accumulates enough dirt to take on the task. She scoops up several handfuls into her rolled-up T-shirt, draws in a deep breath and reassures herself she can do it. She considers her baseball bat but decides to leave it, then darts towards the rocky outcrop.

She spots them. Three guards, Archimedes, and the new guy, Cadmael.

She doesn't pause for a moment.

At the speed of light, Edra douses the fire of one of the pits with her load. She escapes, unseen, then darts back for more.

As she leaves, she hears an outcry. A commotion follows. She needs to hurry. From what she saw, there are another two fires to put out.

Back at the mound of dirt, frantically reloading, Edra fails to notice the sudden appearance of another presence. Without warning, she faceplants the ground. She whips around to see Cadmael. The brute stands over her, his axe raised, ready to strike. Her reflexive response to kick him in the groin saves her. Her attacker falls to his knees, drops the axe and cups the injury. Edra kicks away the axe, seizes her baseball bat and rams the end of it into his face. A sickening crunch and a howl of pain follows. A gush of blood spurts from his nose, saturating his linen tunic. He vanishes.

No time to waste. Edra needs to extinguish those fires to snuff the smoke shield.

With a sufficient dump rolled up in her T-shirt,

she grabs her baseball bat and sprints towards the passage. Again, Cadmael appears before her. She springs high to avoid him and races to the passage. This time she encounters guards, standing shoulder to shoulder, protecting the remaining fires. This doesn't deter her. She acts swiftly, snuffing out another fire before the guards realise what's happening.

She makes a hasty getaway. But Cadmael obstructs her once again, appearing from thin air, his bloodied expression demonic, his intention clear. He swipes at the congealing red liquid and spits out a mouthful of tainted saliva.

Edra swings her bat. Cadmael vanishes; she misses. He reappears a few metres from her, crying out for reinforcement. The trio of guards approach, their footsteps thundering. Edra takes off and hurries to reload. The final fire needs to be extinguished. If she doesn't succeed, Jaeger can never return.

And then she remembers the painted image of the hamsa. Her heart sinks. Will the strength of the talisman prove to be the one and only obstacle to their safe passage home?

Edra needs to deface it somehow. But how? She needs to mask it or smear it with something. But with what? And then Cadmael's bloodied tunic comes to mind. There just might be enough blood soaked in the fabric to render it sufficient.

Now to get that tunic!

As Edra shovels the soil, her mind races. Cadmael needs to reappear for this to work. She tightens her grip on the baseball bat and darts to the passage, only to find it abandoned. She stops.

Strange.

Her senses ignite.

She dumps her load; the task is complete. Smoke billows for a moment before it's taken by a soft breeze. The air clears. She listens for Jaeger's return. With the smoke barrier gone, he and their ghost friends should be able to approach. She stops, her guard up, waiting for Cadmael to reappear. Waiting to pounce.

But all is quiet. *Too quiet!*

Edra scans the area. No Cadmael, no Archimedes, no guards. No obstacle for her to leave. Her heart pounds. And then a sudden thought comes to her. *Where's Vyvian in all of this?* She looks skyward. Best be on her guard. *Never underestimate Vyvian.*

Without warning, a voice of pure evil resounds in her head and threatens to upend everything.

Archimedes!

She's swift to draw on a song of empowerment to block him out. *Fight Song,* by Rachel Platten.

This is my fight song
Take back my life song
Prove I'm all right song

Archimedes appears from the shadows of the forest, a smirk on his face. Cadmael and the three guards flank him. Edra swallows hard. She's outnumbered. She draws in a deep breath and strengthens her resolve with the words of the song strong in her mind.

Archimedes' smile vanishes. He frowns. Then the lines of his brow furrow deeper. At his side, the others appear perplexed. One of the guards nudges him. Archimedes shrugs him off and tries again. Cadmael shoves Archimedes aside. The disgraced Invincible stumbles. And since he's not built for mortal combat, he turns tail and flees.

Edra's brow raises. *One down, four to go!*

She studies the brutes in front of her and reinforces her hold on the baseball bat, ready to use it. And if her reflexes weren't as sharp as they were, Cadmael's sudden appearance mere centimetres from her would've been her downfall. But they are, and Edra's swift action blocks his attack. His fist contacts the bat instead. While he's doubled over in pain from his mis-hit, Edra grabs the given opportunity to knee him in the face. Cadmael stumbles, trips and falls back, cracking his head hard on a rock. The bully doesn't recover.

Edra's eyes narrow. *Two down, three to go!*

She examines her three remaining adversaries, each built like a brick wall, each ready to annihilate her. She braces herself, the baseball bat firm in hand.

I've still got a lot of fight left in me!

Like enraged bulls, they charge. But Edra has the jump on them before they realise what's happening. With the grace of a gazelle, she leaps high in the sky to avoid them. They turn as one, grunt, then charge again. And again, Edra springs into the air over the top of them. She grins. She could do this all day. What was she worried about?

The guards suddenly stop and fall back, cowering behind their shields. She frowns, not quite understanding their reaction.

She hears laughter come from behind her. It's Jaeger. She turns and almost cries at the sight of him.

The guards take off, screaming.

Jaeger crows. 'Wimps! And don't bother coming back!'

He then whooshes to Edra's side. 'Are you okay?'

Edra beams, overjoyed to see him. 'I am now! What took you so long?'

Jaeger chuckles. 'Seriously, we tried getting back,

but that barrier was too much. It was impossible for us to return.'

His gaze goes from Cadmael's unconscious body at Edra's feet to the bloodied baseball bat at her side. His eyes pop. 'Looks like you didn't need our help, anyway. How the heck …'

She grins. 'Don't ask.'

Again, he chuckles.

Her heart flutters. It's good to hear him laugh.

But now's not the time to let their guard down. There's much to be done. Edra falls to Cadmael's side and yanks at his tunic, stripping him naked. 'Keep an eye out for any further threat. Especially Vyvian,' she calls over her shoulder.

Jaeger gasps at Cadmael's bare form. 'What the hell, Edra? What are you doing?'

But Edra doesn't stop to explain. She mops up as much of the fresh blood the fabric can absorb from the brute's face and the back of his head, then climbs the boulder alongside the entrance to get to the painted talisman. She swipes at the icon with everything she has, smearing it with blood.

Realising her efforts, Jaeger cries out encouragements.

Soon the image is no more. She pauses to assess her work and draws in a breath. She prays that what she's done will make the difference needed for them all to return home, because there was never any guarantee they could. The painted amulets are, after all, a superstitious belief and nothing more. She turns to Jaeger, hesitant to test her theory.

He shrugs. 'There's only one way to find out.'

Edra looks at the defaced painting and then at the smokeless firepits. Has she done enough? And has she overlooked something—something more obvious and less prophetic?

Jaeger's lip curls. 'Edra, stop overthinking it.'

She grins. He knows her too well.

He waggles his eyebrows. 'Come on, let's see if all your handiwork has paid off.' Jaeger looks skyward at the ghosts hovering above and gestures for them to prepare to leave. They jostle one another, eager to be the first to go in.

Edra takes a few steps, enters the passageway and stands stock still. Her eyes close in silent prayer, begging that the others are able to follow.

Then, without restraint, one by one, her new friends float past her—hesitant at first, then with enthusiasm when they can see they can.

It worked. She's done it!

And then, with an almighty whoosh, each ghost races to be the first to cross the threshold.

Edra shields herself from the flying debris and laughs. She turns to Jaeger and grins. 'Last one through is a rotten egg!' She takes off to beat him.

'Hey! Not fair!'

Jaeger hurries after her, and together they reach the portal and plunge through to the other side.

37

CRAZY

PEANUT

Peanut plonks himself down and rests his head on the rock wall behind him, waiting for Jack to reappear. He takes a moment to recover, his energy levels sapped. 'Why the heck are we even bothering?'

Ruby frowns. 'What do you mean?'

'This pile of rocks! We're killing ourselves, and for what? I reckon if we die, we die. So what? The way I see it, we'll turn into ghosts, like Jack did. And then we can just float through this frick'n wall instead of breaking our backs doing *this*!'

He sits forward, his eyes suddenly bright, a huge grin on his face. 'Imagine it! Us as ghosts!' He laughs. 'Now, being able to vanish is pretty cool, but being a *ghost* … well, that's just next level!' He rubs his hands together, his eyes sparkling. 'Rubes, just imagine! We'd be able to go anywhere. Have a snoop around. Cause a bit of mischief. And when we go home, we'll come back to life.' He turns to Kenny. 'Ain't that right, Kenny? Win-win!' He leans back against the wall, wearing a smirk on his face. 'I can see the headlines now. *Teenagers die in prehistoric world, then come back to life.*' Suddenly, he sits taller as a thought comes to him. 'Hey, we'll be the only ones in the world who've *really* walked with dinosaurs.' He snorts. 'David Attenborough, eat your heart out!'

Ruby clicks her tongue and shakes her head. 'Yeah, but who wants to die? You twit! I definitely don't.'

'Me neither!' Shaun adds.

Liam jumps up from sitting. 'And what's the guarantee it'll work?'

Kenny glances at Max for the briefest moment, then looks away. He clears his throat. 'Liam, there is none. But,' he adds quickly, 'going by what's happened in the past, the chance of it happening is pretty high. Take Jaeger, for example. He died in the ancient realm a few years ago, but came back to life when we brought him home.' He looks at Peanut, his brow furrowed. 'I, for one, am not ready to take that chance. Although somewhat tempting, I don't think I'd like to be stuck here forever.'

'Ditto,' Shaun adds. 'I think I've seen enough dinosaurs to last me a lifetime.'

'I'm with you, Kenny,' Bec says. 'If I have to go through the pain I just went through to die, count me out. O—U—T, out! Maybe you should ask Jack what he went through before he—' Bec stops short. She whips around to look at Max, and her hand flies to her mouth. 'Oh crap! I … I really didn't mean to say that.'

Max squeezes Bec's hand, a forced smile on her face. 'Hey, I'm not that precious.' She sighs. 'I pray to God Kenny is right. But as far as us dying to prove his theory'—she gives Peanut a stink-eye—'I don't think so.' She clicks her tongue. 'Peanut, you and your warped way of thinking … I don't know where these wacky ideas come from.'

Peanut grabs Max in a headlock and ruffles her hair. 'Didn't you know? There's a whole heap of *wacky* going on in this head of mine, Max.'

They all laugh.

The mood changes.

38
CRITTERS

RYKER

Submerged in the deep darkness of the lake, Ryker darts towards the glow of the portal at a speed he never imagined possible. It's effortless. Within seconds, he's reached the gateway to what he can only guess is a world filled with roaming giants from an era long gone—a prehistoric world. He briefly looks upwards to where he's come from. No, there's no turning back. He's determined. He won't allow himself to reflect on the decision he had to make to get to where he is now, or the repercussions of what that decision will do to Aelianna. His friends need him, and the only way he can save them now is by dying first.

Now poised before the floating veil, Ryker prays that the magical powers of the portal that brought Jaeger back to life will aid him too in his time of need. At his side, Albert beckons him to follow. They push forward.

The instant he passes through to the other side, he knows he's come back to life. The chill of the water seeps straight into his bones. He's careful not to gasp.

He adjusts the goggles and looks about. Albert is nowhere to be seen. But what he *does* see is a large, dark mass coming at him. Fast. His heart skips a beat. He needs to get out of there. He looks towards the brightness of what he imagines is the sky above and plans his escape. With his legs firmly pressed together, using swift, powerful, dolphin-like movements, Ryker propels himself upward.

He takes a quick glance behind. The mass is gaining speed. Ryker's chest tightens. This thing is massive—the size of a humpback whale. And knowing that he's just entered a realm full of primordial beasts doesn't placate him in the least. He hasn't come this far to be snacked on by a ravenous ancient reptile. He propels harder and finally breaks the surface. He removes the goggles, swipes the water from his eyes, and does a quick scour of his surrounds. He sees land. There's no time to waste. He drags a few life-saving gulps of air before darting towards the banks of the large lake from which he's emerged.

Suddenly, the sensation of an immense swell beneath the surface alerts him of an impending change. The hairs on the back of his neck bristle. He's not going to make it. The swell is going to swallow him whole. He turns, draws a deep breath and braces himself. In the split second he gets before being dragged under, he sees something shocking enough to knock the wind out of him. Mere metres away, a beast of majestic proportions emerges above the water's surface and thrusts itself into the air. And riding high on the snout of the gigantic whale-like creature is his new friend Albert.

Drawn under by the force, Ryker tosses and turns in the surge of the whitewash. He battles to find stability and prays he doesn't die trying. Finally, the pressure of the swell subsides. He rights himself and rises to the surface. Gasping for air, he spots the mischief-maker on the bank of the lake, doubled over laughing.

'Cooee! What a hoot!' Albert hollers. 'Better than the rollercoaster ride at Wonderland City any day of the week!'

Ryker grits his teeth and swims towards him, vowing to wring the kid's neck as soon as he reaches him. But by the time he gets there, he's wasted. Both physically and emotionally. He drags himself to lie quietly by Albert's side and takes a moment to catch his breath. He drapes his forearm across his eyes to shield them from the bright sun, processes what just happened and chuckles. 'So … I see you've made a friend.'

Albert slaps his thigh and laughs. 'Ho, Ho! Scared ya, didn't I?' He laughs some more. 'Isn't she a beauty? L'il ol' Nellie! She and I are mates. We go way back.'

'*Little?* I'd hate to see what you'd call *big*!'

Albert chokes on a splutter. 'Oh man, you ain't seen nothin' yet! Wait 'til ya see the big 'uns!'

A rush of adrenaline forces Ryker to sit up like a shot. He looks around, taking in their surroundings for the first time. Everything around them looks like it's been magnified ten thousandfold. The trees are gargantuan, the ferns massive. Suddenly, he feels the size of an insect in an oversized world. And lurking in its depths, he can only guess, is a multitude of dangers. His guard hikes up to the max. This situation is nothing like he's ever experienced before. Vigilance has suddenly taken on a new meaning. Staying alert is one thing, but keeping his wits about him while in this precarious, unknown world is key. There's no room for panic.

He draws in a calming breath. 'So better than a rollercoaster ride, huh?' he asks in a quiet and calm manner, while scrutinising the area for potential threats.

Albert chuckles. 'Yeah, waaay better!'

Ryker's senses heighten, every sound, every movement, amplified. Every muscle in his body twitches. He's ready to react. 'And where did you say this ride is?'

Oblivious to Ryker's focus elsewhere, Albert carries on. 'Oh, Wonderland City? It's in Sydney. Do you know it? On Tamarama Beach. Dad took me there when I was a little 'un. Boy, was that the best day ever!' His face lights up, recalling the memory. But very quickly, the sparkle in his eyes fades. He shrugs. 'But I guess it's gone now. Good stuff always gets trashed in the end. Don't it? Just like the orphanage.'

Ryker turns his attention to the boy and studies him for a moment, now with a clearer understanding of who he is. Not only did Albert lose his parents at a young age and end up in an orphanage, but also, over the decades, he's witnessed the destruction of the home he once knew. From what Ryker can remember from the information Kenny had sent him about the orphanage, the building barely stands now. A crumbling, dilapidated relic of the past. Ryker reaches over and ruffles Albert's hair. There's no wonder the boy's been causing so much monkey business.

Ryker gets to his feet and gestures to Albert to lead the way. 'Come on, let's keep moving. Show me where this cave is.'

Apart from the sound of them moving through the lush vegetation, the rainforest is eerily quiet. He'd expect to hear birds chirping in the treetops and small animals scurrying in the underbrush, but he doesn't. He looks skyward and wonders whether birds even existed at this stage in evolution. He shrugs and continues. *Even if they did, these trees are so huge you'd never hear them anyway!*

As they move from the lake, the forest darkens. Rays of light filter through in slivers. The temperature drops. Ryker follows as Albert navigates an unseen path under ferns the size of houses and hard, stiff-leaved palm-tree-looking plants that seem familiar, but their name escapes him at the moment. Cycads come to mind. But the size of these cycads is nowhere near anything like the ones he'd read about in the paleoecology course he studied. They're massive.

Ryker tries to familiarise himself with the direction Albert is taking them. He snaps and tears the fern branches in his path and scuffs the earth with his boot. From one of his cargo pants' pockets, he pulls a compass, then looks up at the sun to gauge the time. The arrow settles to navigate itself, locating magnetic north, but then he wonders, *Does the sun rise in the east and set in the west in this world too?* He shakes his head, feeling suddenly stupid. *Of course, it does! It's the same world, only millions of years younger.*

His vague recollection of the prehistoric periods, a time when *T. rex* first roamed the earth, tells him it was approximately ninety million years ago. His eyes widen.

NINETY MILLION years ago!

He blinks a few times as the immensity of that fact sinks in. But enough of that; he needs to remain vigilant. Ryker focuses on keeping up with Albert. His jaw clenches. *I hope he knows where he's going.*

Thankfully, Albert's pace indicates that he does. Ryker reminds himself to have faith and believe in the boy. It's taking everything he has to take a back seat in all of this. Following someone else's lead is foreign to him. He struggles to hold back from taking over, putting it down to his concern for his friends. He has no idea what state he'll find them in. What if they're hurt? He thinks of Max. *Of course, she'll be all over that already.* He looks down at his bloodstained shirt, now faded from the water. *I'll get her to have a look at this mess too.* The arrow to his chest smarts like nothing else, but he won't let something like that slow him down.

But what if Max is hurt? He shudders to think what'll happen then and shakes the disparaging thought from his head. He needs to believe that they're all safe under the protection of Ruby's uncompromising shield.

The same shield he suddenly wishes he had a claim to. For there's movement up ahead. Ryker grabs Albert by the arm and tugs him closer. They halt to listen. Albert stares at Ryker, ashen faced. He looks ready to run. Ryker's seen that look of terror before and knows the knee-jerk reactions that typically follow will only end badly. Therefore, he tugs Albert to him and muzzles his mouth. Albert struggles against the restraints. Ryker tries to convey to him that all will be safe if he remains still.

After a period of indecision, Albert submits.

They squat low and listen. Ryker barely allows himself to breathe. In the near distance, he senses a presence. How close it is? He can't gauge. Its size? He can only guess at it. Is it alone? It sounds like it is. If only he could see something, but the dense foliage around them doesn't allow it.

His ears prick at the distinct sound of something breathing … something sniffing out a scent. Ryker looks down at his bloodied T-shirt. Could it be him? Ever so slowly, he reaches down to his boot and unsheathes his hunting knife, his hand tight on the handle grip.

And then the vegetation before them parts. A scaly, leathery snout pokes a path to them, and suddenly they're face to face with a beady-eyed, half-metre-tall reptile. Or is it a bird? Feathers covering its upper body suggest it might be. Albert lets out a muffled cry and fights to get away. Ryker looks at it with less trepidation. It's the size of a dog. This he can handle. He stops to listen if it's alone, having no idea if these creatures travel in packs. The critter inches closer, its head angling to take them in, one eye at a time. Ryker looks down at its feet and spots two extremely large sickle-shaped claws on each of the second toes. He frowns. Those talons could do some real damage. He'll need to keep a close eye on them.

Before letting him go, Ryker gestures to Albert to get behind him. His finger pressed tightly to his lip stresses the importance of moving without provoking the critter. Albert looks at him with wide eyes. He nods. Ryker releases his hold, and Albert scrambles to safety. The beady-eyed dinosaur steps closer, bares its teeth and hisses. Ryker tightens his grip on the blade. *Vigilant at all times. Expect the unexpected!*

Ever so slowly, Ryker gets up from his crouched position, ignoring the pins and needles prickling his calves and thighs. He waits, his arms raised in defence.

'Watch his feet,' Albert warns in a barely heard whisper. 'They're deadly.'

Adrenaline courses through Ryker's veins. His heart throbs. He makes no movement, not even to blink, his eyes locked with the enemy.

Without warning, the overgrown lizard-bird lashes out with its upper feathered claw. Ryker's reflexive response to strike at the attack saves him from being carved like a roast dinner. The dinosaur screeches in pain as the blade amputates its right upper limb in one fell swoop. Ryker repositions the blade and prepares to go again. But the dinosaur retaliates. Using the strength of its long tail to maintain balance, the beastie lashes out with the sickle-shaped claw on its foot, slicing a sizeable gash on Ryker's forearm. The blade flies out of reach. The animal attacks again before Ryker has a chance to regroup, this time gouging a fleshy chunk from his leg. Ryker bites down on his lip. He holds back from crying out and uses the surge of adrenaline coursing through his veins to lunge at it. He grabs it in a headlock, struggles with it, then with an almighty effort, pries open its jaw until it snaps. The animal squeals before falling limp to the ground.

Ryker turns to look for Albert. He spots the boy off to the side, the retrieved knife in his shaking hand. His eyes unblinking.

'Holy heck! Look at you!'

Ryker briefly assesses the damage. A profuse amount of blood oozes from the gaping wound on his arm, and the ripped leg of his cargo pants darkens with the fluid saturating it. He holds up his hands to inspect them and knows the blood there isn't the dinosaur's alone. Those razor-sharp teeth left rivet holes in his fingers. Ryker peers a little closer and plucks out what appears to be a tooth. He then takes a moment to apply pressure to the wound on his leg with his hand. He gestures to Albert for them to make a move. 'There'll be more of them any minute.'

Albert takes the lead. Ryker follows, his hand now firm on the gash on his arm.

'You're right, we need to get'cha outta here,' Albert tells him on the run. 'Those ones don't usually travel in packs, but there'll be others. Mark my words. They'll pick up on your scent in no time,' he says breathlessly. 'You know what? It's a wonder you're still alive. I've seen those critters rip their victims to shreds with those claws. They might look cute and harmless, but, boy, are they deadly!'

Ryker knows he just dodged a bullet. He only hopes that'll be the worst they'll encounter. But he'd be delusional if he believed that. This is only the beginning. If a dinosaur the size of a dog can do that to him, imagine what would happen if they came across a *real* one. He picks up the pace.

The sooner they find their friends, the better.

39

Holy Ghost

Jack reports back his findings of the cave-in—the news, bleak. The wall of rubble is way too thick to get through. And to top it off, the cave is now a hive of activity, courtesy of the feasting dinosaurs. His friends look defeated. Peanut cusses and walks away. Kenny runs his hand through his hair repeatedly and says nothing. Max looks ready to cry. He needs to fix this. He tries to channel his superpower of positivity to salvage the situation, but the familiar heat in his core doesn't stir. He tries harder—concentration cranked to the max. But nothing. No heat, no burning sensation in his belly, no radiating warmth to his limbs … not a skerrick of difference. His eyes fly open. *What's going on?*

He gestures for Kenny to step away from the others. 'Kenny, I can't tap into my superpower.'

Kenny shrugs. 'Mate, it's a no-brainer. It's because you're dead.'

Jack winces. *Of course it is!* He groans and gives himself a mental kick, then looks at Kenny, a smile tugging at the corner of his mouth. 'Geeze, kick a dog when it's down, why don't ya.'

Kenny chuckles. 'Sorry, buddy, but it *is* what it is. When you died, your superpower died with you. But look on the bright side, you're intangible now.'

Jack frowns. 'Intangible?'

Kenny grins. 'Mate, you can pass through solid objects!'

Jack frowns. He gestures to the group. 'Yeah, but a fat lot of good that's gonna do us. Just look at them! It's as if they've given up! They need someone to boost their morale, not go back and forth through a wall of rubble. Who's gonna do that now?'

Kenny looks at him sideways and clicks his tongue. '*You* are! Mate, you don't need a superpower to turn this around. You're Jack! And the Jack we know isn't a quitter. And in my eyes, never will be. It's not in your DNA. Buddy, just talk to them.'

Jack studies Kenny for a moment, a crease etched in his brow. Kenny's unwavering belief in him gives him the strength he needs to make it happen.

He pauses to think and work out what to say. The success of it will depend on three things: one, his delivery—he needs to tell them he has a plan and convince them it's solid; two, his reassurance—they need to know that, although unnecessary, he has a backup plan; and three, his confidence—there's no room for doubt. They *will* find a way to get out of this place, and it's up to him to make them believe it.

And so after revealing his hatched plan, Jack soon has his friends buzzing with hope.

'Okay, the strategy is for me to slip past the monster in the lake—easy enough since I'm a ghost— and return to the orphanage through the portal,' he explains. 'Once there, I'll call on the help we need.'

He dusts his hands. 'Done!'

Ruby studies him closely. 'And what's this plan B of yours?'

Jack gulps. There *is* no plan B. He banked on not needing one. Pinning his stock on his one and only plan seemed viable enough. But the vibe he's getting from Ruby says it isn't. And it seems she's not alone. Peanut, at her side, stands with an identical expression on his face.

Jack grins. 'Guys, trust me. It's in the bag. We won't even need to go to plan B, so there's really no point mentioning it.'

'Hah!' Peanut cries out. 'It's because you haven't got one. Have you?'

Jack feigns wounded.

'Peanut, if Jack says there's a plan B, then there *is*,' Max says pointedly.

Jack's lip curls. *That's my girl!*

'Anyway, I agree,' Max continues. 'We won't need a backup plan. Jack's idea sounds solid. We just need to stay here.'

Peanut groans. 'And in the meantime, we die from starvation waiting for Gerard Thompson and the taskforce to get their act together!'

Liam elbows him. 'Come on, Peanut. Cut Jack some slack. How hard could it be? The place is probably swarming with cops, anyway. He'll be back with help in no time.'

Peanut snorts. 'Buddy, don't hold your breath. Based on their track record, by the time they cut through all that ludicrous red tape they stick to, we'll be goners. Wasted away to noth'n!'

Peanut plonks himself on the floor in a huff. His stomach growls. 'Great! And now all this talk of food has made me hungry.' He licks his lips and swipes the wetness from his mouth with the back of his hand. 'Boy, I could go a Big Mac right now!'

Bec rummages through her calico bag, finds something and throws it to him. 'Here, eat this. If you're anything like me, you can't think straight when you're hangry.' She turns to Jack and frowns. 'When can you leave? The sooner, the better. I don't know how long I can put up with his whining.' Her eyes roll. 'I know what a pain in the neck I can be when it comes to food.' She gestures to her bag. 'And I've only got a handful of this stuff left.'

Peanut gingerly holds up the dried-up, crab-like morsel by one of its legs, takes a sniff of it and gags. His hand shoots up to cover his mouth and pinch his nose. 'Oh, man, that's totally gross! What are ya trying to do to me? Kill me?'

Bec chuckles. 'Believe it or not, they're actually quite tasty. A little chewy, but they do the job. They're from Albert's stash. He trades them with the guards at the *fortress* … wherever that is.' She shrugs. 'Apparently, they're a delicacy.'

Peanut pulls a face. 'Reminds me of the time the Ancients served us that *blood soup*. They called *that* a delicacy too. *Bleh!* I'm gagging just thinking about it!'

Kenny reaches into one of his cargo pants' pockets, pulls out a crumpled protein bar and tosses it to him. 'Go easy! I've only got a couple left.'

Peanut's eyes light up. 'Ho, ho! *Legend!*' He rips open the wrapper and holds the flattened bar up at eye level, divides it equally into two, lobs one half into his mouth and offers Ruby the other. Two minutes later, he's back on track. One hundred percent Team Jack.

Jack grins as he prepares to go. Being caught out on a lie doesn't surprise him. Peanut knows him too well. Well, it wasn't exactly a lie. Of course, there's a plan B. It's just that he hasn't come up with it yet.

40
PLAN B

JACK

Once again, Jack braces himself to pass through the solid barrier of rock. He prays he can do this—return in time to save his friends. Peanut's earlier dig at Deputy Director General Gerard Thompson and the taskforce assigned to the ancient portal wasn't that far off the mark. Previously, despite the urgency, time was wasted. They spent days jumping through bureaucratic hoops before anything happened. Jack hopes this time will be different.

He looks at Max, who's biting her fingernails, her expression worried. She sees him studying her. Her lip curls, but her smile doesn't reach her eyes. He tries to reassure her with a wink, but it makes no difference. He's not surprised. She's worried. And truth be told, so is he. She's more than likely sensing it. Yes, he can go through solid walls, and yes, he can dodge the giant, man-eating monster in the lake, but how the heck is he meant to locate the portal? In all the confusion, the goggles have gone awol, so unless by some miracle he's able to develop the ability to detect heat without the use of thermal-imaging goggles, he's in deep water … literally. It'll take him forever to find it.

Suddenly, the plan doesn't seem *so* solid.

And then a thought comes to him: *Albert! Albert can help! He knows this place inside out!* But where to find him? *The kid took off like a startled rabbit. He could be anywhere!* Locating Albert becomes Jack's main objective, and he needs to get going. He stops briefly to see what more he can do before leaving. He looks at Bec's calico bag and considers their meagre rations. *And there's no water!*

Kenny watches him and frowns. 'There's nothing else you can do here. Stop wasting time.' He lets out a troubled breath. 'Jack, provisions are the least of our problems. The air in here is thick with gases. Carbon monoxide, hydrogen sulphide, methane, carbon dioxide …' He stops abruptly and presses his lips shuts, ending the pointless rambling. He sighs. 'Look, Jack, bottom line, with or without a fire, we're running out of oxygen, and there's a cocktail of gases in here that isn't good for us. We're gonna run out of air before anything else. The only thing you can do is get help. And fast. This torch can't hold out much longer. We'll be in complete darkness soon.'

The look of alarm in Kenny's eyes speaks volumes. Jack doesn't waste another second. He braces himself and flies through the wall.

Once past the barrier, he pauses a moment, only to inspect the situation with the *T. rex*. The half-eaten carcass still maintains a solid interest. Although the three smaller dinosaurs spotted earlier are nowhere to be seen, a pack of larger dinosaurs are now indulging in their place, as predicted. *Deinonychus.* There must be at least half a dozen of them grappling to get their share. He imagines they'll continue to feast until they've had their fill, which could be awhile—going by the size of the *T. rex*. Or until a larger flesh-eating dinosaur comes to stake its claim.

But that's something he'll deal with later. First, he needs to find Albert, then locate the portal and, finally, get help. What the taskforce does once they get here is their problem. His mission is only to get them here.

Jack flies out and hovers above the majestic forest, surveying the surrounds. He takes a moment to orientate himself, seeing the sun high, the sky cloudless. All appears tranquil. So tranquil and so surreal, his breath catches. He hardly believes where he is.

From his elevation, he spots the lake—the passage back home. Movement among the vegetation in the far distance draws his attention. The trees part and ferns quiver as something paves a path through. He can only imagine the size of the beast capable of making such a stir. And then a head emerges from the canopy of trees—smooth-skinned and attached to an enormous anaconda-like neck. Wads of large leafy foliage dangle from its relatively small mouth. And what Jack initially suspected was a small bare hill behind it turns out to be the dinosaur's enormous back.

Of all the toy dinosaurs he owned as a kid, Jack's favourite was *Brachiosaurus. Or was it Diplodocus?* He smiles. Either one. These and *Stegosaurus.* Being less ferocious than the more popular meat-eaters like *Tyrannosaurus rex, Megalosaurus* and *Allosaurus.*

He watches on as the majestic beast ambles along, taking its time with its meal. If he wasn't witnessing it with his own eyes, he'd never believe it.

He's tempted to fly closer to have a better look but remembers the urgency of his task. He takes one last look back towards the cave entrance, spots movement, and flies closer to investigate. He stops suddenly when he catches sight of Ryker. 'What the hell! Where did you come from?'

Ryker's blade whips out in front of him like a shot, his stance suddenly ready for battle. When he sees Jack—as a ghost—he stumbles backward and falls flat on his rear.

'What the hell yourself, Jack! You're *dead*?'

'WHAT?' From out of hiding, young Albert, the elusive troublemaker, jumps forward. His hands fly to his mouth. 'Oh no! What have I done?' He falls to a squat, hugging his knees. Tears stream down his face, leaving tracks on his grimy skin. 'This is *all* my fault!'

Ryker crouches by his side, tugs him into an awkward embrace and shushes him.

Momentarily taken aback by Ryker's gesture, Jack remains silent.

'Yeah, for now he's dead,' Ryker tells the boy, trying to comfort him. 'But he'll come back to life when we get back home. That's how it works. Remember?'

Albert stops, sniffs, then nods. He peeks a look at Jack. 'I'm really sorry you died.'

Jack should be livid about what's happened, but he can't bring himself to be that person. He shrugs. 'Hey, no biggie. In a way, it's kinda neat.' He smiles. 'I just spotted a *brachiosaurus*!' His eyes widen. 'Never in a million years would I have ever thought I'd hear myself say that! A real pinch-me moment. It was so cool!'

Albert smiles.

Jack's focus turns to what needs to be done. 'But as cool as that is, being dead has its limits.' He looks at Ryker. 'Mate, we need your help. There was an avalanche, and the guys are trapped behind a wall of rubble. Physically, I can't do a thing to get them out. I was on my way to get help. And I think I've just found it. Come on!'

After briefing them on the situation. Jack guides Ryker and Albert through the cave opening, cautioning them to remain silent, and leads them to a safe place furthest from the feasting dinosaurs.

'We need to get these overgrown lizards out of here,' he tells them. 'That way we can start on the wall.' He stops when he notices, for the first time, Ryker's mauled and bloodied fingers and the gashes on his arm. He looks down—the stain on his cargos hints at carnage too.

'Mate, I didn't realise …'

Ryker shrugs. 'It's nothing. I'll live. Anyway, once we tear down that wall, Max will fix me. Let's just focus on what we're up against here.' He leans forward and peers around the boulder. 'And you said there are six or seven of them?'

Jack nods.

Ryker frowns but says nothing. He then looks

at Albert with a sudden gleam in his eye and grins. 'Buddy, we just need a diversion.'

Albert's hands fly out in front of him. 'Hey, whoa! Don't look at me. I'm no one's lackey!' He points his finger at Jack. 'Pick him! He's already dead!'

Ryker chuckles. 'I wasn't thinking of *you* being the diversion, Albert!' He chuckles some more. 'Look, I have an idea. And I think it's a good one.'

Ryker pats down the bulges of his cargo pants' pockets, then reaches into one of them and retrieves two short lengths of electrical wire and a chocolate-bar-sized slab of something that looks very much like putty or modelling clay, dirty-white in colour. 'I can make explosives from these,' he tells them. 'All I need are the detonators. There are two … somewhere …' Again, he searches his pockets. He stops and looks up with a grin. 'Got 'em!'

Jack has a fair idea where Ryker's going with this, and it alarms him—his friends are on the other side of this explosion. But he remains open to whatever plan Ryker has—he needs to trust him.

He watches on with keen interest as Ryker splits the plastic explosive into two—one slightly larger than the other. He then rolls them into separate balls, pockets the larger of the two, then secures a wire into the one in his hand. With the other end of the same wire, he attaches it to the detonator. 'We won't need a huge bang,' he tells them. 'Just enough to get them running.'

He pats down his pocket. 'This one …' he says with a curl on his lip, '… this one's for later.'

If Jack could sweat, he'd be sweating buckets right now. 'Man, I hope you know what you're doing.'

Ryker looks at him knowingly and waggles his eyebrows. 'Piece of cake!'

Jack laughs. He knows that if Peanut were here, he'd be rubbing his hands with glee.

Ryker looks about them, then gestures towards a large boulder a few metres from the cave entrance. 'Perfect.' He grasps Albert by the arm and takes him behind another boulder—one deeper into the cave. 'You stay here and don't move. Got it?' He presses him down with his hand, forcing him to squat. 'And keep your arms over your head. Like this.' Ryker shows him. 'There'll be shrapnel.' He hands him his goggles. 'Here, wear these—they'll stop the dust going into your eyes.' He then turns, gives Jack the once over, and shrugs. 'I guess you'll be fine as you are.'

Instinctively, Jack squats next to Albert and shields his head. He almost laughs at himself when he realises what he's doing.

Ryker initiates the timer on the detonator— programming the explosion to go off in thirty seconds. He then slips from their refuge and secures the putty at the base of the chosen boulder. After adjusting the detonator to rest against the rock, he starts the timer.

Silently, Jack begins the countdown. His breath held.

Ryker retreats from the imminent blast with the calm and confidence of an explosives expert. For Jack, perhaps too calm. He holds back from calling out for him to hurry. Within moments, Ryker has reached them. He tugs Albert to his side and covers him protectively.

Meanwhile, Jack continues with the countdown. Five, four, three, two, one …

KABOOM!

On impulse, Jack ducks.

Ryker squats lower, his broad frame sheltering Albert. Bits of rock and debris shower their safe place, but they cause no harm.

They hear a scrambled commotion as the dinosaurs vacate in a panicked rush.

'Right. Let's go!' Ryker shoots up like a well-sprung coil. He dusts off the fragments of rock and moves forward with readiness. Jack whooshes ahead of him. Albert trails at the rear, the goggles dangling from his neck.

Ryker comes to a halt before the wall. 'How deep does this go?'

'About three metres,' Jack tells him.

Ryker walks the length of the wall, randomly testing it at various intervals. He stops, then pulls from his pocket the other ball of the plastic explosive. He releases a sigh and clicks his tongue.

'What's wrong?' Albert asks, alarmed. 'Don't ya have enough?'

Ryker looks away and scans the space around them. Again, he studies the ball before looking at Jack. 'Three metres, you say?' Again, he sighs.

Jack chews his lower lip. What if Albert's got it right? What if Ryker hasn't kept enough of the explosive to tear down the wall? His heart sinks. *We're screwed!*

Jack turns away and curses under his breath. He should've followed his gut instinct and been more proactive in the decision-making. He rubs the back of his neck. But it's done. They need to get on with it. Somehow.

He looks at Ryker and draws a deep breath. Ryker is military trained—he's been pivotal in the past, and he can help again. Jack takes a moment to remind himself of this. He can trust him. His shoulders straighten. 'So, buddy, what's the problem? Is there anything we can do?'

Ryker scratches his head. 'I'm worried about the resistance we'll get from it being so thick. The impact of the blast may not be enough to do the job.

I should've kept more of the plastic explosive.'

The plan is no longer solid. Jack bites back a cuss. His mind races with what needs to be done.

Ryker frowns at his reaction and shrugs. 'Hey, no worries. It just means we'll need to dig the rest of the way.'

Jack looks at Ryker's bloodied hands, his fingers dimpled with puncture wounds. It looks like he's had a fight with a crocodile. *How the hell are we sposed to do this? It's practically a small mountain of rock we've got to move … correction, Ryker's got to move. But with hands like that …*

'I'll help!' Albert pipes up. 'I'm a whole heap stronger than I look.' But then his smile wanes and his chin drops. 'After all, it's 'cause of me you're in this mess.'

Ryker chuckles and ruffles his hair. 'It's okay, buddy. We'll get them out. You'll see.' He gives Jack a wink.

41
Totally Smok'n!

JACK

Fading light from the torch at the foot of the wall of the cave-in gives off enough of a glow to stop them from being in total darkness. Jack's stress levels heighten. He prays the batteries hold out a little longer … long enough to buy the time needed for what they have to do. Kenny takes a few measured steps back and forth in the confined space of the passage, mumbling to himself. He stops every now and then to scratch his head—his thoughts private. Jack can tell he's working on a plan, and although anxious to hear it, he waits.

Again, Kenny stops. He rubs his chin and gives Jack a sideward glance. 'Three metres thick, you say?'

Yet again, the question of its thickness. Jack sighs and nods.

Kenny continues to survey the space, then looks back at him. 'And Ryker has plastic explosives?'

Peanut jumps up, fist-pumps the air and hoots. 'Woohoo! My man!'

Jack wishes he had his confidence. He tries to, but can't sustain a grin. He answers Kenny with a nod.

Kenny paces back and forth a few more times, then stops once more. 'Okay, so if my calculations are right, we can make this happen. It *is* doable.'

Jack lets out his breath. Finally, there's hope.

Kenny turns his attention to Ruby and smiles, but says nothing.

Ruby frowns.

Kenny nods and gestures for Ruby to do something.

Ruby's frown deepens.

Kenny's smile vanishes. His head tilts to one side; his brow puckers. And then the penny drops. 'Oh! Did I forget to mention that we need *you* for this to work?' He clicks his tongue and chuckles. 'Hey, my bad. Yeah, Ruby, you're the *key* to this happening. We can't do it without you.'

Ruby blinks a few times.

And so too does Jack. Did he also miss that memo?

Ruby jumps to her feet, plants her balled-up fists

on her hips and stares Kenny down. 'WHAT?'

Kenny has the decency to look abashed.

'Kenny, you can't just drop something like that on someone and think it's okay! *Okay?*' She whips around, her gaze piercing. She looks from Max to Jack, then Bec and Liam, and finally from Shaun to Peanut. She struggles to put two words together. Her hands fly about, animated. In the end, she throws them in the air in utter frustration. '*ARGH!*'

They all take a step back.

And then her shoulders slump, her head drops, and her eyes close. 'That's a lot of pressure for one person.' She turns to Peanut, her eyes pleading. 'You've seen what I'm like when it's too much. I *choke*!'

Peanut steps to Ruby's side and drapes his arm across her shoulders. And then, to Jack's mortification, instead of consoling her, Peanut has the audacity to agree. 'Yep, you're right. You *do*.' He turns to their new friends. 'She does, you know. She's chucked a few doozies in the past. Choked beyond anything *I've* ever seen.'

To add insult to injury, he grabs hold of his neck and pretends to strangle himself.

Jack groans. The others snort, trying, but failing, to hide a laugh.

Ruby stares at Peanut, wide-eyed and open-mouthed. Instinctively, Jack floats a little further back.

And then, to Jack's horror, Peanut continues. 'It's true! You can't deny it. We've all seen it!' But then he grins, eyes sparkling. 'Yeah, the *old* Ruby would choke in these sticky situations, but the *new* Ruby'—he pauses and waggles his eyebrows—'the new-and-*improved* Ruby—man, is she HOT or what? And I mean *sizzling*!' To add emphasis, he pokes her shoulder and makes a hissing sound. 'Yeow, girl! Totally smok'n!'

He looks at their new friends and points his finger at them. 'I'm doing you a solid, you hear? There's no mess'n with this one! She's *frrreak'in* Wonder Woman!'

Jack shakes his head and chuckles. *Peanut to the rescue!* He should've seen it coming. As amazing as Ruby is, sometimes even *she* needs reminding.

Peanut pulls Ruby into a hug. Fighting him at first, Ruby soon melts and snuggles against him. They share a moment.

Back to the plan. Jack can't wait to hear it. 'So, Kenny, what's *Wonder Woman's* role in all of this?'

Ruby rolls her eyes. Her shoulders straighten. 'Okay, let's hear it.'

Kenny's eyes light up. 'Awesome! You can do this, Ruby. The plan's almost foolproof.'

His grin is infectious. Jack rubs his hands. Kenny's got this.

'It's all got to do with physics,' he begins. 'So with

your shield, Ruby, pressed hard against the wall in here, and the pressure created by the explosion out there, the impact of the blast should force the rocks outwards. And just like that, the job gets done.'

He turns to Jack. 'And as long as Ryker and Albert are well out of the way, no one gets hurt.'

Jack grins. Too easy. He can see the plan is a good one. He hopes Ruby sees it too.

Ruby clicks her tongue. '*Is that all?* Kenny, had you said it was going to be that simple, I wouldn't have overreacted.' She groans. 'Come on, quit wasting time. Let's do this.'

They're back on track. Jack dives through the wall to fill Ryker and Albert in on the plan. He's excited. Unless Kenny's mistaken—which never happens— this should work.

As soon as they've made the necessary preparations, they put the plan in motion.

42

Never The Weakest Link

PEANUT

Peanut closes his eyes and lets out a sigh of relief. He shakes his head and runs his fingers through his shaggy mane. There was a moment there where he thought Ruby was going to lose it—to forget how totally awesome she is, crawl away, deep into herself, and give up. With Jack void of his superhuman ability to calm, Peanut was sure their goose was cooked. But he realised he didn't need Jack. He could do it himself. He'd done it before; he could do it again. And just like that, the problem was solved. Ruby just needed a nudge to remind her.

He tugs her into his side for a hug and places a kiss on her brow. 'You're not the weakest link, Rubes,' he whispers in her ear. 'You never were, and you never will be.'

She turns to face him, her eyes softening, and she reaches up to cradle the side of his face. No words are said; there's no need. He smiles. He gets it.

With instructions now relayed back to them from Ryker, Peanut prepares for what's coming.

Jack darts back through the rubble one last time to check if Ryker is ready. He returns moments later and reports the detonator is in place and the timer is ticking.

That's it. Time's up. There's no turning back.

Her eyes narrowed, her focus steeled, Ruby is ready. She throws her weight behind her shield, pressing it hard up against the wall of rock. Peanut mechanically mimics her, but knows his actions will make little difference. He looks back. The others squat, protected as best they can further in the passage. He prays the impact of the explosion on the other side of the wall does exactly what Kenny's calculated it to do and nothing more. He believes in Kenny, and has faith in Ruby and Ryker, but he still draws in a shaky breath. They're about to find out if this'll work.

And then suddenly the ground shakes. Simultaneously, the shield bucks from the blast, the impact forcing them back a short distance. Peanut gasps. But Ruby's got this. With nothing but determination etched on her brow, Ruby fights against the weight of the explosion.

Peanut watches in awe as the wall of rock collapses before them, giving way to slivers of daylight peeking through the newly formed cavities. Dust particles litter the air.

There's a moment of stunned silence before everyone breaks out into triumphant cheering. Peanut hollers and hoots the loudest.

Ruby steps back, her face aglow. Peanut pulls her into a huge bear hug and swings her around. 'Damn, girl! Freak'n *Wonder Woman*!'

They laugh.

He leans in and whispers. 'Told ya! You're the bomb!'

Her eyes fill with tears. So too does Peanut's.

Coughing from the other side grounds them.

With visibility poor, Peanut squints to see Ryker. And at his side, Albert. Both working fiercely to tear away the rocky barrier. The shield vanishes, and the others join in with equal enthusiasm.

Soon they have an opening large enough to set them free.

Albert sniffles and wipes the tears from his eyes, leaving dirty smear marks on his cheeks. 'Boy, am I glad to see you guys!' He swipes his runny nose across his torn shirtsleeve. 'You've got no idea how bad I feel about this cock-up.'

'And so you should, you little creep!' Peanut yells at him, suddenly angered. All the adrenaline pumping through his veins explodes. 'What the hell were you thinking? I've half a mind to beat the crap outta ya for what you've done!'

Bec shoots Peanut an angered look. 'Put a sock in it, will ya?' Her gaze softens towards Albert. 'What you did was pretty crummy, Albert, but you went out on your own, and on a limb, and got help. To me, that's pretty cool. And look! I'm all better.' She turns to Max and gives her a wink.

Breath heavy, stomach in knots, Peanut stops his rant and looks around. Bec's right. And now's not the time, nor the place, to play the blame game— danger lurks beyond the temporary safe place they're in. They're too exposed.

With their numbers now at nine, the chance of being detected has dangerously multiplied. He turns to Ryker for instruction and notices for the first time the state he's in. His clothes, drenched in blood, mask wounds that are by no means superficial. His hands, caked with blood and grime, allude to the mammoth struggle he's undertaken to get here.

He turns to find Max, but she's a step ahead

of him, pushing forward to be at Ryker's side. She draws back at the sight of him. 'Oh my God! What happened?' Her head whips around to locate Jack. 'You never said anything!'

Jack cringes and makes a hasty exit. 'I'll go check out if we're safe.' He whooshes out of the cave before Max gets a chance to react.

Ryker braces her by the shoulders. 'Settle down, you little spitfire. I'll explain everything later. Right now, all I need is for you to patch me up.'

She crosses her arms and growls.

Ryker chuckles. 'Please.'

She huffs. Her shoulders slump.

So while Max busies herself tending to Ryker, Peanut takes in the state of the cave since they were last there. That's when he spots the remains of the *T. rex* half buried beneath the avalanche of rubble. He goes to investigate, and what he sees leaves him dumbfounded. He lets out a slow whistle. 'Will ya get a load of that?' He moves closer to examine the beast's half-eaten remains, its thick scaly skin ripped open, insides devoured, the flesh stripped to the bone. A total bloodbath.

The others gather to look.

'Whoa! It's massive!' Liam says, his eyes wide.

Bec and Shaun lean in closer to see. Ruby appears happy to keep her distance. Max continues giving her attention to Ryker and his multitude of injuries.

Kenny studies the carnage with obvious interest. He estimates the thigh bone alone to be around a metre and a half long, which, after delving into his mental Google search, he declares is in accord with prehistoric archaeological findings of the present time.

Peanut pokes a little nearer. If only he could see its head—he remembers how huge its teeth were and is hoping to take home a souvenir to show the guys in the hockey team. But unfortunately, its enormous head is buried under the mound of rock. He kicks away some of the stones. Perhaps he can get to it if he digs a little. But Ruby's look of disapproval instantly nips that thought in the bud. He chuckles. Clearly, she saw the direction his thoughts were heading. He shrugs.

She rolls her eyes.

Meanwhile, Jack returns with an update, having scoped the outer area. 'Listen, we need to get out of here while the coast is clear. I'm guessing there's only a few hours of daylight left, so we've gotta hustle.'

Ryker starts to go, but Max yanks him back. 'Not yet! I haven't finished!'

He frowns. 'Steady on. I just wanted to check something out. I was thinking that if we can figure out which direction the dinosaurs went, we'd have a better chance of staying clear of them.'

Liam's hand shoots up. 'I'll have a squiz! I've done a bit of bush tracking with my grandfather. Could be useful.' And before anyone has a chance to argue, he darts off to investigate.

Jack is quick to follow.

Peanut debates whether or not to go after them, but gets distracted by the conversation Ryker and Kenny are having while Max heals Ryker's wounds.

'Ow, that looks painful, Ryker. What happened? What attacked you? Jack said the ones here, earlier, were *Deinonychus*,' Kenny says enthusiastically. 'And we know they travel in packs, which, believe it or not, is a good thing. We'll hear them coming—less of a chance of them sneaking up on us.'

Ryker describes in detail the feather-covered dinosaur he encountered. It stood at about half a metre tall and was approximately two metres long. He then goes on to say that, at first, it appeared harmless. It wasn't until he saw what those sickle-shaped talons on its toes could do that he realised he was in deep trouble.

'From what you're telling me,' Kenny says with a frown, 'my guess is you were attacked by a *Velociraptor*.' His focus wanders elsewhere for a moment, clearly deep in thought. 'And according to my search,' he continues, '*Velociraptors* are more likely to hunt solo.' He pauses to look at them. 'Guys, that's *not* a good thing. They could sneak up on us without us knowing.' He pauses as more information comes to him. 'Oh, and they're fast, running at speeds of forty kilometres an hour. Faster than the fastest human.' He stops and shakes his head. 'Small, yet devious. They're the ones we need to keep an eye out for.' He bites his lip. 'But we shouldn't have a problem if we stick together. One on its own wouldn't attack a group, I guess.'

Just then, Jack returns with Liam. 'Hey, guys, Liam's been able to track the dinosaurs. They've taken off, deep into the forest. Away from where we need to go. I don't think we'll be seeing them again any time soon.'

Peanut scratches his head. 'Are you sure? No offence, Liam, but how d'ya work that out?'

Liam shrugs. 'Dunno. It just came to me. A switch just flicked on in my head, and suddenly everything Galoonoordoo ever taught me about tracking in the wild came back and smacked me in the face. It was like I'd been doing it all my life.' He grins. 'You couldn't stop me! I spotted everything. Every broken leaf, every scuffle mark, every upturned rock ...'

Jack laughs. 'He did, you know. He's a complete freak at tracking.'

Peanut recollects that Liam has indigenous heritage. He smiles, knowing Liam's found his superpower.

Jack continues. 'So while Liam looked for the signs, I flew ahead to make sure he wasn't in any danger. And as far as I can see, we're good to go. But we've gotta go now. We can't risk hanging around any longer.' He turns to Max. 'How's Ryker? Are you done?'

Max nods.

Peanut looks about, draws a deep breath and holds it. It's all too surreal. But as amazing as it is, he's seen enough of this prehistoric world to last a lifetime. He turns to Ruby and holds out his hand. She smiles, steps closer, takes it and gives it a squeeze. She pauses a moment, takes a breath, then looks at him.

She's ready.

Ruby activates her shield to encompass them safely, and they enter the forest. With Jack hovering high above them, ready to warn of danger, the journey home begins.

43

And That's How It's Done!

RUBY

Peanut's words of encouragement and support earlier just about reduced Ruby to tears. His unwavering belief in her makes her heart swell. She looks at him, *really* looks at him, and wonders where that goofy, never-serious, commitment-phobe has gone. His warm, hazel eyes speak to her. They tell her he's there for her, no matter how hard, how far or wide … he has her back and always will.

Ruby shakes off the warm, fuzzy blanket of sentiment. There's work to be done … they're about to enter the prehistoric forest.

She activates the shield to safely encompass her friends, takes Peanut by the hand and forges ahead. Albert leads the way, with Ryker a close second. Trailing behind her and Peanut are Max, Kenny, Shaun, Liam and Bec.

Although Jack had assessed and reassured them of a clear passage to the lake, Ruby's eyes are peeled. Anything can happen, and at any time.

She looks skyward, sees Jack and feels confident he'll lead them well. She breathes easier, knowing he's there. Free to focus on the plan, she wonders what's going to happen once they've reached the water's edge. Their success will rest with her; escaping this treacherous world and returning home in one piece will fall on her shoulders—again.

She stops. Her pulse races. This is way too familiar. *No!*

She shakes it off. She won't allow herself to think about the giant, water-living monster that could potentially foil everything.

That's not gonna happen! Albert will make sure Loch Ness Nellie doesn't make an appearance. That's his job!

And hers is to get them to the portal. She racks her brain, trying to come up with a way of doing that. Ordinarily, a sphere filled with air, once submerged, will only catapult to the top of the water, just as it did when they first entered the prehistoric lake; one second, they were immersed deep in a voluminous reservoir of water, catching their first glimpse of Nellie, the *Mosasaur*, the next, they'd torpedoed skyward to the lake's surface.

So how's this supposed to work?

As they battle the overgrown forest and inch closer to their destination, the question rolls around in Ruby's head on repeat.

Along with the question, the word *torpedo* pokes at her subconscious like a burr in a sock. She pays no attention to it—her focus remains on keeping her friends safe in the shield. But eventually, the persistent prickle becomes too much to ignore, and an idea comes to her. She may have her answer!

What if I create a torpedo with the shield? We could propel our way through the water.

In the past, she's moulded the pliable barrier into many things—a boxing glove, a stretcher, a cherry-picker. So why not a torpedo? She frowns. *But how?* She needs to imagine it in action for it to work, but she has no idea how torpedoes function.

Ah, but Kenny does!

And so, not so delicately, Ruby yanks Kenny aside. 'Kenny, I need you to give me the 101 on something, and fast!'

Surprised by the sudden urgency, Kenny splutters.

'Tell me what you know about torpedoes.'

The others, curious to hear, stop to listen.

Kenny begins, mechanically reciting a spiel of hi-tech, scientific information—nothing Ruby can understand nor utilise in making this happen. Data overload. She clamps her hand over his mouth to stop the verbal vomit and looks at the others apologetically. 'Um, my bad.'

She tries again. 'So, Kenny, tell me what I need to know in order to get from A to B using a torpedo. And *please* keep it simple.' She forces a smile.

'Yeah, Kenny,' Peanut says, frowning. 'It might help if you repeat all that stuff in English. Ruby might be onto something here.'

'Fair call, Peanut,' Kenny chuckles. He then pauses and appears to refresh his Google search and explore the information coming to him. He informs them that in order to achieve a forward projection, *thrust* is key. And to direct that thrust, propellers are needed. 'We need coaxial, contra-rotating propellers,' he tells Ruby, using his hands to demonstrate, 'to counteract the torque of the torpedo.'

'*Again,* without the techy talk?' Ruby frowns.

Kenny's hands shoot up defensively. He has the decency to look sheepish. 'Oops, sorry.'

Kenny looks at Peanut sideways. 'So, in *plain English*, it just means that to steer the torpedo, the propellers need to share a common shaft, and for them to spin in opposite directions.'

Ruby thinks on it for a moment. Again, she frowns. 'Okay, so we've got the propellers, and they're spinning the way you said they should for us to guide it, but you said we need *thrust*. What's giving us *thrust*?'

Kenny blinks a few times. 'You are! You're the engine.'

Ruby's eyes widen. 'Say what?'

'Well, not you alone,' he adds, 'we'll all be helping. Together, we'll be creating the driving force behind the shield to propel it forward. The displacement of the water caused by the spinning propellers is the *reaction force*, called *thrust*.' He grins. 'Simple!'

Ruby grimaces. *Yeah, right! Simple.* 'Come on,' she says. 'All this talk is giving me a headache. Let's at least get to the lake in one piece, and then we can check out this theory of yours, Master Google.'

Kenny chuckles.

Now back on track, the nine friends move on. Rays of light filtering through the huge-leafed vegetation indicate the day is still young. The sun is bright; the sky is clear. Navigating their way is no issue. Every now and then, Ruby gazes skyward, peeping through the gaps in the canopy of leaves to monitor their situation. Each time, Jack signals all is well. They move on.

'We're nearly there,' Albert tells them in a lowered voice. He turns to Ruby. 'Just be ready. Make sure the shield is strong. We'll be in the open, and there's no guessing what's waiting for us.'

Ruby looks up to find Jack, but there's too much foliage to see him. Her pulse quickens. She doesn't hesitate. She reinforces the protective barrier.

At her side, Peanut nudges her and smiles. 'You'll ace it. Don't worry.'

They inch closer, careful not to make a sound. And then, through gaps in the leaves, they see it; the lake, mere metres away, beckons them. Finally, they can be rid of this place.

Using the edge of the shield, Ruby pries open a break in the leafy screen and nudges them forward. Ryker pulls Albert back behind him. Without warning, Jack whooshes down and appears before them. They all jump.

'What the hell, Jack?' Peanut cries out, clutching his chest and gasping for air.

And he's not the only one trying to recover. Ruby takes a moment to remember to breathe.

'Sorry about that,' Jack says with a smirk.

As a group, they exit into the opening.

'Guys, we need to get cracking while the coast is clear,' Jack tells them. 'Albert, you know the way to the portal, so we'll follow you. And remember, if we come across Nellie, it's up to you to divert her. Right?'

Albert nods.

Ryker clears his throat. 'Um, hold up a sec.' He stops. 'I'm sorry to have to throw a spanner in the works, but my journey with you ends here.' He turns to Ruby. 'Ruby, let me out.'

His out-of-the-blue announcement startles Max. She grabs his arm. 'What!'

He squeezes her hand. 'Look, I need to get back to Aelianna and fix up the mess I left there. I'm sorry I don't have time to explain, but you're in good hands with Albert, and what I need to do takes priority.'

Again, he looks at Ruby. 'And you can let Albert out too. He's got no issues swimming the lake unaided.'

Ryker turns to Albert, takes from him the thermal-detecting goggles dangling from his neck and hands them to Ruby. 'And better you keep these—just in case you lose Albert.'

He turns to Albert. 'You need to come back for me after you've shown them the way. Okay? Without the goggles, I'm stranded. Got it? I'll be here waiting for you.'

'We'll send him straight back,' Jack promises. 'Be careful. Stay hidden and don't do anything stupid.' He grins. 'Because I don't wanna have to come back for you. All right?'

Ryker chuckles. 'You've got no worries there, Jack. I'm done with this place.' He looks at Albert questioningly and shakes his head. 'It's beyond me why you keep coming back. You must be nuts!'

Albert shrugs. 'Beats being dead!'

Ryker ruffles Albert's hair and chuckles. 'You know what? I know what you mean.' He gives him a wink and they share a knowing look.

Max looks at him sideways.

He coughs. 'So, um, Ruby, are you ready?'

Ruby blinks; her heart rate hikes. She takes a moment to run through everything she and Kenny talked about earlier, then takes a deep breath.

It's show time!

Her eyes close as she envisages their escape. The cigar-shaped missile, her friends enclosed within it, a single axle, two propellers rotating in opposite directions, the acceleration, the *thrust* ... and finally the portal. Her eyes pop open—the shield has now taken on the shape of a large torpedo. Her lip curls. She's ready.

In single file, Ruby, Peanut, Max, Kenny, Bec, Liam and Shaun approach the lake's edge and enter. Albert stands aside and prepares to guide them. Once they're half-submerged, Ruby concentrates on creating the contra-rotating propellers. To her thrill, they form, but more importantly, they start to spin—

just as Kenny advised they should. She pauses. Now for the acceleration and *thrust*. She grins and turns to Ryker. 'You couldn't do us a favour, and give us a leg up, could you?'

Ryker returns the grin and gives her a wink. 'Ruby, it'd be an honour!'

He prepares for what needs to be done. He rolls his shoulders, squats and lunges a few times, swings and stretches his arms, then cracks his knuckles. He's ready.

'Guys, I'll be here for you,' Jack says. 'And I'll do everything I can.' He shrugs. 'Which won't be much, I guess—being a ghost an' all.'

'Jack, just being there will help,' Max tells him with a wink.

It's time. Ruby braces herself. 'Okay, on my word, we push. And I mean *push* like you've never pushed before! I want legs, arms and backs. I want teeth clenched. I want to hear growling. We need to keep the momentum going once Ryker's given us the kickstart. We need to maintain the *thrust*!' She fixes the goggles on the top of her head and gives Ryker a nod that she's ready.

Ryker positions himself behind, ready for the run-up. And then, without a moment to spare, he comes at them with speed. Ruby prepares for the impact. Suddenly, they're under water, darting forward, accelerating deeper.

Ruby urges everyone to push. And they do. Shoulders pressed hard up against the wall of the shield, they each strive to keep up the driving force. Max groans. Peanut growls. Liam curses. Bec cries out. Shaun grumbles, and Kenny's face screws up with the effort.

From the sideline, Jack spurs them on. Gesturing for them to keep going.

Like a flash, Ruby watches Albert sail past them, motioning that they follow. He's like a fish. It's effortless. It then dawns on her that Ryker was right—Albert has absolutely *no* issues swimming the lake because he can breathe underwater. That's his *superpower*.

She makes an effort to keep up with him, but then, in the depths of the murky water, she sees it—and it's coming straight for them. Her worst nightmare. Nellie. It's huge! Ruby can't remember it being so big. She swallows a cry and reinforces her focus. She needs to stay strong, to protect her friends.

Thankfully, Albert is onto it. He's quick to tackle the problem and turn things around. He steers Nellie away from the course she's on and redirects her. For a moment, there's turbulence—the shift in the current causes their vessel to rock. Ruby loses her footing, and the others stumble to right themselves.

Soon, the motion stabilises, and surprisingly, the effort needed to maintain their momentum lessens. Ruby could squeal with elation. Masterfully, Albert has used Nellie to create a slipstream. And if they continue in the wake of the giant, they'll reach the portal in no time.

Ruby turns to Kenny and grins. Kenny wipes tears from his eyes.

Peanut fist-pumps the air and hoots. 'We're home and hosed, baby! Mahlee, here we come!' He throws a kiss into the vast abyss. 'Thank you, Nellie!'

Ruby smiles. *And thank you, Albert!*

44
MOVING FORWARD

AELIANNA

The day is coming to an end. The forest floor darkens in the ominous Valley of Lost Souls. Visibility, already reduced, diminishes further. Aelianna shivers, wraps herself tighter in the animal hide draped over her shoulders and reinforces her hold on the sizeable dagger Ryker had bought for her. She remains vigilant. She must leave now but cannot bring herself to move from the cold rock she's perched upon, hoping against hope that Ryker may present himself. She needs to see him, even if only for one last time.

Just a few more moments.

She thinks about the string of confusion in

Medwin's premonitions of late—mostly those of Ryker. No death; no life. Unclear and bewildering. Ryker's demise, a mystery to him.

How is it possible? She herself witnessed his death. His lifeless heart silent against her ear. And yet, defying all that is known, Medwin continues to catch whispers of the future with Ryker in it. Aelianna clings to this ambiguity. It gives her a splinter of hope.

She wipes the wetness from her cheeks and sniffs. She looks skyward, yearning to catch sight of him. Needle-like prickles once again sting her eyes. Tears return to mar her vision. Her lower lip quivers.

Why has he not appeared?

But ample time has passed. She sighs and drags herself to her feet, resolved to return at daybreak. One final look before she goes. The wispy silhouettes of the poor lost souls trapped in eternal oblivion float aimlessly above her, insensible to her being there. Not one of them resembles her lost love.

Perhaps he will appear tomorrow.

As she turns to leave, the space around her suddenly changes. A gentle caress from a wisp of a breeze suggests a familiar presence. She stills. She can hardly breathe. Her eyes close.

'Aelianna?'

The sound of his deep, warm voice breaks her fragile composure. She falls to her knees, cups her face and cries. She feels his presence at her side.

'Aelianna, look at me. Please. You'll see I'm okay.'

Torn between the need to look at him and the pain she'll feel seeing him no longer alive, she parts her fingers. Slowly at first, enough to take a peek. She falls back, aghast.

Ryker holds his hands up, alarmed. 'Hey, I'm not in any pain; I promise you. I'm just not … well … as I was before. That's all.'

Tears threaten to fall again, but this time she won't allow them. Aelianna draws in a sharp breath. ''Tis only the shock of seeing you like this, my love.' She shakes her head, sits taller and sniffs. 'I am not insensible about what has happened. You have passed, and now … well, now you are no more. You have returned in a spirit form.'

Ryker moves in closer, his hand poised to cradle the side of her face. The all-too-familiar tenderness she sees in his warm, green eyes casts aside her pain. Her eyes close, but the chill she feels from his touch surprises her. She gasps and draws back. Too late, the pain she sees in his reaction just about destroys her.

'I had no choice,' he says hurriedly. 'Aelianna, you've got to believe me. Had I known the depth of the tarn, I would've found another way.'

She swallows hard. 'And our friends needed you,' she says in a whisper.

But I need you too!

She shakes off the melancholy and strengthens her resolve. 'Ryker, I understand. Truly I do. And if it were me, I would have done the same.'

He sighs. 'You've no idea how much I want to hold you right now. I can see your pain, and it *kills* me!'

Her eyes widen. She presses her hand to her lips to mask a smirk.

He frowns.

Her chin dips, and she looks at him sideways. 'But my love, how can it kill you? Already you are dead.'

With that, the mood changes. The crease on Ryker's brow softens; his shoulders fall back. He smiles.

Aelianna commends herself. A chance to take away his hurt presented itself, and she took it. Moving forward, she remains mindful to mask all future emotions that reveal her pain.

And now to discover what has happened. 'Please tell me your efforts were not for naught. Our friends are safe, are they not?'

Ryker's eyes brighten. 'Thanks to Albert, they're back home, safe and sound.'

With excitement in his voice, Ryker goes on to describe the world they'd stumbled upon—the unfathomable forest and the enormous, ferocious beasts that resided within it. Aelianna listens on in amazement as he takes her on his perilous journey.

'In the end, once we knew we were safe to leave the cave, Albert led us back to the lake, distracted his overgrown water-dwelling friend, Nellie, and allowed Ruby the time and space needed to bring them safely back home. And they *did* make it home. Albert reported it when he came back for me. They're all safe. And as for our mischievous friend, he too has returned to the orphanage. Once he showed me the way back to the portal, he went home.'

'And so Albert has returned as a spirit?' Aelianna asks, her mind processing the information, and her heart racing at the prospect of Ryker also returning, full of life. 'Ryker, is there hope for you too?'

He moves in closer and smiles. 'Yes, my warrior princess. If I'm not wrong, I should return as I was before.'

Aelianna remains impassive. She won't allow her hopes to cloud what may potentially never be.

'Look, there's no guarantee,' he tells her hurriedly. 'But Kenny thinks it'll work.' He shrugs, his grin confident. 'So if Kenny believes it will, then that's good enough for me.'

Although having much faith in Kenny's knowledge, Aelianna holds back from rejoicing just yet and forces a smile … for Ryker's sake. She reaches out to him. 'Then all is not lost.'

He smiles. 'Hey, what happened to Edra and Jaeger?' Ryker asks quickly. 'Have you left them with your family?'

Aelianna shakes her head. 'Jaeger honoured his promise to those who aided us in our time of need. He and Edra have returned home with them.' She smiles. 'Many broken families will be healed from their return, I am certain.'

A sudden chill reminds Aelianna where they are. She tightens the hide on her shoulders and looks about them. 'We must take steps to leave,' she tells him. 'Father will be troubled by my absence.'

Ryker smiles. 'Come on, then, let's get you home.'

45

OPTIONS

RYKER

Ryker thinks on the task that Edra and Jaeger must've taken on—returning home with a multitude of missing persons. He hopes all has gone to plan and that they've reached the portal without complication. All those misplaced ghosts would've come back to life, if Kenny's theory is right, so he can only imagine the dilemma Edra and Jaeger had to face with the authorities and the media when they returned. As will he when *he* returns. That is, *if* he returns. He watches Aelianna climb the steep incline of the valley and calls to mind her extreme happiness at being home again. It was clear she'd missed her family terribly. And although professing her happiness living in the modern world, Ryker can't help but think she'd be happier here.

He draws in a deep breath and weighs up his options.

Of course, choosing to stay in the realm with Aelianna will mean he'll remain as he is—a ghost. Never again to hold her, or even touch her. Never again to taste the sweetness of her lips or know the fragrance of her hair. Is that too much to sacrifice? To leave his family and friends to be with her … forever in a state of lifelessness? His heart sinks. He doesn't think he could do it. Not even for the one and only love of his life.

Granted, being a ghost has its benefits, but do those benefits outweigh ever feeling the warmth of the sun on your skin or the tenderness of a caress? He's in a mess of emotions, torn. What he knows for certain is that a decision this big won't be an easy one to make.

Why does everything have to be so hard?

The eeriness and chill of the deep dark valley start to dissipate as they emerge into the warmth of the sunlit forest above. Not that Ryker can feel any of it. The colour in Aelianna's skin and the sparkle in her eyes reappear to tell him so. He remembers that gloominess only too well.

She turns and smiles at him. And suddenly, that

smile reminds him of how much she means to him. She is his world. And he could never be anywhere without her. He returns her smile. His decision is now clear. Wherever Aelianna chooses to remain, so will he.

They move on in silence.

As he floats behind her, he wonders what Aelianna might be thinking. He's anxious to know. Has she also made a decision? Will it be that they remain in this ancient realm forever? If so, is she hoping he'll be okay with that?

He looks about the forest and sighs. *Well, if that's what she wants, then this is my future.*

Aelianna rests a moment to remove the animal hide she uses to shield herself from the bitter cold. She rolls it and secures it under the strap of the holster tied to her waist that houses her sizeable blade. He notices her small backpack. Ryker knows what's in that pack. He smiles with pride. She came prepared.

But then, movement caught from the corner of his eye alerts Ryker of potential danger. 'Stay here!' he instructs before whooshing skyward.

He scans the area to locate the culprit and spots her in the near distance. Vyvian. She flies high, then dives low before vanishing.

Suddenly, Ryker realises his mistake.

He's left Aelianna on her own.

46

VYVIAN

AELIANNA

Aelianna dives for cover. Her hand tightens around the handle of the hunting dagger. Ryker's alarm came from something he caught sight of skyward. She can only guess it to be one person—Vyvian. Will Vyvian seek vengeance on Ryker by attacking *her*? What better way to seek retribution? Vyvian, once professed a great beauty, now gruesomely disfigured at Ryker's hand; her revenge will be sweet. Destroy what Ryker loves best—the lowly forest girl, now gifted a privileged life.

Aelianna remains vigilant, prepared for the attack. Vyvian may swoop at any moment, her deadly arrows targeted only at her. Aelianna recognises her vulnerability, for she is not ignorant. Apart from her dagger and the forest for her cover, her defences against a flying villain are pitiful. If only she had her bow and arrow. Then it would be an even battle.

And then she remembers something Ryker had her pack for the journey. Her eyes brighten. Without a sound, she reaches for it, prepares it, and waits.

A skyward movement suddenly catches her eye. Aelianna spots her assailant dipping and swooping, hunting for her prey. Aelianna dares not move. She hardly breathes.

And then Vyvian disappears from view.

Time passes. Aelianna cranes her neck. If only she could locate her. She steps away from the safety of her concealment to inspect. A twig snaps underfoot. She gasps. And suddenly, Vyvian is before her—no more than a few strides away.

Aelianna freezes.

Vyvian grins. Half her face showing her pleasure in uncovering her prey, the other, frozen in time from heavy scarring. Her once-thick, black volume of tresses, now matted and singed. In its place, patches of puckered and raw, reddened skin.

Aelianna almost pities her.

Almost!

She dropped her guard once; she won't drop it again.

Vyvian raises her bow, an arrow secured in its place. 'I should take from you all that Ryker took from me,' she hisses, 'and leave you, as he left me, pitiable and grotesque—too hideous to be looked upon. Of worth only to lay fear to.'

Aelianna watches as Vyvian draws tight her bow with fingers that were once nimble, now bleached from mutilation. She very nearly gasps at the sight of them, but reins in her focus and stands firm. She must act now or die.

And then the arrow finds its release. And with such speed, Aelianna has time only to dive from its path. The motion propels her down a deep escarpment. As she tumbles and rolls, she compels herself to cling to the weapon in her hand—this is her only hope. Flashes of green streak past her as she falls, and misdirected arrows strike the earth. If it were not for her accelerated pace down the slope, Aelianna would be dead.

A harsh and abrupt stop prevents further movement. Winded and disorientated from her contact with the obstacle, Aelianna struggles to place herself. She staggers to her feet, only to stumble to her knees as she fights to find equilibrium. A cry of terror from above buys her the crucial seconds she needs to adjust. She looks skyward and spots Ryker in the throes of haunting Vyvian.

But Vyvian is quick to recover. Very soon, Ryker's attack on her proves futile.

Vyvian locks eyes with Aelianna and prepares her bow. Aelianna must act now before it's too late. She takes aim, and with Ryker's instructions foremost in her thoughts, fires. A jet of noxious fluid streams from the metal device and hits her target with precision.

Vyvian shrieks in agony. Her hands tear at her face.

Aelianna has managed to buy some time. Now to escape. She turns to take on the steep incline down which she fell and uses everything she has to claw her way up the slope. Ryker cries out encouragement at her every step.

Fingers, bloodied from her exertions, grapple with the obstacles and seize hold of the crutches the forest has to offer her. Shrubs, tree roots, branches, boulders. Anything that'll take her far from Vyvian and back to safety. She pauses briefly to glance up the slope. Not far to go now. She digs deeper.

'Keep going! Don't stop!' Ryker cries out.

And then, at last, Aelianna reaches the top. Breathless and weakened by her efforts, she staggers to her feet and stops to catch her breath.

Ryker beckons her to move onward. 'I'll go back and check where Vyvian is,' he calls out to her. 'I can't depend on the wasp spray being enough to put her off.' He whooshes off to see.

Now orientated and never more determined to escape this danger, Aelianna races through the forest, her destination fixed and clear in her mind—her safe place, her home. But she cannot allow herself to believe she is totally secure. If Ryker has reservations, then so too must she.

She moves on with urgency, her senses heightened. There's no reprieve in her efforts. Tree roots trip her up and branches tear at her limbs, but Aelianna does not stop. Glancing often over her shoulder, she races on. And, finally, she finds herself on a familiar path. Still, she urges herself to keep going. She needs to make it home safely.

With Vyvian nowhere in sight, and her destination within a reachable distance, she pushes harder.

Finally, she's there.

She stops and looks about.

But where is Ryker?

47
THE DECISION

RYKER

Ryker spins around on the spot, then flies higher to locate Aelianna. He scratches his head. She's nowhere to be found. He doesn't understand it. He wasn't gone that long, was he? He pauses to reassess. He'd rocketed back to where he'd left Vyvian. She hadn't gotten far, groping blindly on all fours, crying out for help. Right or wrong, his good nature got the better of him—Ryker couldn't leave her like that. Not even after all she'd done to him, and all she threatened to do to Aelianna. Though by no means ever a saint, Vyvian's evil intentions, now manifested to gargantuan proportions, were a direct result of the suffering *he* had inflicted on her. This, he takes full ownership of.

Vyvian may have had her sights set on revenge—and now he easily could too—but Ryker is not that person. Not anymore. Once upon a time, tortured by the circumstances of the ancient realm, yes, most definitely. But now, with his heart filled with love? Never again.

He'd found her defenceless and flew down to help her. Of course, she rejected his offer, vowing to destroy him a thousand times over. He laughed. 'How do you kill something no longer living?' he asked her.

She flew at him in a rage and clawed out blindly, screeching like a banshee.

'Let me help you,' he told her. 'I've tormented you enough.'

'HELP ME! I would rather DIE!' she hissed.

'If I can lead you to water, you'll have half a chance to see again,' he said. 'If not, you'll go blind. And what use would you be as an Invincible then?'

Vyvian cursed him a hundred different ways before she allowed him to guide her to the stream. And that's where he'd left her.

Mindful of the stretch of time he'd been gone, Ryker whooshed back to join Aelianna. But now, even from his place circling high in the sky, she's nowhere to be seen.

Where could she have gone?

He imagines she would've headed home, so he heads that way. Within seconds of reaching her small village, he finds Molan sitting at his doorstep. The poor fellow topples over at seeing him. He clutches his chest and takes a moment to recover.

'Forgive me, Molan, but I'm desperate to know that Aelianna is safe.'

'*Aelianna?*' Molan jumps to his feet, his eyes suddenly wide. 'Son, my daughter is not here, nor have we seen her. Against our wishes, she spends much time in The Valley of Lost Souls, awaiting your return.'

Ryker stops. Did he miss spotting her in his rush to get here? No, he can attest to being thorough in his search. *But where is she? Surely, she was heading home.*

Clearly, she wasn't.

Then something must've gone wrong! His gut clenches. 'Molan, I've got to find her!'

'Ryker, you must consider …'

But Ryker doesn't delay. He whooshes off, cursing himself for his stupidity. Because of his pathetic moment of charitable weakness, Vyvian is on the loose again. He needs to get to Aelianna before Vyvian does.

Ryker retraces his path. He flies back to where he'd left Aelianna. Still, she's nowhere to be seen. He combs the forest in search of her. Nothing. He darts to the creek where he left Vyvian. She, too, is no longer there.

Good God! What have I done?

Tortuous images flash before him as he imagines his worst fears realised.

But then his ears prick to the sound of movement in the near distance. He goes to investigate and finds Vyvian, crawling on all fours, heading blindly in the direction of the fortress.

Ryker draws back. Clearly, Vyvian poses no threat to anyone in this state. So if Aelianna isn't where he'd left her, and she hasn't returned to her village, then where is she?

Suddenly, clarity dawns. His eyes brighten. All tension dissipates. His lip curls at the corner. He knows exactly where she is. Spirits soaring, he rushes to catch up to her and, soon enough, finds her.

Aelianna's face lights up the moment she sees him, and just like that, his world is set to rights.

His instinct was right in thinking she was making her way home, because she was. His only mistake was in thinking *which* home.

And now, mere metres from The Forbidden Passage, he knows for sure.

Aelianna was heading home … returning to *their* home.

48
Cooee!

PEANUT

The protective sphere surrounding them disintegrates with a pop as soon as they pass through the portal connecting the prehistoric realm to the real world. They scramble to exit the shallow body of water they've entered with Ruby streaks ahead of Peanut. He grabs a hold of her shirt to slow her down, needing to keep her close.

Liam and Shaun are the first to drag themselves from the creek. They fall to their knees and collapse in a heap on the sandy bank.

Peanut and Ruby come a close second. Peanut takes a moment to help Ruby settle before plonking down by her side. He stops to catch his breath and watches

Kenny and Bec emerge from the water, followed by Max and, thankfully, a returned-to-life Jack.

Peanut can't help but grin. His chest explodes with gratitude that Kenny was right. His best buddy is back and whole.

Liam sits up, hugs his knees and breathes out a huge sigh. Shaun bowls him over, laughing. 'Look at us! We bloody well made it!'

Liam gets to his feet, cups his hands to his mouth and cries out at the top of his lungs. 'Cooee!'

Beaming from ear to ear, Bec races over to join them. She tackles Liam to the ground. All three hug and roll about excitedly.

Peanut tugs Ruby to his side. He needs to hold her. They sit for a while, silent in each other's embrace. Never has he felt so connected with anyone as he does with her right now. She pulls away and looks at him. He brushes aside a strand of hair from her face, needing to look at her face—all of it. She smiles. His heart stutters. He never wants to let her go. And he never will.

He looks over at Jack. He and Max are sharing a similar moment. 'Oi!' he calls out, his smile twisted. 'A little too much PDA going on there!'

He chuckles but sobers quickly when he spots footprints mysteriously emerging from the bank, heading his way.

Ruby laughs. 'Hey, Albert, you made it. Welcome home!'

Ruby's hair flies about her face in an inexplicable manner, making her laugh. Peanut watches on with a frown. And then a wayward strand magically moves and gets tucked behind her ear.

Colour rises and flushes Ruby's face. She touches her cheek and giggles. 'You're welcome.'

It doesn't take long for Peanut to realise what just happened. He jumps up. 'Oi! Back off, buddy! Find your own girl.' He folds his arms. 'This one's taken. Got it?'

Peanut gets an unexpected whack at the back of his head. He stops. His eyes narrow. His hands curl into fists. He's poised in a boxer's pose, his chin jutting out. 'D'ya really wanna do this?' he says, dancing on the spot. 'Come on! Let's go, *buddy*, you're on!'

Peanut gets another whack to the back of his head. This time, harder. He almost sees stars. 'Why, ya pain in the neck!' he says, seething. 'How's that fair? Show yourself, ya little coward!' The air around them whirls about without warning. Dust and debris enfold them. Peanut shields his eyes and splutters. 'Okay, okay! You win, ya creep!'

Ruby laughs. 'Call it payback. How does it feel to be on the receiving end of not being able to see someone coming?'

Peanut yanks Ruby up by the hand, and before she's had a chance to protest, he pulls her to him and kisses her.

Cheering and whooping from the sideline eggs him on. He dips her in a dramatic fashion and deepens the kiss. By the time he's finished, Ruby struggles to remain upright, swaying unsteadily in a disorientated daze.

Peanut's lip curls. 'And let's just call that *your* payback, Miss Arlington!'

Peanut turns to Jack and gives him a wink. Jack gives him a thumbs-up sign and pulls Max closer to his side. Max laughs and snuggles into him.

'And you know something, *girl?*' he says to Ruby with a grin. 'You, my friend, are my newest hero!' He applauds her and gives her a kiss on the cheek. 'What d'ya reckon, guys? Is she a *legend* or what?'

The gang crowd around them, cheering and clapping Ruby's efforts.

Kenny claps the loudest. 'Ingenious! Ruby, you definitely bested anything you've ever done with that torpedo. Who knew you had it in you?'

Peanut gives Kenny a friendly nudge. 'I knew!'

He gives Ruby a wink.

She smiles.

'Oh, man, what an adrenaline rush!' Shaun cries out. 'I tell ya what, though, when I saw that humungous water-living giant coming at us, I didn't know whether to cry or crap my pants!'

'Same!' Max laughs. 'And I agree, Peanut, as a hero, Ruby can't be beat.'

Once more, the air around them whips up a cloud of dust and debris.

Coughing and spluttering, Max motions for it to stop. 'Okay, okay! And a big thanks goes to Albert and Nellie for their part in bringing us home. *Yay* for Albert, and Nellie the *Mosasaur*!'

They all hoot and applaud.

Again, the dust rises, spins into a funnel shape, then settles.

The sound of voices in the near distance alerts the group that someone's approaching. And then someone calls out. 'Kenny! Max! Hey, is anyone there?'

Shaun cries out excitedly, 'Riley? Is that you?'

'SHAUN?'

'RILEY!'

And then there's pandemonium.

The sound of people slashing through the overgrown thicket to get to them fills the air along with excited voices of authority communicating news back and forth over two-way radios. There's a whirring sound in the distance, and then suddenly a helicopter overhead eclipses the sun. The kids shrink back and shield their eyes from the debris it disturbs.

'Stay where you are!' an amplified voice booms through a megaphone from above. 'This is Captain Dean Logan. Reinforcements are on their way. Are there many casualties?'

Peanut waves his hands in the air, reassuring him they're all okay.

'You are to remain where I have a visual on you,' Captain Logan instructs.

All of a sudden, several armed, uniformed military personnel appear from the brush. Commands are hollered, reports relayed, and then familiar, and some not so familiar, faces emerge from behind them.

Wails of disbelief and elation fill the air. Brothers are reunited, families become whole, and friends huddle. Tears stream down excited faces.

Peanut pulls Ruby to his side, his throat thick with emotion. 'Will ya get a load of what's going on? *We* did this … *we* made this happen!'

Ruby wraps her arms around his waist and looks at him, her deep amber eyes sparkling. She reaches out to touch his face. '*You* made this happen, Charlie. You! You came up with the idea of forming The Triple C and made it happen. And I'm super proud of you.'

Peanut's stomach does a flip. He tugs Ruby closer. Their foreheads touch.

'Oi!' Jack calls out, laughing. 'Too much PDA going on there, Mr Brown!'

Peanut chuckles. 'Is that right, Braden? And your problem is …?'

Ruby pulls Peanut in close to her, kisses him and grins. 'Absolutely nothing at all!'

Peanut smiles. 'Nope. Not one iota.'

Just then, Peanut's stomach growls so loud, they all hear it. He breaks from Ruby's embrace, looks at her questioning expression and shrugs. 'Nah! It's all good. I've got all I need right here.'

And this time, Ruby's eyes don't roll.

49

THE SACRIFICE

AELIANNA

Aelianna waits in perfect silence within sight of The Forbidden Passage concealed beneath the huge lush leaves of the forest. A forest that has protected her in the past. A forest she has known all her life. A forest she may never know again. Tiny prickles sting her eyes. A decision needed to be made, and she made it. Not that the decision was a difficult one, for it was not. And if need be, she would do the same, time and time again. But to leave, as she is now, with no farewell to her family, no promise of ever returning … the ache in her chest gnashes at her resolve.

But the image of Ryker, a smile on his face,

playfully ruffling Albert's hair—he as a father figure, Albert, a son—softens the pain, and only deepens her conviction to do this.

She sits taller—her decision now unwavering. To remain in the realm would be a mistake she would regret on many levels. Not only would her presence here be a constant challenge—for Vyvian is sure to regroup—it would endanger her beloved family and dear friends of the forest.

Aelianna peeks skyward searching for Ryker, her concern mounting. He has been gone from her too long. Has something untoward occurred? The instant she thinks it, she dismisses it. She almost laughs at the absurdity. What harm could come to a ghost?

But where is he? Did he not foresee me returning to the Gateway?

Suddenly, she sees him, and he sees her. The relief on Ryker's face tells her that he did not. This confuses her.

He gestures for her to remain hidden, and darts out of sight. Aelianna knows he goes, most likely, to assess the safety of The Forbidden Passage before proceeding.

Her earlier investigation revealed the portal was manned—two guards standing sentry at the entrance. Aelianna recognised them from her time within the fortress walls. One, called Lucius, although intimidating in both nature and appearance, has been said to have a profound aversion to guarding the portal from fear instilled by childhood tales of the mysterious passage. The other, Marcus, is one she would often avoid. His imposing form and scarred-up face petrified her.

A commotion at the passage entry signals for her to be ready. She hears cries for help and panicked screams, and then there's silence. Aelianna peers out from the safety of her hiding place to find the guards nowhere to be seen. In their stead, and to her joy, is her adored husband.

But something is wrong. She senses unease. Even from this distance, she can see the furrow of his brow. He motions for her to come.

She races towards him. Efforts must be made to remove that scowl and replace it with a smile. And she does. Ryker softens as she approaches.

'Thank God you're safe,' he tells her. 'I've been out of my mind worrying about you!'

Her lip curls at his over-protectiveness. Not much has changed. That, she tells herself, is something she needs to work on. 'But why? I am here, and as you can see, I am unharmed. Where have *you* been? I had expected you sooner.'

'I went back to the village. I thought you would've returned there.'

She shakes her head. 'The forest is no longer my home. I belong on the other side of the Gateway with you.'

Ryker's face lights up. And so too does her heart.

She gestures they leave. The sooner they pass through the portal, the faster she can hold him whole in her arms again.

And he will *return whole!* she tells herself.

Ryker trails as they enter. She notices him pause once they've rounded the bend in the rocky passageway. She frowns and wonders why. Before them lies the way home. Aelianna looks at him. She sees apprehension in his eyes. It alarms her.

'All will be as it was. Will it not?'

Ryker says nothing.

But Aelianna won't have any of it. She straightens her back, rolls back her shoulders and juts out her chin. 'For certain it will. I have faith in Kenny and his unfathomable knowledge. You shall pass and return as before.' And without another destructive thought, Aelianna draws in a breath, marches onwards and plunges through to the other side.

50

ENDLESS LOVE

RYKER

Ryker groans. He truly doesn't deserve her. Again, he's underestimated Aelianna's strength of character. When will he learn? And now she's on the other side, waiting for him. So he'd better make a move. He drags in a shaky breath and wonders, for the millionth time, what comes next. *Whatever happens, happens!* There's no changing anything now. In a worst-case scenario, he'll remain a ghost. And if that's the way it's got to be, then so be it. There's always the option for them to go back a few million years in time, and live among the dinosaurs …

Ryker stares at the wispy curtain and wills it to work in his favour. His eyes close, and then he takes a leap of faith and stumbles through to the other side.

Aelianna squeals. She just about bowls him over with her excitement.

His eyes fly open. He pats himself down and laughs. He's back, and he's whole. Ryker tightens his hold on her. She has his heart and always will.

Never has he been so happy to be alive. He cups her face in his hands and looks at her. In her eyes, he sees the true gift he's been given. She's a wonder, a paradox to all he imagined her to be. Soft and diminutive on the outside, but built with a strength that equals his own.

And one day soon, he'll show her that he finally gets it—that he finally understands and values her. An impromptu return visit to the realm should do it. And that way, Aelianna can spend time with the people who know her and love her just as much as he does.

51

THE LOCKET

MAX

Max holds tight the silver locket dangling on a chain around her neck—her seventeenth birthday present from her father. Her family and friends surround her, singing *Happy Birthday*. She looks upon their happy faces with vacancy, her thoughts elsewhere. A niggling notion lurks in her subconscious, distracting her.

She looks again at the heart-shaped pendant in her hand and frowns. In her mind's eye, a scene plays before her. It's dark. So dark she sees nothing. And then there's a voice—an angelic, comforting voice, urging her to wake. The locket, pressed against her chest, becomes animated, wriggling with energy. She grabs it and gasps. It very nearly singes her fingers.

Max studies the hand the pendant had burned. Had she imagined it? She shakes her head. No, she definitely hadn't. Without question, there was an unnatural warmth to it. A strange and inexplicable heat. The very reason why she remembers it so clearly.

The locket, now cool and lifeless in her hand, feels different—detached and altered in some way. It's not the same. Max sighs. For some reason, she now wishes it *was*.

Someone clears their throat and breaks her state of reflection. At her side, her father gestures that it's time for the birthday cake. Max notices the look of concern on Annuska's face and smiles to reassure her.

She was miles away—totally lost in her imaginings. She shakes away her thoughts and makes an effort to focus on being present.

Her friends wait—Jack, Kenny, Peanut and Ruby, all with questioning looks on their faces. The candles are alight and flickering with life, waiting for her too. She needs to make a wish. Her lip twitches. There's no mystery there; it's been the same wish for the last five years. With her breath drawn, she pauses a moment before releasing it to blow the small flames away. Wisps of smoke drift upward. There's applause, and then the room is filled with excited chatter. Annie busies herself with the cake, cutting it into servable portions.

Jack draws near, leans in and gives her cheek a kiss. 'Happy birthday, Max.' He takes from his pocket a small, flat, square white box and places it in her hand. 'I hope you like it.'

Max looks from the mischievous look on Jack's face to the box. Her stomach does a flip.

Ruby runs to her side and claps her hands in excitement. 'Oooh! Max! Open it!'

She doesn't need to be told twice. Max pries the lid open to reveal a beautiful, delicate silver bracelet, and dangling from it, a small, heart-shaped locket— one very much like the one given to her by her father, only smaller.

Jack takes it from the box, unclasps it, and secures it around her slender wrist. 'Open it,' he says with a grin. 'Look inside.'

Unlike the locket from her father, this one isn't sealed—it has a hinge. Max can only imagine it holds a photo. She smiles. *Perhaps a photo of Jack.*

She struggles to open it one-handed. Jack leans in to help. With a click, the heart springs open to reveal a tiny portrait of her mother.

Max's breath catches. She wasn't expecting that. Her eyes prickle, and she blinks a few times.

Jack gently wipes a runaway tear from her cheek. 'I figured you'd like to have her with you always.'

The gesture, so full of heart, melts her. Max reaches up and wraps her arms around his neck and kisses his cheek. She couldn't love him any more if she tried.

Max's father clears his throat. 'Um … funny you should say that, Jack,' he says, sounding suddenly guarded.

Max releases her hold on Jack, looks at her father and frowns.

Edward can't hold her gaze. He lets out a drawn breath and appears to prepare to say something, but says nothing. There's silence.

Max crosses her arms. 'Dad?'

Again, Edward clears his throat, and again, he struggles to put words together. Instead, he reaches for the pendant around Max's neck and places it in the palm of his hand.

'This'—he stops and draws a sharp breath—'This, in actual fact, is a pendant too … of sorts,' he tells her. 'But … but it's one made especially to hold something special inside.'

Again, he pauses.

Again, Max frowns.

He loosens his collar. 'Okay, there's no delicate way of saying this. Max, the pendant holds some of your mother's ashes. It's what you call a cremation keepsake.'

Kenny splutters. His eyes widen. 'Sick!'

Jack and Ruby draw back as one. Ruby's hand shoots to her mouth. Jack appears two shades paler.

At their side, Peanut flinches. His hands shoot up in front of him. 'Whoa! You're kidding me! Right?'

Max draws back. She's lost for words.

'So,' her father continues, 'it would appear that Jack and I are like-minded—each wanting you to have your dear mother close to you … always.'

There's silence. And then, unexpectedly, there's sudden clarity. Max gasps—she can hardly believe it. She almost laughs with giddiness. She jumps about excitedly. She was right. She wasn't going nuts. It was her mother's voice she heard in the cave—*her* voice, coming from within the locket.

'Be my brave girl. Fight!'

'Find that strength within. You can do it!'

It was *her*! She was *there*!

Max's eyes sting. Her breath catches.

She thought it was a dream! *But it wasn't a dream at all! It was real!*

She tightens her hold on the pendant, willing the warmth she'd felt in the cave to manifest itself once more. But sadly, the shiny, silver-heart locket sits lifeless in her hand. Cold. Empty.

She stops.

But why?

'Max, honey, are you okay?'

She looks at her father and blinks a few times, unable to answer. She can't understand it. And then suddenly she can. She gasps. Her mind races. Her pulse accelerates.

'Max? What's wrong?'

She sees the look of concern on her father's face and holds up the pendant. 'Dad, Mum's been with me the whole time. She came to me and helped save us!'

Edward frowns. He exchanges a look with Jack. Jack shrugs.

But Max is far too excited to stop and explain. She darts away and into the formal living room, where, on the mantle above the fireplace, among family photos, sits an exquisite, ornate vase—an urn sealed with her mother's ashes.

Ever so carefully, Max takes the urn from the mantle and hugs it to her chest. She smiles the biggest smile. Her heart suddenly full. After all this time and so many birthday candles, Max's one and only birthday wish might finally come true.

To be continued …

A Note From The Author

If you enjoyed this book, I would be very grateful if you could write a review and publish it at your point of purchase. Your review, even a brief one, will help other readers to decide whether they'll enjoy my work.

If you want to be notified of new releases from myself and other Alkira Publishing authors, please sign up to the Alkira Publishing email list. In return you'll get a free ebook of short stories and book excerpts by Alkira Publishing authors. You'll find the sign-up button on the right-hand side under the photo at www.alkirapublishing.com. Of course, your information will never be shared, and the publisher won't inundate you with emails, just let you know of new releases.